Great Rea

for

INTO THE BLUE

I thoroughly enjoyed this book. It weaves an interesting tale, which spans from Russia, to Lancashire, to the south coast. The characters are identifiable and you find yourself on a journey with them as they try to make sense not just of a crime mystery, but of their own personal circumstances, which are cleverly interlinked with each other. The plot is compelling enough to make this book a real page turner. It is by no means the plodding, slow and sentimental crime dramas that you so often get from British authors but is a fast paced adventure. I look forward to reading more from the talented author.
Holmes Fan. (Melksham, Wilks.)

The characters, plot, and the story progression could have been from a seasoned writer. I read a lot; Cornwell, Archer, Cole, Smith, Heller. This Author will be a contender.
D. Valentine. (Oldham, Lancs.)

A very exciting and enjoyable read, a real page turner, look forward to the next book by this author.
B. Cooper. (Dorchester)

Great plot, couldn't put it down, more please.
F. Duffy. (Lancs.)

Good read, good plot and strong characters.
D. Shellard. (Whitworth.)

J M Close was born in Oldham. His first career, in accountancy, lasted a few short months, terminated when the company he had joined from college went into liquidation, along with the industry it serviced. Like many unemployed young men he turned to the military for employment. Studied electrical engineering at the Royal School of Electrical & Mechanical Engineering, Chatham. Upon leaving the Army he spent some years working as a TV service engineer, before moving into Office Equipment and Data Management technology. *Into The Blue* is his debut mystery novel

www.jmcloseauthor.com
twitter: J M Close @closecall21

By The Same Author

Long Ride On A Ghost Train

One boy's voyage of self-discovery through the black and white world of the 1950's: an age when the teenager was invented, Rock 'n Roll was king, and the good really did die young.

**Due for publication in *JMP* paperback
Autumn 2016**

INTO THE BLUE

\#

J M CLOSE

First published in Kindle books 2014

USA edition first published in paperback 2015

This edition published 2016
by
J M Publications

Copyright © J M Close

The right of J M Close to be identified as the sole author
of this work is asserted by him in accordance with the
Copyright, Designs & Patents Act 1988

No part of this publication may be
reproduced, copied, or transmitted, in any
form, visual or audio, without the written authorization of
the publisher and copyright owner.

This book must not be lent, resold, hired out or
distributed, without the publisher's consent, in any
cover or binding other than that in which it is published

ISBN 978-0-9933267-2-1

Printed and bound in the UK by Clays Ltd. St Ives plc

All characters and events portrayed in this book are fictional.
Any resemblance to real people or occurrences is purely accidental.

New York 2009

The Buick cruised to a stop outside the junk-yard. Behind the closed gates stood a steel cabin, its door shut tightly against the winter chill. The single window was frosted over with condensation through which flickered the pale, white, light of a fluorescent tube. The whole cabin vibrated noisily to the thumping, bass, beat of heavy metal music.

An impatient blast of the car's horn cut off the music. The cabin door opened. An armed security guard stepped out. Recognising the car he opened the gates and waved it through. He re-locked the gates then followed the car down a wide alleyway, between bales of scrap metal stacked three-high.

The car moved slowly. The driver anxious to avoid the worst of the metal detritus that littered the ground. Reaching the far end of the passageway, he nosed the car into a brightly illuminated compound and stopped. He turned to the woman beside him.

'Stay here!' he ordered. 'This won't take long.' Leaving the engine running he climbed out. Pushed the door shut and stood waiting for the guard to catch up.

It was a cold night, but he didn't seem to notice. Under a thick, woollen overcoat he wore a stylish suit.

Around his neck hung a long silk scarf, more a statement of fashion than a useful weapon against the cold. The handmade leather shoes on his feet were so highly polished they would have reflected starlight, had there been any around to reflect.

A thin, freezing mist drifted across the compound. It made the man's pale, Slavic, face look paler still. Turned his breath into wreaths of white vapour. Reaching up he pulled the flaps of the Russian trapper's hat he wore, over his ears. Made from mink fur, the hat had been specially imported from Moscow.

When the guard came up to the car the two men walked together, across the compound.

'You sure 'bout this, boss,' asked the guard, uneasily.

'What - you got a problem?' asked the other, sharply.

'No no boss! No problem. But takin' out a Fed? That's some serious stuff, man. Gonna bring down a whole shit-load of trouble on us, for sure.'

The driver stopped. Regarded the other steadily. 'Let me tell you how it works here, Danny! Some guy tries to bring us down, he's a dead man. Whoever - whatever he is, he's a dead man. Now this guy? No one asked him to stick his nose into our business. But he did. So he gets what he gets. You ain't happy with this, you're welcome to join him. You got that?'

The guard nodded submissively. Said nothing more.

'When we're through here, throw him into a trunk. Sanitise the place then send the car to the crusher. By the time they notice he's missing, there'll be nothing left of him.'

'You're the boss.'

'You got it!'

The guard walked on across the clearing, making for the modified shipping container that served as the yard office. He went inside. Came out seconds later with another security guard. Between them was a man in his mid twenties.

Wearing only Levi's and t-vest, the man shivered in the chill air. Bare-footed, his ankles were hobbled with loose chain, his wrists bound with wire. He fought furiously against his captors as he was dragged into the compound.

From inside the car the woman watched fearfully. Something bad was going to happen here. Something she did not want to see. But she could not take her eyes off this struggling young man who refused to go quietly to whatever awaited him.

Roughly the prisoner was hauled before the waiting driver. Forced down onto his knees.

'Hello Frankie,' smiled the driver. 'Been hearing bad things about you. Seems you're not all you make yourself out to be. Got anything to say about that?'

The young man said nothing. Words would not help him now. Nor would he give them the satisfaction of hearing him beg for his life.

The man with the silk scarf strolled over to a small wire cage on the edge of the compound. He reached inside, came out gripping a piece of angle iron about thirty inches long. Carrying the bar he returned to the prisoner. Then, without warning, began raining down blows on the helpless man's arms, legs, and body.

His victim roared with pain. Curled himself into a ball to protect himself. At a nod from the driver, the two security men joined in the assault. Laid into the prone body with their booted feet, inflicting damage everywhere but the head. Knocking the man senseless was not a part of the plan. He had to feel the pain.

From the front passenger seat the woman looked on in horror. Appalled by what she was witnessing. Her hands rose to her mouth. A flood of emotions welled up inside her. Unable to contain herself she erupted from the car. Stood by the open door, visibly shaking.

'Enough!' she screamed at the men. 'Enough, for god's sake! What are you, animals?'

The driver paused in his murderous assault. Turning his head he stared at the woman, eyes bright with rage. He started towards her, panting heavily from the exertion of pounding his victim. When he came close he raised a gloved hand and struck her, savagely, in the face.

The blow knocked her back against the side of the car. Her knees gave way and she slid to the icy ground. For a moment she felt only numbness. Then the pain rushed in, so intense it felt like someone had thrown boiling water into her face. Stunned, she lay there, blinded by tears. The taste of warm blood filled her mouth and throat.

'What part of *stay there* do you not understand?' barked the man angrily. 'Now get back in the car! Keep your eyes, your ears, and especially your big mouth shut. Do you understand that?' The woman nodded, dully.

Returning to his task the man began beating the prisoner even harder, glancing from time to time at the woman as if to say 'this is down to you now, because you made me mad!'

Slowly she climbed to her feet. Gripping the car door and pillar she pulled herself up onto the seat. Swung her legs inside. Reaching up she lowered the sun visor to examine her face in the mirror. Seeing the damage somehow made the pain worse. She pulled a wad of paper tissues from the glove compartment and held them gingerly against her bloody nose.

'Hey, you look cold Frankie?' The voice of her assailant rang out clearly. 'Looks to me like you need warming up a little? We can do that, can't we guys?'

The security men laughed. One of them stepped forward with a gasoline can. Began to splash the contents over the body of the man lying on the ground. Their victim stirred as the liquid soaked into his clothes.

Through the open door of the car the woman heard his pitiful pleas. Asking his attackers to spare him this and shoot him instead. The sound of a striking match removed all hope of this. A flame arced through the air, quickly followed by a *whoosh* as the gasoline ignited.

The victim screamed as he was engulfed in flames. He tried to climb to his feet but was knocked back down by a swinging blow from the iron bar.

The woman turned her face away. Closing her eyes she placed her hands over her ears to shut out the screams. Tears ran down her cheeks. They mingled with her own blood to fall as soft, pink, rain-drops onto the velvety surface of her new Cashmere coat.

Tarasan: Kazakhstan:

Five Years Later

Yana Nabiev did not even look as she stepped onto the old highway. The big road, as it was known locally, carried nothing in the way of traffic these days. At night it was virtually a ghost road.

The ancient highway effectively cut the village in two. Geographically, and socially. On the high ground to the west, in their fine houses, lived the more affluent members of the community. To the east, where the ground was soft, muddy, and prone to flooding in spring, the less fortunate huddled inside a sprawl of tiny hovels that were cold in winter, hot and airless in summer, and damp the rest of the time.

The big road had doubtless been a fine piece of engineering in its day. Strong and wide, it had carried the troop convoys from Kustanay, in the north, to the southern borders of the Soviet empire. But that was years ago. Now it was badly worn. Neglected. The surface strewn with dangerous potholes. Its edges eroded by years of winter frosts. It was badly in need of some serious maintenance. But who had money to spend on road repairs, these days?

The Russians had built the highway, of course. Back in the days when Stalin was using this country as a dumping ground for any ethnic group he found unacceptable. There had been a great many of these.

Yana was too young to remember life under the despot. But she was old enough to remember the Soviet State: and its war. Oh, she would never forget its war. Nor the husband she lost to the Afghan Mujahedeen, leaving her to raise two children on a worthless pension. Life had not been easy in those days. Now it was better. Not great, but better.

As she angled her way across the road, large round spots began to appear in the surface dust. Heavy drops of rain began falling on her head and shoulders. Yana quickened her pace. She needed to reach home before the full downpour struck or she'd be soaked.

A gusting wind came out of nowhere. Caused her loose coat to flap about wildly. Expertly, she wrapped and belted the coat tightly around her plump figure. Pushing her hands into the deep pockets her fingers came into contact with the letter. They caressed the smooth paper of the envelope and she smiled broadly. She could still seeing the look on Rosa Beyanev's face as she had read its pages.

Showing the letter to her friends gave Yana almost as much pleasure as reading it herself. Not that she would ever aspire to call Rosa a friend. But the woman's family had some standing in the small community, and she would have felt both slighted and offended had she not been given the same opportunity to read it, as everyone else. Yana knew only too well that it would not do to offend the Beyanevs.

The dirt track leading up to her small dwelling was only metres away when the front edge of the shower swept in, instantly turning the surface dust into thin, black, mud. Yana broke into a shuffling trot. She didn't even see the ancient Zis farm truck parked up without lights a little way down the big road.

Stepping off the concrete she entered the narrow track. Allowed herself a moment of relief. Soon she would be home. Drinking tea in her warm kitchen. Reading the letter again. She never tired of reading the letter.

She had almost reached her door when a short, broad, figure stepped out onto the track to block her way. Yana stopped. She peered nervously through the rain at the man standing before her. Recognition, when it came, brought a stab of fear.

'Hello, Yana Nabiev!' There was no warmth in the man's greeting.

'Stand aside old man,' she said, more boldly than she felt. 'We have no business, you and I.'

The man's shoulders shrugged carelessly. 'Oh but I think we have? Important business. Family business. Business concerning the letter you have been showing to everyone.' He moved in closer. Held out a calloused hand. 'Perhaps you would be kind enough to show it to me?'

The hand in her pocket instinctively gripped the envelope. She stepped back as the man advanced, only to find her retreat blocked by two younger men who had silently approached from behind.

'The letter!' demanded the man.

'I give you nothing,' she spat out, defiantly. 'You will have to take it from me. And I will scratch out your eyes while you try!'

The man smiled. Nodded briefly. Yana was seized from behind. She started to scream but a thin rope was looped around her neck and pulled tight, cutting off her breath. The rope continued to tighten until, at last, the woman's struggles ceased and her lifeless body sank onto the muddy ground.

A brief search soon discovered the letter. It was passed to the old man who slipped it into his pocket. Without another glance at the dead woman the three men hurried back to the road. They climbed into the Zis truck and drove off into the rain, carefully avoiding the water-filled potholes.

London

Three months later.

The man in the dark grey suit sat at a table in Starbucks. He slowly chewed an egg-mayo sandwich. A confirmed vegetarian, egg mayonnaise was about as adventurous as he got.

The coffee with which he swilled down the food was black. He preferred it that way. Black coffee was the beverage of a man who didn't run with the pack. A serious drink that marked him out as a serious man.

Lying open, on the table, was a book on the English Lake District. This year he was determined to visit the National Park. See first-hand the sweeping fells, the craggy landscapes, and the tranquil tarns. Perhaps in early October, he thought, when the crowds of summer tourists had gone.

Closing the book he finished off the sandwich and drained his cup. Checked his watch and debated whether or not to have a second coffee. There was just time.

The door of the café opened. A man entered. He wore an ill-fitting blue suit over a ghastly yellow shirt with a red tie. Looking around, the stranger spotted him. Came straight to his table and took the chair opposite.

The newcomer was short and slim, with close-cropped dark, hair. His face was mean. Thuggish. The face of a man with little or no regard for the feelings, or wellbeing, of others. Pale, watery, eyes stared across the table. Regarded him with silent amusement and a hint of cruelty. He nodded a silent greeting.

'Do I know you?' snapped the man in the dark grey suit, irritated by this invasion of his space.

'I know you!' the other replied. From his pocket he pulled an envelope. Tossed it carelessly across the table. 'Here, take a look!'

Grey suit ignored the envelope. Dismissively, he picked up the book. Reached for his coat on the seat beside him. The stranger quickly leaned forward and wrapped a strong hand around his wrist. The grip tightened. Hot pain shot up his arm, making him gasp.

'Open it!' He was ordered.

The man in the dark grey suit let the coat fall back onto the seat. His wrist was released and he rubbed gingerly at the white nail-marks left embedded in his skin. Reluctantly he reached for the envelope and shook the contents onto the table top.

Six photographs fell out. Face down. Impatiently he flipped them over, then froze. His eyes went wide. His jaw dropped, and his stomach lurched sickeningly. He stared at the top photograph with a rising sense of dread.

The other man reached out. With the dexterity of a card dealer he spread the photographs so they could all be seen. Then he deftly swept them together again, and slipped them back into the envelope.

'Been a naughty boy, haven't you sonny-Jim?' he smiled. 'The question is, does your family know what you like to do with little boys? Do your employers?'

Grey suit closed his eyes. He took a deep breath and tried to regain his cool. A shake-down, he decided. This had to be a shake-down. He looked at the man sitting opposite and strove to keep his voice even. 'Well, you don't look like a cop. So what do you want? Money? Is that it?' He gave a half smile. 'If it is, you're going to be pretty disappointed. I don't have very much.'

'I'm not surprised!' Grinning cheekily, the man waved the envelope. 'This is one seriously expensive hobby. But don't you worry, kiddo. This is not about money. It's about this job we want you to do, for some friends of ours. A job that shouldn't be too difficult for someone in your position - and believe me, we know exactly what your position is.' The stranger paused to let this sink in. 'All you need do is say yes, and all these photographs - and the video they were taken from - will disappear. Like forever.'

'And if I refuse?'

'You won't!'

The man in the grey suit took time to consider his response. He thought about what would happen if these pictures were released. His carefully controlled life would be over. He would become a pariah amongst his own family. His well-paid job and the lifestyle it brought, not to mention his pension, would also be gone. The man was right. He had no option but to agree. His shoulders sagged in defeat.

'So, who do I have to kill?' he joked sourly. At least, he hoped he was joking.

'No one,' smiled the stranger. 'Someone else will do that.' He produced a photograph of a woman. Passed it across the table. 'Your job is to find her. That's all you have to do. If you're really lucky, she might even find you.' He passed over a flash drive and cash-card. 'The memory stick has all the details you need: and a contact number. If there's anything you don't understand, call the number. Any problems, call the number.'

'And the cash card?'

'Expenses. Finding her will cost money. Use the card.' The man leaned back and smiled. 'You can even cream off a little for yourself, for personal expenses. But don't go getting all members of parliament on us or some people might get upset. You wouldn't want that.'

'How long have I got?'

'As long as it takes.'

'And if I can't find her?'

The man climbed to his feet. Smiled coldly. 'Then, my friend, you will find a whole world of shit hitting your fan.' With a small nod, the stranger turned and walked from the Starbucks.

1

MONDAY

Dutton:

I rarely see the television news. Don't ever feel I've missed anything, either. Politics and tragedy. That's all you get. The first, pure soap opera. The second - well, who needs to hear about other people's troubles? Not me, that's a fact. I've had more than enough tragedy of my own, thank you very much.

This said, nor do I make a conscious effort to ignore news programmes. It's just that by ten o clock, most evenings, I am comfortably asleep in my recliner. Head back, feet up, and snoring with the best of them.

I have a long day. It begins at six, with a shave and a shower. Then I dress and take my dog Lucy for a walk, trying hard to avoid the local yob and his pit bull. I say pit bull, he claims it's a Staffordshire. But then, don't they all?

Each morning the yob is there, on the beach. Letting his dog run freely. Always wearing dark blue shorts and a green tee-shirt (the yob, that is, not the dog). I often wonder what he does for a living? And if he does it in dark blue shorts and a green tee-shirt. He must do something. No one is out walking their dog so early, unless they have somewhere to go.

By seven-thirty Lucy and I are in the car, setting off for work. On the way in we call for breakfast. Eat it in the office. Egg and bacon sandwich for me, two sausages for Lucy. Lucy is fat. I'm getting there.

I like to be in the office early. You never know when someone might open their eyes to a new day, only to find they are in urgent need of a private investigator. If they do, then the first agency they will see in the local directory will be Abacus.

Abacus Investigations. That's me. I did consider using my own name, but *The Terry Dutton Detective Agency* sounded a touch pedestrian. Also, Abacus is a good marketing ploy. The name makes it number one on the list of agencies which, as lists go, is not very long anyway where I live.

One-man detective agencies, like mine, are a dying breed. An endangered species. Today, most agencies are large city, or regional, operations. Well staffed, they can offer a whole range of services from high tech surveillance and car tracking, to snooping on dishonest employees. Plus, mobile phone and computer hacking. Only they don't call it hacking any more. Not since Leveson.

They still offer services to individual clients. But their bread and butter business is corporate. That's where the real money lies. The bigger the Company, the more lucrative the contract.

I have never had an appetite for commercial work. It's not what I want. I much prefer working for real people who need my help. But being a one man business is fairly limiting, so I have to specialise. I offer only two services. Tracking down missing persons, and providing proof of infidelity.

The first is my speciality. It's what I did for some years in the police force. The second is rarely needed in divorce courts these days. But some people like to be sure they have all the facts, before they throw their partner's belongings into the street.

Most of the work I do is not very romantic, though it can be rewarding. Nor is it dangerous. Unlike most fictional private detectives I have never been shot at, beaten senseless, or involved in a hundred-mile-an-hour car chase through the streets of London. Not yet anyway. But life's full of surprises, isn't it?

My home is on the South coast. Isle of Portland. From there I drive into Weymouth each day, to my three-roomed office suite above a local estate agency. I say suite, it consists of a reception area, my office, and a small kitchen equipped with kettle, fridge, microwave, and sink. There is also a loo. But this is too small to be included in the room count.

I do not work alone. I have a receptionist-clerk. A twenty-five year old reformed drug addict with a pierced eyebrow. Her name is Bianca White - honestly! She tells me there are other piercings about her body, but she keeps these to herself and her occasional boyfriends.

When I interviewed Bianca I was impressed by how intelligent she was. My previous experiences with druggies, and I've had some, were not good. But I followed up her references and spoke to her drugs councillor. She assured me that Bianca had been clean for eighteen months. That she was back living with her parents, in an effort to stay that way. Suffering an attack of social conscience I gave her the job. I was glad I did.

The building in which Bianca and I work belongs to me. The estate agency downstairs pays me rent, which is a little like living off immoral earnings. The house in which I live is also mine. I bought both properties with the inheritance I received from my father. He was a man I never liked very much, but I'm not too proud to enjoy the money he left me.

Much of my working life is spent sitting at a computer, compiling reports. Or making telephone calls to various parts of the country: sometimes, even, the world.

Occasionally I spend time away from home chasing up leads. On these trips I take Lucy with me. I always look for 'dog-friendly' accommodation, but if I can't find it she sleeps in the car. Sometimes we both sleep in the car. Lucy is a ten-year-old Lakeland Terrier. Just one of the many things my wife left behind, the day she sailed off into the blue and never came home.

After my day's work I arrive home about nine. Turn on the TV and open a bottle of Pinotage. I then drink myself to sleep in my reclining chair. Stay there until Lucy jumps onto my lap at around eleven o clock, ready for her bedtime walk. This routine went out the window on the night that everything changed. With it went my monotonous and egocentric lifestyle.

It began with a phone call. The warbling chimes pulled me from my doze. I checked my watch. Five minutes to ten. Few people have my home number. None of them would call me at five to ten at night, unless it was serious. Climbing from the chair I walked into the hallway and picked up.

'Terry Dutton?' asked a voice with an American accent. Not too many of those in Dorset?

'That's me,' I admitted.

'I think you should watch the BBC news, Terry,' he went on in a friendly, familiar, manner. 'You'll find it pretty interesting. Especially the piece about your old hunting ground. And there's a great shot of your wife in there, by the way. I have to say, she's looking pretty good, considering?' Abruptly, the man rang off.

The call left me puzzled. Then angry. If this was someone's idea of a joke they had played it on the wrong guy. I hit 1471. '*We do not have the caller's number*' the robotic voice informed me.

'Fat lot of use you are then,' I complained.

Back in the lounge I discovered Lucy, curled up on my recliner. I didn't have the heart to move her so I made sure the television was tuned to the BBC, then perched beside her on the chair arm. Draining my wine glass I waited for the news to begin, still feeling more annoyed than curious.

It didn't take long. The lead story was about a number of arrests made by anti-terrorist police in Manchester. When the figure of the studio anchor man made way for an outside broadcast report, I leaned forward with interest.

The reporter was standing in a paved shopping area that I vaguely recognised. In the background was the sports outlet store where one of the terrorist suspects was employed. He had been arrested by armed police, when he'd arrived at work that morning.

As the journalist gave out details of the arrest, the camera slowly panned in on the store front. It was then that something quite unbelievable happened.

Next door to the sports outlet was a glass-fronted cafeteria. As the camera zoomed in, the door of the cafeteria opened and a woman stepped out. Turning right she walked hurriedly across the front of the store, in full camera shot, until disappearing off-screen.

The shock was physical. I gasped asthmatically. My legs became rubber. My stomach dropped so fast and so far it must have gone through the floor. What I had just witnessed was not possible. Not even remotely possible. It had to be some kind of illusion. For I had just seen my dead wife step out of a cafeteria and walk up the street, two hundred and fifty miles away in the centre of Manchester.

2

Altyn:

The painting brush fell from the woman's hand. Deposited a splash of yellow ochre onto the tiled floor. Frozen in shock she stared at the television screen. Appalled by what she had just witnessed.

Altyn had never considered herself cursed. Unlucky, perhaps, but not cursed. Now she wasn't so sure. Not content with making her life as difficult as possible, it seemed that the fates were determined that never again would she get the chance to live any kind of normal life. What was that if not a curse?

Only twice in her lifetime had she known real contentment. The first was during those swiftly flowing years of childhood. Years filled with the love and companionship of family and friends.

Then, a few years into her teens, it all came to a brutal end. Her life changed unimaginably when she was cast into a kind of slavery from which she feared she would never escape. But escape she had, and she had used the precious gift of freedom to seize a second chance at happiness.

But those days, too, had been lost - no, not lost, she reminded herself, thrown away: and now the cycle was about to start up all over again. There had been many times in her life when Altyn had known despair. But the depth of misery she felt right now surpassed all of these. Tears ran, unheeded, down her face.

For a long time she stood there. Unmoving. Unable to work up the nerve to do what must be done. Then slowly, from somewhere deep inside her psyche, a new resolve began to emerge. A new strength. Telling her that all might not yet be lost. That perhaps she could still have a life somewhere. Drying her eyes she took several deep breaths. Prepared herself mentally to face up to the probability of yet another upheaval.

She walked into the kitchen. Made herself a coffee. She rarely drank coffee before going to bed, but tonight she would not sleep anyway. Back in the lounge she sat down with the drink and watched the rest of the news, her mind anywhere but on the screen.

When she heard the words *'And now for the news from where you are!'* she stared more intently. Watched the re-run from the BBC's North West studio, hoping she might have been mistaken. She was not. Once again she saw herself walk across the screen, totally oblivious to the damage she was doing.

A new thought struck her. One that made her heart sink even further. What if *he* was sitting at home right now. Watching this very same scene - more in shock than she was? The thought brought even more tears, and an overwhelming sense of shame.

With a fierce effort she pushed such thoughts aside. Refused to allow her mind to go there. What was done was done. There was no going back. This was not a time for regrets. The important thing here was survival. Which meant she must now call the only person who could help her.

Opening the phone she hit number one on speed dial. The call was answered immediately. 'Did you see the news?' she asked at once, breathlessly.

'Hello Altyn. I was expecting your call,' he told her. 'Yes, I did see it. The whole world must have seen it. This is very unfortunate. Did you not see the cameras? The police cars? All the activity?' He was not angry. But his words were filled with a regretful weariness that was more painful than any admonishment.

In truth she had barely registered the scene that morning. With too much time spent on the distribution, and in the cafeteria, she had been running late, with a meeting to attend. Hurrying to find a taxi, she was too wrapped up in trying to save a few precious minutes to notice what was going on around her.

'I am so sorry, Peter, I wasn't even looking. I've ruined everything, haven't I?'

'I don't know? But we must work on the assumption that you have. Not to do so would be very dangerous.'

'So what do I do?'

'What you must not do is panic. Manchester is a big city. Half a million people live and work there. Finding one amongst so many will not be easy. Not even for professionals: and they are not professionals, are they.'

'No they are not. But it's not just them I worry about. What if *he's* seen this television broadcast and comes looking for me? If anyone can find me he will. You know that! I cannot allow this to happen Peter. How could I possibly face him?'

'You may be worrying for nothing, Altyn. He might not even have seen it. But if it helps I'll go to Dorset.

Find out what I can. Then I'll see what can be done to salvage the situation. But I must warn you, our options are fewer than before. We might have to consider an alternative course of action. You understand this, don't you?'

She knew what he was saying. 'Peter I'll do whatever you feel is best. I'm in your hands.'

'Good. Now, are you comfortable with staying in the apartment?'

'For tonight, yes. I don't expect anyone to come kicking down my door just yet. But tomorrow I must move out. I'm linked to this place, through my work. This link must be broken.'

'You have somewhere to go?'

'I think so.'

'Call me when you move. Let me know where you are. How are you for money?'

'I'm fine. Money's not a problem.'

'Draw as much as you can from your account, as soon as you can. Then destroy your cards before they lead someone to you. If you need anything else call me at any time.'

'Thank you Peter. I am sorry to be so much trouble.'

'You are not trouble Altyn. Not now. Not ever. Do not think this.'

The call was ended. For a moment she sat there. Considering what he had said and the implications of it. Then she reopened her phone and called another number. After several ring tones a man answered.

'It's Kat,' she said. 'I'm sorry to disturb you at this time, but I need a favour: and there's no one else I can ask.'

3

Dutton:

Dorset is not my birth county. I'm a Yorkshire lad. Born in Dewsbury, West Yorkshire, in 1979. My mother, Ruthy, was a clerk at the ICI plant, up the road in Huddersfield. My father was Harry Dutton. A nineteen year old brick-layer from Lockwood.

Harry was an ambitious lad. By the age of twenty-five he had his own building company. He also had his first mistress, his *fancy woman* my mother called her, but there was nothing fancy about Pauline Barnes. She was short and plump with big frizzy hair, a hooked nose, and enormous breasts. When she wasn't lying on her back underneath my father, she ran the office for him.

Ten years down the road from there, and my father had become a property millionaire. Pauline had been replaced by a succession of giggly young things and we lived in a big house, way out on Scammonden Moor. Very Wuthering Heights.

During this time I was at Rishworth school. Studying for my A-levels. My father was hardly ever home. My mother, who couldn't drive, spent most of her time rattling around inside the big empty house, bored out of her skull. I didn't know it then, but already she was a hopeless alcoholic.

Two years into my degree course at Manchester University, Harry stopped coming home altogether. He divorced my mother and moved into a penthouse flat in Leeds, with his latest girlfriend. He let mother have the big house, which she sold at once. She moved back to Dewsbury to be close to former friends and family. But her life was already over. Within a few short months, a ruined liver carried Ruthy Dutton off to an early grave.

Harry came to the funeral. Large as life, with his latest fancy woman. She actually looked younger than me. Probably was, too. As we walked away from the grave he put his arm around my shoulder, like he thought a real father would. I elbowed him in the guts and walked away. Left him doubled over in pain. That was the last time I saw him alive.

I left university with a degree in archaeology. Married a college librarian, and joined the Greater Manchester police force: like you do. My university education brought me rapid promotion, my busy career a broken marriage. By the age of thirty-one I was a divorced Detective Inspector. Running *Missing Persons* out of Chester House.

Then, quite unexpectedly, my father died. He suffered a coronary whilst taking a holiday in the Seychelles. The penthouse went to his girlfriend, along with just over a million pounds to keep her in short skirts. The rest, for some reason, (conscience probably) he left to me. Over three and a half million pounds, after death duties. Suddenly I was a multi-millionaire, and my father had his revenge for the elbow in the guts. My career was blown right out of the water.

You can be lots of things and still be a policeman. Musician. Comedian. Sportsman. Even a wife beater (I've known a few). What you cannot be is a multi-millionaire. The police force, like most places of work, is no place for the obscenely rich. So, with a failed marriage and an aborted career behind me, I left Manchester and moved to Dorset.

This was not just a whimsical move on my part. I had been to Weymouth as an eight year old. On holiday with my parents. My father was messing about with other women then, although I didn't know it at the time. All I knew was that we felt like a real family, as we strolled through the town and played on the beach.

We visited Portland Bill. Climbed to the top of the lighthouse. Then sat down to strawberries and cream in the café. Afterwards we walked along Chesil Beach, collecting cuttlefish shells to take back to Yorkshire.

During that seaside holiday I fell in love with the whole area. Twenty-four years later, and ridiculously rich, I decided that this was the place I would most like to live, given that I could now afford to live more or less anywhere I chose. So I moved down to Dorset and bought a house on Portland.

Deciding to take up sailing I bought a dingy. Took lessons from a retired lobsterman who claimed he'd been born on a paddle-steamer, somewhere between Weymouth and Bournemouth.

Once my seamanship and navigation skills were up to scratch I invested in a small yacht called *Sweet Ruby*. Had it re-registered as the *Sweet Ruthy*, in memory of my mother. Some of the old hands shook their heads at this. Muttered darkly about changing boats' names bringing nothing but bad luck. Perhaps I should have listened to them.

I joined the yacht club, and the golf club. Quickly fell into a routine of assured idleness. At first I enjoyed every minute of it. But soon discovered that a life of constant leisure can become irksome and dull.

I became bored. Restless. What I needed was something more to fill my days. I needed a job. But police work was all I'd ever known, and I wasn't going back to that. Nor was I about to forge a new career for myself filling up supermarket shelves, however worthwhile.

After much thought I decided to set up my own detective agency. This way I could continue doing the job which, as a policeman, I had found the most rewarding. So I purchased a commercial property in Weymouth, with a sitting tenant on the ground floor, and opened Abacus.

4

I met Alex at the yacht club. On a dark, February, afternoon. I stepped out the door, walked to my car, and there she was. Her small van was in the bay next to mine. The bonnet was up, and she was staring at the engine like it was covered in Egyptian hieroglyphics.

'Can I help?' I asked, secretly hoping she'd decline my offer in favour of the RAC. Not that I didn't want to help, of course. It's just that the only thing I know about cars is how to drive them. So I didn't want to end up looking both oily, and stupid. But when she turned and awarded me a smile of gratitude and relief, it felt like someone had just turned on the sun.

Her name was Alexana Morel. Alex to her friends. She was a florist. Having delivered flowers to the club for someone's birthday, she had left the car on the car park and gone off to lunch. 'Now it won't start,' she explained, in an accent that lay somewhere between Eastern Europe and mid-Atlantic. 'It just clicks when I turn the key.'

Now I might not know much about cars. But I've been driving long enough to recognise the symptoms of a flat battery when I hear them. 'You didn't go off and leave the headlights on, did you?' I asked.

A small tongue briefly appeared between her lips. She lowered her eyes, guiltily. 'Probably,' she admitted. Reaching into the car she turned off the headlight switch, and sighed.

'Don't worry. I'll get Andy. He'll sort it for you.' Andy was the yacht club's resident mechanic. He arrived with his super-booster-charger gizmo. Had the engine running in seconds.

'Don't stall it,' he warned her. 'Not for a while anyway. You might not get it started again.'

She gave me a faintly worried look.

'How far are you going?' I asked.

'To Swanage.'

Swanage was miles out of my way. But when you're playing knight in shining armour, you just don't care do you?

'I'll follow you,' I said. 'Just in case!'

She made it home without stalling, then invited me in for coffee. She ran a flower shop in Station road. Lived in the apartment above. The place was warm, cosy, and filled with Ikea furniture. Strangely at ease with each other we sat in the tiny lounge, chatting and drinking coffee.

Alex was a former flight attendant with Air Baltic. She had come to England three years ago to open her own flower shop. I asked her why Swanage? She told me she had once met someone who came from Dorset, and they had recommended the area. After visiting to see for herself, she had fallen in love with the county and its coastline. Like me, she had decided that this was the place for her.

By seven o clock we were still swapping life stories. She asked if I'd like to stay for dinner. Having heard nothing good about Eastern European cuisine, I wasn't sure I wanted to. But I was enjoying her company too much to refuse.

In the event the food turned out to be Italian. We shared a home-made lasagne with warm ciabatta bread, washed down with a Sicilian Rosso. The food was delicious and I drank far too much wine to drive home. When I said I'd call a taxi she said I could stay the night if I wished. Sleep on the settee.

So I stayed the night. But I didn't sleep on the settee.

We had a June wedding at the register office, in Swanage Town Hall. Abacus Investigations was still in its infancy and Alex couldn't just up and leave the flower shop in the hands of her young assistant. So we settled for a weekend honeymoon in Cherbourg. Then on Monday morning, it was back to work.

We lived in my house on Portland. Spent the long summer evenings (when it didn't rain) walking by the sea. We strolled along like two soppy teenagers. Often huddled together against the Atlantic winds that swept the island. Life was good. Then, six months after we married, Lucy arrived.

Lucy's owner had died. When the niece of the deceased woman called into the flower shop to order a wreath, she had Lucy with her. Very clever, I thought. She asked Alex if she knew anyone who might give the little terrier a good home, and of course she did - us! So then there were three of us taking an evening stroll.

Most weekends we went sailing, taking Lucy with us. Not too far, mind. Just along the coast. I'm not the most confident yachtsman so I never sail out of sight of land. I taught Alex how to sail, and navigate, and she picked up the skills like she was born to them. Even started going out alone whenever I was busy, or working away. Alex came to love sailing. She quickly became a far more accomplished yacht handler than I'll ever be.

We had fifteen happy months together. After a disastrous first marriage I felt I had, at last, found the woman with whom I wished to spend the rest of my life.

Then I lost her.

I was in France. Following up a reported sighting of a client's missing sixteen-year-old daughter. The girl had run off with a fifty-year-old choir master, whom everyone had thought was gay - which just goes to show, doesn't it?

The couple had been spotted on a caravan park, close to the city of Arles. It was a long way to go, but the client was a lawyer. Lawyers are a good source of business for private investigators. So on that Thursday morning I said goodbye to Alex and Lucy. Drove to Bristol and flew from there to Marseille. I expected to be back Saturday afternoon.

The next day Alex left the shop around lunchtime. She told Jenny she was going sailing. At a little after five she was seen taking the yacht out of the harbour. This was the last sighting anyone had of her. And because I was not at home, no one raised the alarm when she failed to return.

On Saturday morning, wreckage was spotted by the crew of the Guernsey ferry. They reported it to the coast guard who went out and found the remains of the *Sweet Ruthy*. The yacht had been run down by some larger, heavier, vessel. I returned from France to find a full scale sea search under way, for my wife.

Alex was never found. She was declared lost at sea. With no body, a funeral was out of the question. Neither of us were church-goers, so I settled for a simple act of goodbye on the harbour front. I didn't expect much of a turn-out, but the number of people there on that day surprised and moved me.

Jenny, Alex's assistant, was there of course, with boyfriend Paul and a bunch of her customers. The Swanage Businesswomen's Guild was represented. The Yacht Club too. A small group of neighbours from Portland came, their ranks swollen by a large contingent of locals. Good people, who simply wished to show their respect.

I stood with Lucy on the quayside, at the spot where the yacht was usually moored. The Yacht Club chairman read a short eulogy, then I threw my wreath into the grey harbour waters. Said a silent goodbye to the woman I loved.

The weeks that followed the memorial service were the darkest of my life. I stumbled through each day, barely knowing what I was doing. The agency suffered, whilst I sat at home wallowing in grief and self pity. I kept hoping, against all reason, that one day I would wake up and find the whole tragedy a dream. With Alex lying beside me in our bed. But this was never going to happen, and deep inside I knew it.

The months passed. The dark days of winter became a constant reminder of that other, brighter, light that had gone out of my life. Inevitably, the passage of time and the gradual dawning of a new spring, drew a fragile blanket of numbness over the pain. They dulled its sharpness, but never took it away completely.

In April, with the winter behind me, I threw myself back into my work. Began taking on every assignment I could find, to fill the empty hours.

Without even realising I was doing it, I spent less and less time at home. More and more hours in my office. When I did creep home at the end of each day, usually after an evening meal in one of three pubs, I would turn on the TV, open a bottle of wine, and drink myself to sleep in the chair.

This is what my life had become. Until that night.

5

Ballinger:

In a small barn just outside Sherborne, John Ballinger shook his head in vexation. Picking up a steel ruler he measured the distance between the upper holes on the fuel pump flange then checked the blueprint. The holes were five millimetres out.

Five Millimetres. He could not believe it. How could this happen? Perhaps he needed glasses? Stronger lighting above his workbench? A brain transplant? For a long moment he stared balefully at the fuel pump, almost willing it into spec. Then he shook his head and reviewed his options.

The simplest solution was obvious. Elongate each mounting hole by two and a half millimetres, to make it fit. Who would know? With a sigh, he answered his own question. He would know, of course! And he would never be able to drive the car without reminding himself that although it looked very much the real deal, in one very small detail it did not conform to the original specification.

There was nothing else for it. The flange and pump base would have to be re-cast. It would cost time, and money, but it would teach him to be more careful in future. Especially when drilling out mounting holes.

The sound of the telephone disrupted his thoughts. He set down the fuel pump, crossed the barn, and took down the wall-phone. The caller ID showed the name Lucas Devine.

'Yes?' he asked.

'You're not watching Dutton!' complained Devine.

Ballinger sighed. 'We've had this conversation before. If you want Dutton watched twenty-four seven, then you had better come up with some more money. That way I can hire a second pair of eyes. But it isn't necessary. Right now he'll be at home, where I left him an hour ago. Doing the same thing he does every night. Drinking wine and sleeping it off. So what do you want?'

'You're wrong about Dutton. He's not sleeping. Right now he'll be watching his wife on television. Probably sobering up faster than he's ever sobered up in his life.'

'You're saying she's on TV?'

'From Manchester. Do you have a television?'

'Of course I have a television. Sometimes I even watch it.'

'Watch it now. BBC News channel. Record it if you can.'

'All of it?'

'The piece about Manchester. She's on there - you'll see her. When Dutton sees it he'll go ape. My guess is he'll head up there like a bat out of hell. You just make sure you're right there with him. If he runs straight to her let me know. If not, stay with him until he contacts her: and don't let anyone get there before you.

'Anyone? Like who?'

'You'll know the 'who' when I do. After tonight the whole world and it's mother will be heading north. We need to get there first. Find her, and bring her in.'

'What if he doesn't watch the news?'

'Believe me, tonight he will.'

'Ok. Is that all?'

'You watch yourself up there Ballinger. Dutton's ex-Manchester Police so he'll be back on his own turf. Don't get in his sights. He'll have friends there, still serving. They can make life pretty difficult for you if he thinks you're a threat. I'll send his complete file over so you know exactly who you're dealing with. Looks like things are moving at last! So don't let me down on this.'

The phone went dead. Ballinger hooked it back on the wall. He shrugged off his overalls and left them on the work bench. Flicked off the lights and went outside. Locking up the barn he walked around to the back of his cottage. Let himself in through the kitchen door.

Going through to the lounge he turned on the TV. He went to the BBC news channel and pressed *Record*. Upstairs he showered, slipped into his dressing gown, then moved back down into the lounge. He poured himself a whiskey, stopped the recording, and ran it through on fast-play. When he found the item on the Manchester terrorist arrests, he watched it at normal speed.

He ran the sequence twice. Then paused the image as the woman stepped out onto the street. Carefully he compared the figure on the screen with the photograph he had. Definitely her. How unlucky was that?

Picking up his phone he pressed a key. The call went through to voice mail. 'It's Ballinger,' he said. 'Looks like things are coming to a head. He'll be travelling north to Manchester, either tonight or tomorrow. It's important we know where he's staying. Thanks.'

He closed down the phone. Opened his laptop. Looked up hotels in Manchester and decided on the Copthorne. He rang the number, made a reservation, then returned to his computer. The file on Dutton had arrived. Sipping the whiskey, he read it through.

Much of the information he already possessed. The phone numbers. Email addresses. Makes, models, and registration numbers of the man's cars. But there were other things in the file. Things he hadn't known. Including a copy of the private detective's police service record. He read through the file slowly. When he felt he knew as much as he needed to know, he finished his drink and went to bed.

6

Fallon:

Joey Fallon drove to the T-junction and turned onto the unlit road. With the lights off he coasted down past Dutton's house, then pulled to a rolling stop.

Climbing from the car he strolled back up the road. Settled himself into his usual spot across from the house. He checked the time. Ten o clock. It would be another hour before Dutton set off with his dog.

Dutton was a man of habit. His dog-walking routine took exactly thirty minutes. He always took the same route, at the same speed, and got back at the same time. Which was fine. Thirty minutes gave Fallon plenty of time to do what he had to do.

Gazing across the road he could see lights inside the house. Not bright, probably just a few reading lamps. The curtains were part drawn. There was neither sound nor movement from anywhere within the building.

From the nearby coast came the sound of crashing waves, followed by the rolling sigh of a million shifting pebbles as the tide came in along Chesil beach. It was a mournful sound. Amplified by the stillness of the night. For many, the sound echoed the collective death rattle of countless souls lost at sea. To Fallon it was just noise.

He re-checked his watch. By now he was usually on his own time, with Dutton settled in for the night. But not tonight. Tonight, he'd been told, was crunch time. Which meant that at some time within the next few hours he could expect the man to make his move.

In his pocket Fallon carried a tracker. Pre-set, all he had to do was attach it to the car in the drive when Dutton took his dog for a walk. The device should make it easier to keep tabs on him - or so they said. Fallon was not much into technology.

Later,, he decided, he would drive into Weymouth. Find himself a woman. Unlike Dutton, who in all the time he'd been watching him had never once brought a woman home, or gone out socially with one, Fallon needed a woman from time to time or he'd go crazy. And tonight might be his last chance for a while.

He leaned back against the stone wall. Closing his eyes he pictured himself in his London flat, with one of Levkin's girls. He really did miss those perks. Still, with any luck he'd be back there soon enough, now that things were starting to happen.

Again he checked the time. Surely his watch had stopped? He hated this job. It was unbelievably tedious. He should be in the pub now, enjoying a pint and a game of Crib with the locals. Instead he was stuck here in the bloody dark. Next thing you know it would be raining.

Fallon had been up since before six a.m. Bored and tired he began to drift off, falling asleep on his feet. He neither saw, nor heard, the approaching figure until, from somewhere far too close for comfort, came the sharp, angry, yap of a dog.

7

Dutton:

My first reaction to the shock of seeing my wife on TV was to pour myself another glass of wine. Then I tried to make sense of what I'd just witnessed.

The simplest explanation was that I had seen someone who bore a remarkable resemblance to my wife. Certainly this was the most obvious answer. Yet even as I considered the idea, I knew this wasn't the case.

The woman I had seen on the screen was Alex. I had no doubt of that. She not only looked like her, but moved like her too. And whilst it is surprisingly common to see someone's double, or near double, it is unlikely they would have the same height, build, and muscle movement as the person they resembled. Unless they were identical twins. And to my knowledge, my late wife did not have a twin.

I needed to see the clip again. I switched to the BBC news channel and waited for the headlines to be repeated. As soon as the announcer uttered the words, *in Manchester today*, I pressed the *record* button and downloaded the whole sequence. Ten minutes later I had watched it several times over. The more I watched it, the more convinced I became that it was Alex.

She looked slimmer than I remembered. Had lost weight - more than was good for her, I thought. Gone too was the beautiful, long, blonde, hair. She wore it shorter now. Dyed ginger, in an obvious attempt to change her appearance. But to me she was instantly recognisable.

She had something tucked under her arm, on the other side of her body. I couldn't make out what it was. I watched the screen, my mind in turmoil, still unable to believe what I was seeing. Not daring not believe it. After a long and difficult struggle I had finally come to accept that Alex was gone from my life. That I would never see her, touch her, or hear her voice again. Suddenly this notion had been turned on its head.

A torrent of emotions ran though my brain. The strongest of these was an overwhelming urge to drive to Manchester at once. Tear the place apart until I found her. But I resisted the inclination. Told myself I needed to approach this as I would any other missing person case. Systematically and doggedly, without giving way to irrational impulses.

Yet even as I made my plans, a small voice in the back of my mind was uttering a warning. Reminding me that if Alex really was still alive, then she had gone to enormous lengths to convince the world that she was not. In which case she would almost certainly not wish to be found. Least of all, possibly, by me.

I pushed the thought aside. This was something I'd worry about when I found her. And find her I would, I had no doubt about that. It's what I do, and I do it well.

Downloading the sequence to my laptop, I printed off a still shot of Alex emerging from the café. I packed a suitcase with everything I might need for a few days. Then I slipped into my coat and trainers and took Lucy for a quick stroll.

Normally I would have taken her our usual walk. To help clear my head of the wine I'd consumed. But I was in no mood for this. So instead, I slipped out the back door and cut through the garden. Onto the narrow, rutted, access lane that ran behind the house.

It was dark. But I knew every inch of ground and walked it confidently. A hundred yards on the lane swung left, to join the road on which the house stood. Joining the road I headed back towards my front door. There was no traffic so we stuck to the tarmac, rather than risk a broken ankle on the grass verge.

Thirty yards from the house, with the dog leash gripped in my left hand and my house keys in the other, Lucy suddenly stopped. Her rear legs thrown back, nose held high, she peered into the gloom at something she had seen, or sensed. Then she let out a long, low, growl.

I followed her gaze. Across from the house, by the hedge, was a black shape that resembled a human figure. It was so dark I couldn't be sure so I stood there, watching for signs of movement. A long minute passed without any hint of motion. I tugged at the leash to get Lucy moving and we walked on. After a dozen or so paces she stopped again. Her tail ramrod straight, hackles rising along her back, she gave out a sharp warning bark.

Immediately the black shape detached itself from the boundary wall. Morphed into the figure of a man. Hurriedly he walked off in the opposite direction, staying close to the hedge in an effort to merge into the gloom. Moments later the interior light of a car came on as he climbed in. I heard an engine start up and then the car quickly drove away, without lights.

I carried on to the house. When I reached the front door I looked to the spot where the man had been standing. He had to have been watching the house. A burglar, perhaps, seeing the lone house as an easy target? I would get Bianca to call the security company tomorrow. Ask them to take steps to protect my property whilst I was away.

8
TUESDAY

Dutton:

I didn't sleep that night. Didn't even go to bed. I knew it would be a waste of time. I made myself comfortable on the recliner and dozed fitfully. At one point I was aware of Lucy jumping onto my lap. She was still there, sleeping soundly, at six o clock when I decided it was time to move.

Showered and dressed, I watched the news clip one more time. I experienced an odd thrill of delight and longing when I saw Alex step out onto that street. So I watched it yet again.

Putting the photo-shot into my travel bag I took Lucy for her morning walk. Nodded an absent-minded good morning to the yob as I walked back to the house. After loading Lucy and the rest of my things into the car, I set off for the office.

There were two jobs on the books. Missing housewife, Liz Turner, was one of them. Liz had travelled to St. Malo in the family car, taking her toy boy with her. By now they could be anywhere in Europe, and the case had come to a standstill. Excepting divine intervention, it was likely to remain that way for the foreseeable future.

I called tomato-grower Jack Turner. Told him I still had no news. I asked if he would like me to mark the file *stalled*, and review it from time to time in case anything came along. He told me to forget it. Said he was going to divorce her anyway, which didn't surprise me. I'd always felt he was more upset about losing his car than his wife.

'I've cancelled the insurance,' he told me gleefully. 'Reported the car stolen. Just wait until she gets pulled. Thanks for what you've done Terry. But I'm not going to spend any more on this. She's not worth it. Tell me what I owe you and I'll send you a cheque.' I promised to send him the account then closed the phone.

The other case was teenager Mathew Bramleigh. Mathew, a closet homosexual, had been 'outed' on Facebook by some of his friends (who needs friends like that?). Full of shame and confusion the boy had run away from home, and his parents feared for his safety.

I hated to pass this case to someone else. But I had little choice. At eight-thirty I rang Dennis Worrell at Banner Investigations. Asked if I could lay off the job with him. Dennis and I had a reciprocal arrangement for when either one of us had more than we could handle. He immediately took the job off my hands, leaving me clear.

I faxed all I had on the missing boy to Dennis, penned a note for Bianca telling her where I was going, then left the office. Lucy jumped into the back of the car and settled down behind the dog rail. This was a trip she was definitely making. If any creature on God's earth knew the real Alex Dutton when she saw her, it was Lucy.

My first stop was Swanage. I left the car behind the florist's shop and entered through the back door, like I'd always done. The place was now owned by me, and managed by Jenny. I could have sold it, but for some reason I felt unable to let it go.

I hadn't seen much of Jen in recent months. She and Paul were now married. They'd sent me an invitation to their wedding but I hadn't gone. Weddings are lonely affairs when you've just lost your wife. Now we sat in the back of the shop, drinking coffee and playing catch up. When the shop bell announced the arrival of a customer Jen went through to the counter. On her return I steered the talk towards Alex. Asked what she remembered about the day of the accident.

'I remember being surprised when she said she was going sailing,' she told me. 'She never went sailing on a Friday? It's the start of the weekend! Our busiest time. Mind you, she had come in early that morning. Made up all the orders so I'd only have the counter to deal with. She left about eleven-thirty.'

'Did she seem strange in any way? Behave oddly?'

'She was quieter than normal. Not her usual bubbly self. I've often thought about that. Wondered if she had some kind of premonition? When I asked if everything was alright she said she was fine. That she always got a bit down when you were away.'

'Did she have Lucy with her?'

'Oh yes, she always had Lucy with her. I would have thought it very strange, otherwise. How is Lucy?'

I told her Lucy was fine. Asked if she remembered anything out of the ordinary that had happened in the days, or weeks, leading up to the accident. She thought about this, then shook her head.

'It's been some time. But I really can't think of anything. The only thing that ever happens around here is that people come in for flowers - oh?' she suddenly stopped. 'There was mister Sputnik, of course. But you probably know about him?'

'Sputnik?'

'Didn't she tell you about him? He arrived a couple of weeks before the accident. Rented the apartment on a short term let. His real name was Susnik - something like that. I couldn't get my mouth around his name and kept calling him Sputnik. Alex thought it was funny, so we called him that between ourselves.'

'What was he like?'

'Alright, really. Forty-ish I'd say, though you can't always tell with foreigners, can you? He had ginger hair, cut short, and he looked quite fit. He was a friendly soul. Very chatty. Natty dresser, too. A suit and tie man. Said he was over here on business. Something about a waterfront scheme? Alex liked him a lot. She used to chat to him in Russian.'

'In Russian?'

'Well, in whatever language they spoke. It sounded like Russian.'

'How long was he here?'

She thought about this. 'He was still here at the time of the accident. I remember seeing him there at the memorial. But soon after, the *'To Let'* sign was back on the apartment and I never saw him again.'

I asked the name of the apartment's letting agent. She searched it out and I wrote it down. Then I thanked her for the coffee and prepared to leave.

'Terry has something happened, concerning the accident?'

She obviously hadn't seen last night's news item; or if she had, failed to recognise Alex. 'Don't worry,' I said. 'It's just me! Twelve months on and I'm still trying to get my head around what happened.'

Jen sympathised. Asked if I had thought about counselling. She believed the best therapy was to talk about things. She told me to call in for a coffee and a chat whenever I was in the area. I promised I would, but I knew I wouldn't. The flower shop held too many memories for me. Returning to the car I gave Lucy a gravy bone and a drink, then set off for Manchester.

9

Fallon:

Fallon followed Dutton to Swanage. Watched him drive around the back of the florists. After waiting five minutes he left his car and entered the shop by the front door. When the girl came through to the counter he caught a glimpse of the private detective sitting in the back of the shop, nursing a cup of coffee. He asked for a funeral wreath price-list, then left the shop.

He approached Dutton's car. After looking around carefully he attached the tracker to the underside. Once back in his own car he took out something resembling a sat nav and switched it on. A computer-generated map of Swanage lit up the small screen. It showed the red dot that was Dutton's car lying just off Station Road. Fallon was impressed. Leaving the tracker screen on, he sat back and waited for the investigator to move.

Last night had been a close thing. He had been careless. Complacent. Dutton had almost caught him out. There was a lesson to be learned from that. Even the most predictable person can sometimes do the unexpected.

Thirty minutes later Fallon watched Dutton leave the shop and head out of town. He went after him. Followed him through Dorchester and all the way to

Yeovil. When he was certain the tracker was working properly he dropped back. Pulled onto a trading estate.

He sat watching the red dot on the screen until it joined the north-bound M5, just east of Taunton. Satisfied that his quarry was heading north he took the road back to the coast. He was in no hurry. He could pick up the detective's trail anytime.

An hour later he was back in Portland, approaching the gated meadow where he had lived for almost a year. Driving over the grass he stopped the car in front of a small caravan. He climbed out. The caravan rocked and swayed as the dog, locked up inside, bounced around excitedly at his approach. When he opened the door, the animal leapt out and greeted him boisterously.

Fallon had named the dog Robbie, after Robbie Coltrane, whom he thought it resembled. He had bought it from a busker who worked the Dorchester market. The dog was meant to win public sympathy for the street musician, and increase his takings. But it had had grown up so savage-looking, it scared away more people than it attracted. When Fallon offered to buy the animal, the man was happy to take his money.

Inside the caravan he entered his tiny sleeping space. Pulled a suitcase from the small wardrobe and began filling it with his personal belongings. There wasn't much. A few bits and pieces of clothing. His shaving gear. Toothbrush and other hygiene stuff. Closing the case he took down his Billie Piper pin ups. He rolled them up with great care, and secured them with an elastic band.

Outside he placed the suitcase in the back of the car. Laid the pin-ups on the rear seat. Opening up the tracker screen he checked Dutton's progress. The man was still heading north, closing on the Midlands.

He returned to the caravan. Stripped, showered, then dressed himself in shirt, suit, and tie. The shorts and tee-shirt went into a plastic bag, with the battered trainers. Pulling on his shoes he was ready to leave.

Last night's call from London had been a welcome surprise. Things were moving at last. The woman had been spotted in Manchester, and Dutton was probably heading there now.

Fallon felt his employers had been too circumspect with Dutton. Five minutes alone with the investigator was all *he* would have needed to get everything they wanted to know out of him. But he had not been allowed to touch the man. Too well connected, it seemed. Still, it didn't matter now. The woman had surfaced and things were beginning to happen.

Ready to go, he threw his old clothes into the car and took a last look around. Fallon wasn't sorry to be leaving. He was a city man. He hated the countryside - and the coast. Wasn't sure which he found worse, the deafening silence of open space, or the endless murmur of the sea. Given a choice he'd be on his way back to London now, not Manchester. But any place was better than here.

He watched Robbie busily sniffing around the field. A part of him would have liked to keep the animal, but there was no place for a dog where he was going. Climbing into the car he started the engine and turned onto the road. Drove away without looking back. The dog paused to watch him go, then went back to sniffing the ground.

Five minutes later the Honda pulled into the bumpy access lane behind Dutton's house. Stopping the car Fallon slipped on a pair of surgical gloves. He took his Beretta from the modified glove compartment and tucked it into his jacket pocket. Then he checked his appearance in the interior mirror. He looked good. Felt good, too. Just like his old self.

Leaving the car he pushed his way through a low wooden gate into Dutton's back garden. Selecting a heavy stone from the rockery he hurled it through the kitchen widow. He was not concerned about the noise. There was no one living close enough to hear.

He removed the glass shards from the frame then climbed into the kitchen. A quick look around found no evidence of a silent alarm so he began a systematic search of the house.

Fallon did not believe the 'tragic widower' act Dutton had maintained these past months. He was convinced that the wife's, so-called, fatal accident had been an elaborate scam. Orchestrated, no doubt, by Dutton himself. With any luck there would be proof of this somewhere in the house. Perhaps even some clue to her exact whereabouts.

He was acting outside his remit, he knew. But he didn't care. He was bored with following Dutton around. Now he no longer needed to. The tracker would do the job for him. It even had a playback feature so he could not only see where Dutton was, but also where he had been during the last twelve hours.

Two hours later Fallon had searched the house from top to bottom. He had found nothing. There was a computer in the study that might hold what he was looking for but Fallon knew next to nothing about computers. When he switched it on it asked for a password. He tried Terry: then Dutton: then Lucy. Finally he tried Portland. When none of these worked he threw the monitor to the floor. Put his foot through the screen, in frustration.

In the kitchen he found the garage door keys. They were hanging up with a set of car keys. He went outside and opened up the garage. Sitting inside was Dutton's Ford Explorer. Like the house, a thorough search of the car and garage turned up nothing.

Fallon was not someone who gave up easily. He returned to his car to consider his next move. He knew Dutton worked from an office in Weymouth. It was possible that what he was seeking was there, tucked away inside a safe, perhaps. That was fine with him. Computers might be beyond him, but he knew his way around a safe.

He checked the time. Five o clock. The streets would be full of visitors, shoppers, and workers, on their way home. Better to wait until later when everyone was in the pub having a good time. Tomorrow he had to be in Manchester. Watching Dutton and getting things organised for the arrival of the Kozaks. It would mean an overnight drive, but that was alright. A visit to Dutton's office might make it all worthwhile.

Leaving the island he drove into Weymouth. Pulled onto a supermarket car park and chose a parking bay some distance from the store's main entrance. Tilting back the seat he settled down for a few hours sleep

10

Dutton:

On the long drive north I thought about the things Jenny had told me. Alex's sailing trip that day had not been spontaneous. That much was now clear. She had come into work early, specifically to clear the decks. So she must have decided the night before, if not even earlier, that she was going out in the *Sweet Ruthy*.

That she hadn't mentioned it to me before I left for France was not, in itself, unusual. I had a tendency to fret when she was out sailing alone. She knew this, and would not want me worrying about her whilst I was travelling.

But the very fact that she *had* been alone, now looked very telling. I could not remember Alex ever going out sailing, without having Lucy along for company. Nor could I see any reason for her to drive from Swanage to Portland, leave Lucy at the house, then go back to the harbour and take out the yacht?

The timing didn't add up, either. If Alex left the shop when Jenny said she did, and drove straight home, she would have been at the house by one o clock, latest. Yet she wasn't seen leaving the harbour until five. So why the big hurry to get away from Swanage? And what was she doing for over three hours? Preparing to do her disappearing act, now seemed the obvious answer.

It seemed incredible that these things had raised no suspicions at the time. Her death had appeared to be nothing more than a tragic accident. Now, with the wonderful gift of hindsight, they began to take on a whole new significance.

What, too, should I make of this Russian? Some guy from her own part of the world moves into her old apartment, and she doesn't think it worth mentioning? This was not the chatty woman I had married. But then the woman I had married would not have sailed off as she did, letting the whole world believe she was dead. Now, as the miles slipped by, I tried to understand what would drive her to do such a thing.

Thousands of people vanish in the UK, every year. For almost as many reasons. Most of them turn up, sooner or later. Either they work out their problems, or the problems go away.

Of this huge number, very few go to the extreme length of faking their own death. This is something no one does lightly. It is an extreme reaction to an extreme predicament.

An insurance scam is one motive, though this kind of fraud is rare. Most people who 'kill themselves off' are driven to it by desperation. Like the businessman, or politician, whose world is about to come crashing down because of some unsavoury revelation. Or the guy who finds himself in such mortal danger that the only safe place to be is in the grave.

I wondered which of these categories Alex fell into? And how much of our life together had been a lie. I also wondered about a man who watched my house late at night, and an unknown American who called my home and advised me to watch the television news.

I arrived in Manchester, driving straight into the evening rush hour. Since moving to Dorset I had almost forgotten what a real traffic jam looked like. Finally escaping the M60 at the Sale turn-off, I made my way to a pub in the village of Timperley. Back in the day it was run by a retired police sergeant called George Butler. I hoped he'd still be there.

When I arrived at the Tipsy Fox it looked much the same as it always had. The area around it was a little more built up than I remembered. But then nothing stays the same does it? Pulling in behind the pub I went through the back door and into the bar.

It was early evening. The place was quiet. A young barman, with bright green tufts adorning his otherwise blonde hair, stood behind the bar polishing glasses He was watching a dark-haired girl at the other end of the bar, taking food orders from a small group of business types.

'What can I get you?' he asked when he finally managed to take his eyes off the girl. I ordered a beer. Watched him pour the drink then paid for it.

'Fancy her, do you?' I asked.

'The girlfriend,' he grinned, smugly.

'Lucky you! Is George Butler still here?'

'He is,' he said, handing over my change.

'Could I have a word with him?'

He walked to the far end of the bar, gently palming the girl's bottom as he squeezed past her. He opened a door, stuck his head through it, and yelled up the stairs.

'Grandad, you're wanted!' On his way back he patted the girl's bottom again. She threw him a coy smile then returned to her customers. 'Won't be a minute,' he told me, returning to the beer glasses.

Muffled footsteps on the stairs. Then George came through the door. He looked older. Thinner. His tall, erect, policeman's frame was gone. But the eyes that scanned the room were as bright as ever. Briefly they passed over me then came back. Locked onto my face. Recognition dawned.

'Well I'll be! Its Terry Dutton!' He came round the front of the bar. Stuck out a hand. 'How're you doing lad?'

We shook hands. His grip felt weaker than I remembered. He turned to his grandson. 'Darren, this is Terry Dutton. You'll have heard me talk about him?'

Darren nodded at me. 'The millionaire, right?' he grinned.

I smiled at George's embarrassment. Raised a hand in acknowledgement. George told Darren to pull him a beer and asked if I wanted one. I lifted my glass. 'Not just yet.' When his drink was ready he led me to a quiet corner of the lounge. We sat down.

'Cheers,' he offered.

'Cheers!' We touched glasses to old times.

'So what brings you back here, Terry? Spent all your money and looking to get your old job back?'

'I'm looking for somewhere to stay, to begin with.'

'That's easy. You can stay here.'

'I have a dog with me - and not that kind of dog,' I added quickly, cutting off his grinning retort. 'The four legs and a tail kind of dog. But she's no bother.'

'No problem. You can have the single at the top of the stairs. It's big enough for both of you.' He lifted the glass to his lips. I noticed his hand was shaking. 'So go on then!' he urged. 'What's the story?'

'I'm looking for someone. A missing woman.' I fished a card out of my pocket and handed it to him. He whistled.

'Private investigator, eh?' He looked me over. Nodded approvingly at what he saw. 'Can't say I'm surprised. I didn't think you were the retiring type. And you know what they say? You can take the man out of the uniform, but you can't take the uniform out of the man.'

'Who said that?'

He shrugged. 'Some dead bugger. Shakespeare? Wellington? Karl Marx?'

'Groucho Marx, more like,' I smiled. 'But whoever it was they were probably right. I couldn't think of anything else to do for a living, so I'm still looking for runaways. One of them was spotted in Manchester yesterday. So here I am.'

'Well it's good to see you,' beamed Butler. 'The room's yours for as long as you need it. And since your client will be footing the bill, I won't insult you by offering a discount. Now come on, let me get you another drink. We have some catching up to do.'

We chatted for an hour. I didn't tell him about Alex, but I did give him the rest of my life story since leaving Manchester, if only to save me having to repeat it later to my former colleagues. I had no doubt that by this time tomorrow, news of my return and details of my post-GMP career would be all over Police HQ.

George told me about his illness. He had been diagnosed with Parkinson's disease. Hence the tremors. When I began to commiserate he waved away my sympathy.

'It's early days! And I've had a bloody good life so I can't grumble. Besides, I smoke like a chimney, eat all the wrong things, and drink far more than is good for me. Always have done and I'm not going to stop now. So the chances are, something else will get me before this does.'

Later we were joined by George's wife Annie, from the kitchen. While she and I chatted, George went to the office for a set of keys. 'Door facing you at the top of the stairs,' he told me when he returned, placing the keys on the table.

Making my excuses I went out to the car. I let Lucy have a wander around the car park then took her, with my things, up to the room. I fed her, went down for my own dinner then straight back up to my room, avoiding an all-nighter with George.

Opening my phone I called Bianca. When she answered her voice came through against a background of chatter and music.

'Where are you?' I asked.

'The Twisted Rigging,' she told me. 'Where are you?'

'Timperley, near Manchester. I'm staying at a pub called the Tipsy Fox.'

'You're joking me!' she exclaimed. 'They don't have foxes in Manchester, do they? You'll be telling me next they have cows up there?'

'I've met a few,' I remarked, causing her to giggle. 'Listen, I don't know how long I'm going to be here but

I'll keep you posted. Take some time off if you want. I've laid off the other jobs, so there'll be nothing doing until I get back.'

'Thanks boss,' she shouted, over the noise. 'You had a call this afternoon. Just before I closed up.'

'Who was it?'

'Dunno? Wouldn't leave a name. Sounded foreign. Said he needed to see you urgently. I told him you was away up north, and I didn't know when you'd be back.'

'What did he say to that?'

'Said he'd call back in a few days. Couldn't have been so urgent then, could it?'

'Doesn't sound like it. Listen, do me a favour will you. Call the alarm company tomorrow and ask them to put a couple of alarm boxes on my house. Just boxes. They can do a proper job when I get back.'

'Someone try to break in, then?'

'There was someone hanging around last night. Might have been thinking about it?'

'Okay, I'll call them first thing. Listen boss, I have to go now. It's my turn on the Karioke.'

'Please tell me you're not singing *I Will Survive*!'

'How did you guess?'

I ended the call and sat on the bed. Worked out a plan for tomorrow. I needed to call into Police HQ at some point. They had access to resources I could only dream about, and a little help from that direction would be more than useful. But first I had some groundwork to do. Starting at the place where Alex had been filmed. Which meant a trip into the city centre.

11

Ballinger:

Ballinger packed the holdall. Put it into the Discovery with his laptop, and a dark grey samples case. Locking up the cottage he climbed into the car and checked his phone. There was one text message: *'Gone to Swanage, then Manchester.'* He knew the significance of Swanage. Wondered what had taken the detective to his wife's former place of work.

He headed west. Made for the M5. It was a good five or six hours to Manchester. He didn't know if Dutton was ahead of him or somewhere behind. It didn't matter. Until he found out where the man was staying, there wasn't a lot he could do.

Lucas Devine was convinced that Dutton knew exactly where his wife was. Perhaps he was right? The detour to Swanage certainly suggested a lack of urgency in the man's search for his newly-resurrected wife? Ballinger, however, wasn't so sure.

According to his informant Dutton was still grieving for his wife, and he preferred to go with her judgement. For one thing, women are more perceptive about these things. For another, he doubted that anyone could, or would, keep up that sort of pretence for as long as Dutton had.

But whether the investigator was going to meet with, or simply look for, his wife, Ballinger was determined to be right behind him. For if Dutton was half as good as his record showed, he might just find her.

At a little after two o clock Ballinger turned into Clippers Quay. Pulled into an empty space behind the hotel. He reached into the back of the car, dropped the laptop into the holdall and carried it, with his samples case, into the lobby.

'John Ballinger,' he told the receptionist.

His room was on the first floor, overlooking the dark waters of Salford Quays. He unpacked his bag and opened the laptop. Looked up the address and post code of the sports outlet featured in yesterday's TV news report.

Using Google Earth he checked out the area. Noted the close proximity of a huge shopping mall. He shut down the computer, showered, changed, and returned to his car. Driving into the city he left the car on a shopper's car park then spent the rest of the afternoon familiarising himself with the place.

This was Ballinger's first trip to Manchester. The city was larger, busier, and more commercial than he had imagined. If Dutton's wife was hiding out somewhere in this place, she would take some serious finding.

Once he'd seen all he wanted to see, he made his way back to the Copthorne. After dinner he sat comfortably on his bed working through a Sudoku puzzle book. At nine-twenty his phone beeped. Another text. It read *The Tipsy Fox, Timperley.* He opened the lap top. Looked up Timperley.

Fifteen minutes later he was on the Chester road, passing the Old Trafford football stadium. He drove through the township of Sale, towards Altrincham. Soon he was bearing left for Timperley, and a short time later he pulled on to the car park of the Tipsy Fox. There were six cars there. One of them was Dutton's Audi. He took out his phone and called Devine. Left a message on the man's answering service.

'I've made contact. He's staying at a pub called the Tipsy Fox, in a village called Timperley. Half an hour outside of Manchester.' He ended the call and settled down in his seat. Opened a bottle of water and drank half of it. As he screwed on the bottle top he saw Dutton and his dog stroll through the car park, making for the back door.

Dutton was tall, as befitted an ex-copper of another generation. His prematurely grey hair gleamed silver under the car park's floodlights. He was a big man. Well filled out. Looked strong and reasonably fit, with just enough softness to his shape to suggest that the fat was winning and the muscle losing out.

Ballinger stayed on the car park. When the place called time he watched the locals drifting off home, in various states of insobriety. At just after midnight he returned to the Copthorne.

Back in his room he relaxed for a while. Sipped a whiskey nightcap from the dumb waiter. Finally he set his phone alarm for six am. and went to bed.

12

Fallon:

Fallon stood outside Dutton's office. He checked his watch. Ten o clock, and the street was empty. With luck it would stay that way until the pubs and bars turned out.

He studied the front of the building and immediately began to wonder if he'd wasted his time. The office was situated up above an estate agency. Two separate entrances stood side by side at ground level. Both protected by steel shutters. Mounted high on the wall above the Estate agent's show window were two bright yellow alarm boxes. One for each business, he guessed.

Casually he walked around the block. Came up to the rear of the building. He climbed a wooden gate and dropped into the yard shared by the two offices. The door and windows of the estate agency were protected by the same steel shutters as those at the front. The Abacus door was covered in steel cladding and secured by a mortice lock.

He looked for another way in. There was a soil pipe attached to the wall. Thicker and stronger than a drain pipe, it branched off into the building beneath a small, high, window then continued upwards as far as the eves. Fallon shook his head. It was a long time since he'd shinned up a pipe. He had no desire to re-live the experience.

Besides, even if he found a way into the office there was still the alarm to contend with. Fallon was as useless with intruder alarms as he was with computers. There was no way he could disarm it. He cursed aloud. Half a day lost. Wasted. He could have been in Manchester by now.

As he turned to leave he heard the sound of voices. They were coming from the narrow lane behind the building. Silently he melted into the far corner of the yard. Tucked himself behind an industrial waste bin. He heard the gate being unlocked then it swung open. In the faint light he saw a young couple enter the yard.

Fallon watched them close the gate and walk unsteadily to Dutton's back door. He heard the jingle of keys and the sound of female laughter. Then the door was open, and they both went inside. When the door swung shut he listened for the sound of a turning key but heard nothing.

He waited two minutes then followed the couple. Gripping the door handle he gave it a tug. The door swung open soundlessly. Inside was a flight of stairs leading to the upper floor. Taking out his Beretta he started upwards.

Reaching the top he stepped onto a small landing. To his left a partly-open door led into a short corridor, dimly lit by a low-energy bulb. Three other doorways were visible along the passageway. Two on his left and one on the right. He stepped quickly out of sight when he heard the sound of footsteps. A woman's voice rang out.

'I'll put the kettle on, my love. Make some coffee. I don't want you falling asleep on me like you did the last time.'

A light switch snapped on. He heard the rattle of pots and other utensils. Peering around the door he saw bright light spilling out from one of the doorways on the left. He stepped into the passageway and inched his way along. Reaching the open door he peered in.

It was a small kitchen. The woman stood before a sink unit, her back to the door. She was spooning coffee into two blue mugs sitting on the drainer. On the black worktop beside her, an electric kettle was just beginning to whisper.

Fallon crept up on her, the Beretta raised like a club. He was about to bring it down on her head when an angry bellow roared out behind him. He spun round in time to see a big young man rushing at him, a huge balled fist lifted and ready to strike.

Without even thinking Fallon lowered the gun and pulled the trigger. The bullet went through the man's left eye killing him instantly. His body crashed to the floor as the woman spun round. She looked down at the fallen man, and then at Fallon standing there with the gun in his hand.

The coffee jar fell from her grasp. It hit the floor and bounced, spraying coffee over the dead man's outstretched hand. She opened her mouth to scream, but before she had the chance Fallon smacked her across the side of the head with the Beretta. With a strange, almost graceful, motion she slid to the floor.

He knelt beside the dead man. Turned out his pockets. There was a wallet, a phone, a bunch of keys and some loose change. Inside the wallet he found credit and debit cards, and a driving licence, all in the name of Gary Lapworth. There was also a wad of notes that he transferred to his own wallet.

Below the sink he found a roll of black bin-liners. He tore one off and dropped the contents of the dead man's pockets into it. After making sure the woman was still unconscious he went to check out the rest of the offices.

Next door to the kitchen was the toilet. Across the corridor was Dutton's office. What had looked like a blank wall at the end of the passageway, turned out to be a screen. Stepping around it he found himself in the reception area. There was a small reception desk with telephone, keyboard, and monitor screen. Perched on an upturned drawer below the desk was a printer.

Opposite the desk was a door. Standing against the wall beside it was a row of plastic chairs. On one of them sat the woman's handbag. He crossed to the door and pulled it open. Found himself on another landing, slightly larger than the first. A staircase descended into a short hallway that ran to the front door.

Back in reception he moved to the window and looked down into the street. Across the road an old man was creeping along the pavement, holding onto the wall for support. Drunk as a skunk.

Satisfied no one was showing any interest in the property he turned off the light. Collected the handbag and carried it back to the kitchen. The woman was still out cold. He rifled her bag, took what money she had, then dropped bag, purse, and phone into the bin liner, along with the man's possessions. Tying up the plastic bag he carried it along the corridor and placed it at the top of the rear stairs, to pick up on his way out.

He entered Dutton's office. On the modern desk was a computer monitor. With a cordless keyboard and mouse. Also standing on the leather-inlaid top was a framed photograph of the investigator and his wife. Behind the desk a comfortable swivel chair sat with its back to the window. In one corner stood a locked filing cabinet. In the other, a steel cupboard containing a computer and printer.

Fallon ripped out some of the cables from the computer. Carried them into the kitchen and used them to bind the woman's hands and feet. He studied her as she began to stir. Not bad, he decided, except for the Goth look. He filled a mug with cold water. Let the contents splash down onto her face. She opened her eyes in confusion. Her eyes widened in fear when she saw him.

'Who are you?' he asked.

'Bianca,' she answered. The name meant nothing to him.

'Why are you here?

'I work here!'

'You work for Dutton?'

The girl nodded.

'Who's that?' he gestured at the dead man.

'He's a friend.' She looked at the body. 'Why did you do that?' she sobbed. 'You didn't need to do that.'

'His fault,' said Fallon. 'He came at me like a lunatic!' He gently kneaded the girl's left breast with a gloved hand. 'Came here for a bit of nooky did you, while the boss is away?' She tried to push him away with her tied hands and he slapped her across the face.

'There's just you and me here now, sweetie,' he reminded her. 'Better remember that. If you're nice to me I might just let you walk away from this. First, though, we need to have a little chat. When you've told me everything I want to know we can relax. Have some of that nooky you were looking for. I've never had a Goth before. It'll be a new experience for me.'

13

WEDNESDAY

Dutton:

In the small dining room I sat down to what Annie called a real breakfast. It should have carried a health warning. Well fortified, I then joined the busy traffic heading into Manchester. I knew exactly where the sports outlet store was located and drove confidently into the city centre.

Manchester hadn't changed much. More cycle lanes competed with more bus lanes, threatening some very painful confrontations. There were also more traffic-free zones and one-way systems than there used to be. But everything else was much the same as it had been when I worked there.

I made my way to the Arndale multi-storey. Drove up the ramp and left the car in the first empty space I came to. Then I made my way back down into the street.

When I arrived outside the sports outlet store, I positioned myself more or less where the TV reporter had been standing. I looked directly at the store front and followed the line that Alex had taken when she walked out of camera shot. It led straight to a side entrance of the Arndale shopping centre. Two hundred, plus, stores: twenty-five eateries: sixty fashion shops:

and sixteen health and body boutiques. That narrowed it down some.

I crossed the paved area. Entered the cafeteria next to the store and ordered a coffee. When it arrived I gave the waitress one of my cards. Asked if I could speak to the manager. The manager, who turned out to be the proprietor, came at once. No doubt wondering why a private investigator was sitting at one of her tables.

'How can I help you, mister Dutton?'

'Terry,' I said, inviting her to sit. She perched on the edge of the chair opposite. Ready to make a quick escape if this turned out to be some kind of sales pitch. Taking out the picture of Alex I passed it to her. She studied the photograph for a moment then looked at me quizzically.

'Her name's Alison.' I lied. 'A stay-at-home mum, married to a local bank manager. Two years ago she started playing on-line bingo. Boredom, I suppose. From there she graduated to more serious on-line gambling, and very quickly caught the bug. Trouble is, she wasn't very good at it. So she ended up with a mountain of debt.'

The woman gave a brief, sympathetic, nod. I went on. 'When the cards maxed out, the money supply dried up. To keep the card companies off her back, and feed her addiction, she turned to a money lender. A loan shark. Inevitably it wasn't long before she found herself unable to pay him back, either.

The lender was a helpful soul. He suggested that she pay him back in some other way, if you know what I mean. Told her that if this arrangement was not suitable, he could always call into her husband's bank and ask him for the money she owed.

Alison was desperate. So desperate, she just walked away from it all. From her home, her husband, even her children. She left behind a letter, explaining what she'd done. Saying how sorry and ashamed she was.

Her husband was pretty frantic, as you can imagine. He reported her missing. The police were sympathetic, but not very helpful. Unless there is some suggestion of foul play, there isn't a lot the police can do if an adult chooses to leave home.

After hearing nothing for twelve months he was convinced his wife was dead. He could not believe she would leave her children and never come back.' I tapped the photograph. 'Then two days ago he saw that.'

'Who took it?' she asked.

'The BBC. The day of the anti-terrorist raid, next door.'

'Oh, I remember her now! She was on the telly, wasn't she? She came out of here while they were filming.' She studied the photograph again. 'She's a bonny woman. What happens if you find her and she doesn't want to go back? You can't force her, can you?'

I shook my head. 'No one can make her go back: and it's not my job to try. I'm instructed only to give her a letter from her husband, asking her to come home. He doesn't care what she did. He's paid off the debts and just wants her back. So do the children. My guess is she'll jump at the chance.'

She looked again at the picture. Holding onto it she climbed to her feet. 'Stay there and enjoy your coffee.

I'll go and ask the girls. They'll be more open with me than with a stranger.'

I thanked her and did as she said. In less than five minutes she was back, a young waitress in tow.

'Tell him!' she said.

'She was here,' the girl confirmed. 'Monday. I served her.'

'Has she been here before?' I asked.

She nodded. 'A few times. She always comes upstairs and sits in the back corner. That's where my tables are.'

'Back corner? Away from the windows?'

'Yes. Right at the back of the room.'

That made a sort of sense. 'What do you make of her?'

'She's not a shopper. You can tell when a woman has her shopping head on, and she never has any bags. Not even a handbag. I think she's a floor walker, or office worker, popping out for a coffee. She could be a company rep I suppose? But she doesn't dress like one.'

'Does she carry a brief case? Laptop? Anything like that?'

The girl shook her head. 'She has a cardboard tube.'

'A cardboard tube?'

'Like students use. To carry their artwork.'

'And that's all she was carrying?'

'That's all she ever has. She keeps her money in a small purse, in her pocket.'

'Does she talk to you?'

Again she shook her head. 'Not really. Just hello and thank you. She never has much to say, and I don't push it. If a customer wants to talk I listen. If not, that's their business.'

'Does anyone ever come in with her?'

'Not that I can remember.'

'What's your impression of her?' I asked.

The girl didn't have to think about this. 'She looks sad. That's how I recognised her. We give names to our regulars. She's my sad lady.'

There was nothing I could say to that. I thanked the girl and her boss and asked for my bill.

'Have it on the house,' said the proprietor. She sent the waitress back upstairs and returned to my table. 'I hope you don't mind, but would you do something for me?' She handed me a business card. 'If you find her, and she goes back home, will you let me know?'

I put the card in my pocket. 'Of course I will: and if she comes in again will you give me a call? I promise I won't harass her.'

'It's a deal,' she smiled, and then returned to her office.

I finished the coffee feeling strangely guilty about lying to the woman. Sometimes lying is necessary to get people to open up to you. On this occasion it wasn't even a big lie. I had merely changed the circumstances of Alex's leaving. The need to find her and get her back home was no lie.

Mulling over what the waitress had said I found the tube business intriguing? No handbag, but carrying a cardboard tube? This ruled out her being both shopper and business rep. What woman goes shopping without her handbag? And most female reps I've met wouldn't be seen dead without a bag over her shoulder, and a laptop in her hand.

I found myself drawn towards the same conclusion as the waitress. Alex must work somewhere close by. Slip out occasionally for a quick coffee in the cafeteria. But what was with the tube? As far as I was aware, apart from cabin crew there was only one kind of work my wife had ever done.

Leaving the cafeteria I followed in Alex's footsteps and entered the Arndale Centre. Began searching for florists. It didn't take long. There wasn't much to find. Just a few flower stalls in the market area, and there was no sign of her amongst them. Nor did showing her picture bring any response from the stall holders.

I widened my search. Combed the surrounding streets. There were several flower shops and kiosks dotted about the city centre. But no Alex.

At lunchtime I collected a ham sandwich, a cream doughnut, and a coffee. Back at the car I gave Lucy a drink of water, let her stretch her legs around the car park, then shared the sandwich with her. I called Bianca to update her but she didn't answer my call. Probably hung-over.

Back at the shopping centre I began a systematic tour of every shop and store in there. Showed her picture to at least one member of staff, each place I called. If Alex worked in any one of them, she would surely be recognised.

The closest I got to a result was the elderly man on the shopping centre's main enquiry desk. He took a long hard look at the picture. 'I've seen her!' he told me. 'Definitely seen her! Trouble is, I can't remember when? We get hundreds of folk at the desk here, every day. She could have been any one of them. But I'm sure

I know the face!'

I handed him my card. Asked him to give me a call if he remembered anything more, or saw her again. He promised he would but I wasn't holding my breath. I suspected that five minutes after I left, he'd have forgotten all about me.

A long time later I'd visited almost every outlet in the Mall. Showed her picture to countless people. Found no one who recognised her. But it was progress: of a sort. I left the mall seventy-five per cent certain that she didn't work there. Nor in its immediate vicinity. Three to one. Not bad odds.

It was late when I got back to the car. Lucy looked at me accusingly so I took her on another short tour of the car park. A drink and a couple of gravy bones and she was wagging her tail again. She's easily bought that one.

After an exhausting day I climbed behind the wheel. Took the down-ramp into the rush-hour traffic, and headed back to my hotel.

14

THURSDAY

Ballinger:

Ballinger was on the road for seven am. The previous day he had followed Dutton to the shopping centre and watched him at work. The man was doggedly thorough. Doing exactly what he himself would have done, but with little apparent success. In the end it had turned into a very long day. With little to show for it.

There was one positive to come out of it, though. He was now certain that the man had no idea where his wife was. No one would spend so much time and effort on such a futile exercise, just for show.

At some time after midnight Ballinger had called Devine. Left a brief summary of his day on the man's answer service. The American would not be pleased with his assessment, and when his phone sounded as he drove along Chester Road he knew who it would be. He pulled in outside a Dental Surgery.

'Yes?'

'You sure about Dutton?' asked Devine. 'He isn't just playing you?'

'How could he? He doesn't know I'm on him! Look, whatever you want to believe, I look at Dutton and all I see is a driven man, desperately searching for his wife.'

There was a moment's pause. Then, 'I guess the good news is that if anyone can find her, he will. The bad news is, you've got company.'

'Go on?'

'The Kozaks are here. Arrived in Manchester last night, with Janko Petrovich.'

'Janko who?'

'Petrovich. Their bodyguard. They were picked up from the airport by some guy called Fallon.'

'Joey Fallon!' stated Ballenger. 'Didn't think it'd be long before he turned up.'

'You know him?

'A Bethnel Green boy. One of Dooby Levkin's hatchet men. He's been staying in a small caravan - that's a trailer to you - on a farm in Portland. Keeping an eye on Dutton. He told the farmer he's a writer, working on his next book. Should make an interesting read. A short one too.'

'Why didn't you tell me about this guy Fallon?' Devine sounded strangely unsettled.

'You didn't ask: and I assumed you'd know about him. You seem to know everything else. I thought he might be working for you? Watching me, watching Dutton. We all know how devious you Yanks can get.'

'Well he's not working for us. He's working for the Kozaks. And the fact that they're in Manchester means they know at least as much as we do. So you'd better keep an eye on this Fallon guy. On all of them, in fact. I don't want them finding the woman before we do.'

'Where are they now?' Ballinger asked.

'A rented house, just outside a village called Ladymere. A few miles from the airport.'

'Do you have an address?' Devine gave him the address and he wrote it down. 'How do you know all this?' He asked.

'Interpol. They like to keep tabs on the Kozaks.'

'So they're under surveillance?'

'Not constant surveillance. Interpol just likes to know where they are. So they monitor their movements when they travel.'

'Are you telling me you get Interpol reports?'

Devine chuckled. 'We *read* Interpol reports. It's not quite the same thing. But hey, we're all on the same side, aren't we?' He went on more seriously. 'This Fallon guy. What's he look like?'

'Evil little troll. Face like a gargoyle. Dresses like a circus clown. Do you know him?'

'Nah! Just wondered, is all.' On this note Devine ended the call.

Back on the road Ballinger tried to work out how this new development would affect him. The Kozak brothers shouldn't be a problem. Not yet. They'll stay on the sidelines. Let others do the legwork until the woman is found. But with Fallon, and possibly the Serbian bodyguard, joining in the hunt, things were likely to get a little crowded. Dangerous, too.

Ballinger knew of Fallon's reputation. Had even met him once. Not for nothing was he called Loon by his peers. He was a psychopath. Dangerously unpredictable with a keen sense of self-preservation. He was also street smart enough to have avoided arrest, despite a long criminal career. Devine was right. He'd need careful watching.

15

Dutton:

Before leaving that morning I asked George how many of the lads I'd worked with, were still at Chester House.

'None,' he said. 'They closed the place down. Moved the whole headquarters across town to Central Park. That's in Newton Heath. Just off Oldham road. Might have been a good move for them, but it didn't do much for us. Took away half our customers. Left us high and dry. Some days I don't know why I bother opening up.'

'You were busy enough the other night?'

'The bed and breakfast helps. We have our regulars - reps and other visitors to the trading estates. But with business expenses cut to the bone, no one puts much across the bar anymore. Come Friday, and they're all gone. It's like a graveyard in here at weekend.

Then there's our Darren. He can't find a job. So I'm having to pay him money I don't have, just to keep him off the streets. God knows how long that can go on? Perhaps I should sell up. Go and buy a place in Newton Heath?'

'It might work!' I offered. 'Most of the lads I knew would be in there, propping up your bar.'

'There's not many left. Most have been moved out into Divisions. Steve Baker's still there I think, with the drug squad. Dave Rogers - he's in firearms training. Oh, and your old mate Tony Hale. He's still there.'

'Tony?' This did surprise me. 'I thought he was in Canada?'

Tony Hale had been a DI in serious crime when I was in Manchester. A graduate like me, we had climbed through the ranks together. When I left Manchester he was all set to move to Canada, and a new career with the Royal Canadian Mounted Police.

'He never got there,' George informed me. 'His father-in-law died suddenly, and his missus wouldn't leave her mother. So they didn't go. It's Superintendent Hale now, by the way. He's joined the upstairs brigade. Something to do with gang crime. There's one or two of the lads that live over this way, drop in occasionally. Keep me up to speed with what's going on there. But it's not like it was in the old days. You couldn't move for coppers in here.'

Leaving the Fox I drove into Manchester. Joined the inner ring road and followed the signs for Oldham. I headed east out of the city and when I reached Newton Heath, turned into the Gateway. At the top of the avenue was Central Park.

The place was impressive. Very modern. A long way from the concrete obelisk that was Chester House. I pulled onto the small visitors car park and went through the main entrance. Asked for Superintendent Hale.

'Do you have an appointment?' the receptionist asked.

'We're old colleagues,' I told her. 'From Chester House. Can you tell him DI Terry Dutton is asking for him.'

'Are you on the visitors' car park?'

I told her I was. She took my registration number then made the call. Pointed to a row of seats.

'Take a seat, Inspector. Superintendent Hale will be down shortly.' I didn't disabuse her about my current lack of status. It wouldn't help.

Five minutes later a door swung open and Tony Hale came bouncing through. Spotting me he walked across the lobby, hand outstretched. I stood up and we shook hands warmly.

'How are you doing Terry?'

'Pretty good,' I answered. 'You?'

'Keeping busy,' he replied. 'Come on, I have time for a quick coffee.' He opened the doors with a pass-card and ushered me through. As we walked along a wide corridor my phone sounded. I took it from my pocket and shut it down.

'She thinks you're job,' he said, referring to the receptionist. 'Civilians are supposed to have a visitor's pass, but I can't be arsed going through all that. Not with you, anyway. As long as you're with me, no one will bother.'

We entered the canteen. Hale pointed me to a table and went to the service counter. I sat down and studied him as he collected the drinks. He looked heavier than I remembered. Uniforms tend to slim people down but Tony had put on weight since we last met. That's what a desk job will do, I suppose. Carrying a tray he came to the table.

'Coffee, milk and two sugars, and a KitKat,' he said, placing the drink and chocolate biscuit before me.

'Nothing wrong with your memory then?'

'Happy days, Terry,' he grinned, raising his cup. 'Here's to good old Chester House. You know they're pulling it down, don't you?' I didn't know. So we drank to happy days and old friends. He put down his coffee. Waved an arm expansively. 'So what do you make of this place? Feels like I'm walking into a clinic each time I come through the door. It's all so clean, and soulless. Not a hint of stale tobacco smoke anywhere.'

'Nice looking building, though. I'm sure you'll get used to it.'

'I haven't enough service time left to get used to it!'

'How's Kathy?' I asked.

He shrugged. 'All right, I suppose. We're divorced.'

'Oh, I'm sorry!'

'It's been a while. It was that Canada business that soured things. I thought we both wanted the same things from life. Obviously we didn't. But then you've been there, haven't you?'

I nodded. 'I got married again. To a florist.'

'A florist, eh? I'm glad to see all that money didn't go to your head.'

'Did you think it would?'

'No mate! Not in a million years. But people do change with their circumstances. Sometimes it's unavoidable.' This was quite deep for Tony. Then suddenly he grinned. 'But you haven't changed at all, have you? Still looking for lost souls, I hear?' Good old George.

'It's a living,' I smiled.

'An interesting one too, I'll bet. So, go on then?' he prompted. 'Is this a social visit? Or is there some way in which this vast machine that is the Greater Manchester Police force can assist you?'

'How did you know?' I asked, sheepishly.

'Hmm!' He studied me for a moment then checked his watch. 'Tell you what Terry, we've got this big, anti-gang, initiative about to go live. So I need to be somewhere else quite soon. Why don't we meet up later. I'll come over your way. See you in Liners, about seven o clock? We can eat there. It'll give you a break from Annie's cooking. Give me a break from mine, too!'

'Alright,' I agreed, wondering if he really was that busy. We chatted a while longer about the old days then finished our coffees. Tony escorted me back to reception and we shook hands until later.

Back in the car I switched on my phone. Checked my voicemail. There was one message. 'Terry, it's Jenny. Something weird has happened. Call me, will you?'

I called back the number. 'Hi Jen, what's wrong?'

'Terry,' she said, excitedly. 'You'll never guess who was in the shop yesterday?'

'The Dalai Lama?'

'Don't be silly! I had Mister Sputnik in here. You remember, I told you about him?'

'Yes I remember.'

'He turned up yesterday morning. Just walked in, large as life. Asked if anyone had been enquiring about Alex in the last day or two.'

'What did you say?'

'I told him the only person I'd spoken to about Alex

was you. He asked when that was and I told him Tuesday. I hope I haven't spoken out of turn?'

'No, that's okay Jen. What did he say to that?'

'Nothing? He just smiled and walked out of the shop. Didn't even ask how I was. It was so weird.'

'Jen, when this bloke was using the apartment did he and Alex spend much time together? Or was it just polite chat, in passing.'

'I don't know how much time they spent together. I was out doing deliveries half the time. He called in most evenings before going up to the apartment. He was always pleasant. Used to crack jokes. Make us laugh. Sometimes Alex made coffee and they sat in the back, chatting. But I don't know what they talked about.'

'I really don't know what to make of this,' I said, truthfully. 'But try not to worry. He's probably harmless enough.'

'Strange though, isn't it? We were only talking about him the other day?' She hesitated a moment before continuing. 'Terry, what's going on? First you turn up: and now him? What are you not telling me?'

What could I say? Certainly not the truth. I resorted to lying again. 'Alex's family are making waves,' I said. 'They don't believe she's dead. They're suggesting she might have gone off with someone. Used the accident to cover her tracks.'

'Oh that's rubbish!' she asserted indignantly. 'Where have they got that idea from? You don't believe that, do you?'

I didn't answer. There was a silence, and then the penny dropped. 'My god you do, don't you? That's why you were here, asking about that morning? And now he's back, nosing around. Do you think she's with him?'

'To be honest, I don't know what to think. I'm just keeping an open mind, that's all. Perhaps they know something I don't, who can say? But I am checking it out. Looking for anything that might point that way, or not.'

'Well I don't believe Alex would do something like that. But I can understand how this might make you feel. If what they're saying is true, it means she's still alive? Terry you really mustn't build your hopes up on some wicked rumour. The most obvious explanation is usually the most valid. You know that.'

'Don't worry Jen. I'm just looking into it that's all. I don't really believe it. As soon as I've worked it through I'll give you a call. Let you know how things stand. Is that alright?'

'It is. And if I see Mr Sputnik again I'll let you know.'

'You do that Jen, and thanks.' I closed the phone. Although I had lied, I felt a kind of relief. Without giving too much away, I'd prepared Jenny for what might well be the inevitable consequences of my search.

The sudden re-appearance of this Russian was an interesting development, too. It looked like I wasn't the only one prodded into action by Alex's impromptu appearance on TV.

16

More legwork. From Central Park I returned to the city centre. Widened my search area. Canvassed those places I'd missed yesterday, in and around the Arndale Centre. Then I moved on to Shudehill, and the old Royal Exchange shopping complex. Finished up in St. Ann's Square. All were within easy walking distance of the cafeteria. Once again I drew a blank. Late in the afternoon, weary and dispirited, I returned to my hotel.

I took Lucy for a walk then called into the bar. Told Annie I wouldn't be in for dinner and went up to my room. I climbed onto the bed. Stretched out my tired legs, and began to doze. Disturbed by my own snoring I shook myself awake. Reaching for my phone I called Andy Morton.

Andy and I sometimes played pairs golf together. I'm not sure why. He consistently plays a worse game than I do. But he's a big noise in the local planning office, which makes him a good contact to know.

'What's up?' he asked.

'I've just heard the Russians were in Swanage last year. Sounding out some waterfront development. Do you know anything about this?'

'I don't remember hearing anything? Has anyone got

money for that sort of thing these days?'

'The Russians might?'

'Well some of them are pretty loaded, that's for sure. Leave it with me Terry. I'll have a word with someone in Purbeck. See what they know. When are we talking here?'

'September last.'

'September? Wasn't that when - '

' - Alex had her accident,' I finished for him.

'Sorry Terry,' he apologised. 'Leave it with me, mate. I'll get back to you.'

'Thanks!' I closed the phone. Readied myself to go out.

Tony was already there when I arrived at Liners Inn. I was pleasantly surprised. After an unproductive day I'd got it into my head that he wouldn't show. That his 'anti-gang initiative' was simply an excuse to cut my visit short. Save him the embarrassment of having to turn down my request for help.

It was mid-week. The restaurant was only half full and we were immediately shown to a table. We ordered our meals and drinks then spent time chatting about our current careers. The food, when it came, was certainly a step up from Annie's at the Fox. Three courses later we drank our coffees and got down to business. I showed him the picture of Alex.

'Good looking woman,' he studied the photograph. 'This your miss-per?'

'It is,' I confirmed. 'She's also my wife.'

He looked at me in surprise. '*Your wife?* Bloody hell Terry, I wasn't expecting that. Your wife, Jesus! What's the story on that?'

I told him everything. Right from Alex's presumed drowning, to her appearance on television. I told him about the man Susnik who arrived on scene just before the supposed fatal accident: and the phone call I had received alerting me to the newscast.

Tony listened intently. He threw in the occasional question then asked about the cafeteria. 'Have you been there? Talked to the staff?'

I nodded. 'First place I went. She's been there before, it seems. Several times. I spoke to the waitress who served her. She doesn't have her down as a shopper. More likely someone who works, or lives, in the area.

'There's not much living accommodation around there. Lots of shops and offices, not to mention the rag trade outlets.' He looked at me carefully. 'You have considered the possibility that she won't want to be found?'

'I have. But Tony, there's no way she went to all that trouble just to get away from me. She didn't need to. She could have left anytime. I wouldn't have liked it, but I wouldn't have made her stay against her wishes.' I took back the photograph and looked at it. 'I think she's in some kind of trouble: and whatever it is, I think I deserve the chance to help put things right. For both our sakes.'

'And if you can't?'

'Then it won't be for want of trying.'

He studied me for a moment then nodded. 'Alright, how can I help?'

'Somewhere in street surveillance you'll have her on

video that morning. With that anti-terrorist operation going down, the whole area would be covered. I need to know where she went from that cafeteria. This is a big city. I don't mind doing legwork - in fact I've done a lot already - but it would be a big help if your people could narrow things down for me.'

He thought about this. 'Well, you have a starting point? And a time? It shouldn't be too difficult to pick her up. The cameras in the Arndale Centre might be a problem - if that's where she went. They're operated by their own security people. You'll have to get their co-operation to check those?'

'I'll sort that.'

'You know I can't just go and commandeer the videos and a couple of bodies to scrutinize them, just to help out a mate?'

'I'm going to have to make her disappearance official, aren't I?'

'You're going to have to make her either a victim, or a criminal. Since you have no evidence that she is in any sort of danger, then it looks like it will have to be the latter.'

'She faked her own death,' I reminded him. 'That's a crime isn't it?'

'It's a grey area. If it involves fraud then yes, it is. But if there's no monetary gain involved or no criminal intent, I'm not so sure. On the other hand, deliberately setting out to wreck an expensive yacht that doesn't belong to you? Has to be a crime in anyone's book.'

'Serious criminal damage?' I exclaimed.

'You'll need to file a complaint. Show reasonable grounds to believe she's here in Manchester - which you can. That'll give us justification for a camera sweep. You can withdraw the complaint at some later date. Happens all the time in domestics, you know that.'

'Okay,' I agreed.

'Come to Central Park tomorrow. Ask for Inspector Peter Leckonby. Tell him what your wife did, and your reasons for believing she is here. I'll fill him in on the rest, and I'll tell him to keep it discreet. We don't want everyone at Central Park knowing your business.'

'Thanks Tony. I'm very grateful.' I looked at him hopefully. 'There's something else,' I said.

'Go on?'

'A full profile search would be useful. To find out who she has over here in the way of relatives, or former associates. If she saw herself on television the other night, she might have already done a runner. If that's the case, I need to know where she might have run to.'

'How much do you know about her already?'

'Her name is Alexana Morel. She is thirty-two, and comes from Limbazi in Latvia. She has an aunt who was into flower arranging, and she was a stewardess with Air Baltic.'

He waited, but I had nothing to add. 'That's it?' he asked. 'That's all you know about her?'

I shrugged. 'What more did I need to know? Her past is her past. We all have one of those.'

'You must have fallen for her hook, line, and sinker, Terry,' he smiled, sadly. 'For a copper - even an ex-copper - you showed a remarkable lack of curiosity.' He leaned forward. Regarded me seriously. 'She's from Eastern Europe, man. Eastern Europe! They're not the same as us. We have a past. They have history.'

He was right. I had simply taken Alex at face value as, indeed, she had taken me. But isn't that what you do when you love someone? Asking for references is not going to do much for any relationship.

'Does she have any family, back in Latvia?'

'Yes. Somewhere in Limbazi - or so she said. But I don't know much about them.'

He sighed. 'Ok. Give Peter everything you do know about her. If there's anything out there, he'll find it. But don't come in too early. Give me a chance to brief him.'

I thanked him for his help. We exchanged phone numbers, and then left the restaurant.

17

Ballinger:

Ballinger followed the two men from Liners and hurried to his car. Ignoring Dutton he watched the other man climb into a Jaguar then followed as it left the car park.

He stayed with the Jag, past Old Trafford and the Copthorne. When his quarry cut through the edge of Salford Quays he went with it, dropping well back on the empty road. Passing a small Travellers' encampment they turned right, into a wide access avenue lined with tram tracks.

They stayed with the tracks for a while. Lost them when the rails curved off to the left. Keeping straight on brought them onto the A6 and from there they joined the East Lancs Road. Soon they turned off towards the suburb of Worsley. Ballinger killed his lights. He stayed well back as the Jag entered a private housing estate. When it turned into the drive of a small bungalow he pulled into the kerb.

Dutton's dinner companion climbed out. Opened the door of an attached garage. He went back to the car but didn't get back in. Instead he stood there, staring across the roof of the vehicle. Ballinger froze. The man appeared to be looking right at him.

The moment passed. The Jaguar driver climbed in behind the wheel and quickly rolled the car into the garage. The door came down and seconds later lights blinked on inside the bungalow.

Ballinger made a mental note of the address and reversed back down the avenue. He thought he saw a figure appear at the window of the bungalow. Then the place was lost from sight as he rounded a bend in the road.

Back on the East Lancs he headed out of the city. The busy trunk road linked Manchester to its great industrial rival, Liverpool. It was humming with trucks and other commercials, taking advantage of the absence of day-time traffic. Picking up the ring road signs he joined the M60. Stayed with it as far as the Chester road exit then turned off.

Leaving the slip road he drove once more through the township of Sale and headed for Timperley. When he reached the Tipsy Fox, Dutton's Audi was sitting in its usual place on the car park. Ballinger gave it half an hour, then called it a night.

Back in his room he opened the laptop. He typed in the address of Dutton's associate and emailed it off. Then he called Devine.

'I've sent an address,' he told the answering service. 'I need to know who lives there.'

18

FRIDAY

Ballinger:

On Friday morning Fallon showed up. As Ballinger approached the Tipsy Fox he spotted the blue Honda. It was sitting in the lay-by that he himself had been using to watch the hotel. Fallon was behind the wheel.

Ballinger drove on. He passed the hotel then turned left, into an avenue of semi-detached houses. Half way down the avenue he did a three point turn, then drove back up towards the highway. He pulled in to the kerb, just short of the junction with the busy road. From where he sat he would clearly see Dutton's car pass by, and the Honda, as they drove into the city.

Five minutes later his phone sounded. He answered it without taking his eyes off the road ahead. It was Devine. 'That address you sent me. Owner-occupier by the name of Anthony Hale. According to the GMP listings, a Superintendent Anthony Hale heads their South Manchester, gang-related crime unit.'

'They had dinner together,' Ballinger reported. 'Very cosy.'

'Probably fishing for help,' suggested the American. 'With luck he might get it. Any sign of the opposition yet?'

'Fallon's out there this morning. Watching Dutton. I'll be watching them both.'

'Good luck.' The man rang off. Ballinger took a quick glance at his watch. It was almost eight o clock.

Twenty minutes later Dutton's Audi cruised past. Close behind was Fallon. Ballinger eased his own car into the traffic flow and headed into the city, staying two cars behind the Honda. He didn't bother watching Dutton. Wherever he was going, Fallon was going too.

Soon he recognised the route they were taking. Took a guess at where they would end up. Sure enough, he once again found himself driving up the ramp of the Arndale Centre's multi-storey car park. Fallon pulled into a slot, six bays beyond the private investigator's car. Ballinger moved into a parking line further back, from where he could see both vehicles.

Leaving the car he followed the two men down the stairs, into the shopping complex. Fallon stuck closely to Dutton. Too closely, in Ballinger's opinion. Neither man looked back as they walked down the long indoor mall. Both were totally oblivious to the fact that they were being followed.

Halfway down the mall Dutton stopped. He approached a security guard and extended an arm upwards, pointing at the high ceiling. Ballinger followed the gesture. Dutton appeared to be pointing to a security camera. The guard responded by using his hands to give out a series of directions. Dutton thanked him, and abruptly turned back the way he had come.

Ballinger smiled as Fallon was caught out by the sudden about turn. The man quickly looked away from the approaching investigator. He stood gazing into the empty window of a closed down store. If Dutton noticed this odd behaviour he showed no sign of it. Passing Fallon he walked back fifty yards then entered a deep recess. Inside were two banks of elevators and a car park pay station.

From across the mall Ballinger watched Dutton step into one of the elevators. Fallon didn't go with him. He hung back until the door closed, and then moved in. He stood watching the numbers on the floor indicator. When it stopped he called another elevator and set off in pursuit.

Ballinger didn't follow them. With one man off the radar, and the other acting like a keystone cop, he decided to return to his car. It wasn't difficult to work out what Dutton was doing. He was going to the security office to get access to the cameras. Once again he found himself admiring the man's diligence and persistence.

Fifteen minutes later Fallon returned to his car. He looked peeved and frustrated. Ballinger studied the man. He hadn't changed much since they last met. Still an over-flashy dresser. Still short and ugly, with close-cropped hair, Fallon carried the unmistakable aura of a violent career criminal. It didn't need a fortune teller to predict that some day he would come to a bad end.

The private investigator was gone for an hour. Then Ballinger spotted him approaching from a different direction. He climbed from the Discovery, strolled casually across to the stairwell pay-station to pay the parking fee, then returned to his car. He didn't hurry. Dutton always took time out to tend to his dog before leaving.

When the Audi finally moved out he waited. He expected the blue Honda to follow. But Fallon didn't move. Not wishing to lose his primary quarry, Ballinger set off in pursuit of Dutton.

Staying with the investigator he checked the mirror from time to time, looking for the Honda. There was no sign of it. The route they were taking was at once familiar. Dutton was returning to police headquarters. Ten minutes later Dutton's car turned into Gateway and headed for Central Park.

Ballinger didn't go with him. He turned right, then right again, into a narrow roadway and stopped. Across a grass verge, dotted with shrubs, he had a good view of Oldham Road and the wide entrance into Gateway.

Five minutes later the Honda appeared. It entered Gateway and drove on towards police HQ. Ballinger cursed himself. He had underestimated the opposition. The man hadn't followed Dutton from Weymouth to Manchester. He didn't need to. There was a tracker on the investigator's car showing Fallon his every move.

He opened the water bottle. Took a slow drink. The return visit to Central Park suggested that Dutton was, indeed, about to receive some support from the police. Settling down in his seat Ballinger made himself comfortable. He thought he might be in for a long wait, and he was right. A much longer wait than he could have anticipated.

19

Dutton:

The director of security at the Arndale Centre was very co-operative. For a small administration fee he offered up copies of everything the security cameras had picked up on the day of the anti-terrorist swoop. It probably helped that I could claim to be working with the police, and was able to drop Hale's name as a reference.

While we waited for the discs to be cut I was given the grand tour, starting with the bank of manned screens that covered every inch of the huge Mall. The director was very proud of his kingdom, and was happy to show it off.

He explained how his small force of security guards operated. How they communicated with each other. How they co-ordinated their response when gangs of shop lifters, pick-pockets, and other unwelcome visitors, invaded the mall. It was almost an hour before I returned to the car with the discs. Lucy was ready for a biscuit and a drink. So I gave her both, then set off for Central Park.

On arrival I asked at the desk for Peter Leckonby. The Inspector was in his mid-thirties. He was bright, intelligent, and well turned out in an immaculately pressed uniform. Obviously a man who took great pride in his appearance. I'd met a lot of police officers like this. Not all of them had been good cops.

He ushered me into an interview room. Took a long statement about the yacht, and the part my wife must have played in her loss. For the profile search he took as many details about Alex as I could give him, which didn't take long. With this done, he generated the statutory crime and case reference numbers required to start an investigation.

Paperwork completed he took me to the canteen. It was lunch time, and the place was busy. Tony Hale was sitting alone at a table. He was eating chilli and chips, washed down with diet cola.

'All sorted?' he asked Leckonby.

'Yes sir.'

'Good. Thank you Peter.'

Leckonby left us alone. Hale scooped up the remnants of his meal. Swallowed them down, followed by a long drink. He wiped his mouth on a paper serviette and looked at me across the table. 'Are you being followed?' he asked

I stared at him, puzzled. 'Why would anyone follow me?'

'I don't know. But someone followed me back from Liners last night. There was an SUV behind me as I cut through the Quays. It was still there when I arrived home. When I went into the house and looked through the window, it took off.'

'You're sure it was the same car?'

'Fairly sure. He stayed too far back for me to make out the number, but he was with me all the way. I suggest you keep your eyes open for a dark-coloured

SUV. Possibly a Range Rover.'

'The roads are full of dark SUVs,' I pointed out. 'Half of them Range Rovers.'

'I know, I know,' he nodded. 'Just putting you on your guard, that's all.'

'Why would someone follow you?'

'You tell me? But if they're following me, they're following you. Think about it! Suppose you're right and someone is after your wife. They're going to watch you, aren't they. Where you go? Who you meet up with?' He pointed a warning finger at me. 'Just be careful! That's all I'm saying.'

He was right of course. There were other people involved in this. People like Susnik, the Russian. Or the American who's tip-off had brought me here in the first place. It was a serious concern, and a distraction at a time when I needed to keep my mind focussed on the task in hand. But I had to take his warning seriously. The last thing I wanted to do was put Alex in danger.

My phone rang. It was my office.

'Excuse me,' I said, answering the call. 'Yes Bianca?'

'Mr Dutton?' It was a man's voice.

'Yes. Who is that?'

'My name is Ryan. Detective Chief Inspector Ryan, Dorset Police. Where are you Mr Dutton.'

'I'm in Manchester. Why are you in my office?'

'There's been an incident here. I'd be very much obliged if you would drop whatever it is you are doing, and return to Weymouth.'

'Listen Inspector, I'm ex-job. So if you don't mind, would you please drop the cop-speak and tell me what's going on down there?'

There was a long pause. 'You have a receptionist? A Bianca White?'

'Since you're in my office, you'll know that!'

'Miss White has been the victim of a serious assault, Mr Dutton. I am sorry to have to tell you, she is dead.'

I didn't see that coming. I almost dropped the phone. For a moment I sat there, stunned. Tony Hale saw my face. He reached over gently. Took the phone from my non-protesting fingers and spoke at length to the Dorset police officer.

'Leave it with me,' he finally announced. 'I'll tell him.' Then he closed the phone.

'I can't believe this?' I muttered, profoundly shaken. 'First Alex, and now this! Jesus, what's going on?'

'D'you want the details?' I nodded, and he went on. 'They were called to your office an hour ago. Seems your cleaner, a Mrs Moore, found the bodies when she went in to clean the place.'

'Bodies?'

'Two of them. Your secretary - '

'Receptionist!' I automatically corrected him.

'- well, your Miss White and an unknown male.'

'When?'

'It's too soon to tell. Their best guess is two to three days.

'How?'

'He was shot in the head. They don't know about her.'

'Jesus!' I repeated.

'They want you down there, right away. The place has been ransacked. 'Ripped apart' are the words he used. Do you think this has something to do with your wife?'

'It must have. Christ, what has she got herself mixed up in?'

'I don't know? But it's now looking like we need to find her, before someone else does.' He climbed to his feet. 'I'll tell Leckonby to pull out all the stops on this. You get yourself down to Dorset and do what has to be done. With any luck we'll have some answers by the time you get back.'

'I'll fly down - ' I started, then stopped myself. 'Shit, I can't! I've got Lucy with me.'

'Where is she?'

'In the car.'

'Give me the keys. I'll have it moved onto the staff car park. Your dog can stay with me. Come on,' he headed for the door. 'I'll get someone to take you to the airport.'

'The discs!' I told him as we hurried along the corridor, 'from the Arndale cameras. They're in the car. On the front passenger seat.'

'I'll get them.'

He steered me through a series of corridors and out through the back of the building. A uniformed traffic cop was just on his way in. 'Where are you going, constable?' demanded Hale.

'Lunch break, sir!'

'No you're not!'

20

The police driver took me to the airport under blues and twos. Dropped me off outside the Rapidair Transit office. While I waited for the helicopter to be started up I called George at the Fox. Told him something had come up and I was returning to Weymouth for a day or two. I asked him to keep the room for me.

Two hours later I was back in Dorset. Touching down on the Portland helipad. I jumped into a waiting taxi and gave the driver my home address. I needed to pick up my other car.

The moment I walked through the front door I knew I'd had visitors. The door to the broom cupboard under the stairs was wide open. Its contents scattered across the hallway. Inside the cupboard, the vinyl floor covering had been rolled back.

I entered the kitchen. The place was a shambles. The window was smashed, leaving broken glass everywhere. Drawers had been pulled out. Their contents emptied onto the floor. Cupboards stood empty, with everything swept from the shelves. Even the fridge-freezer had been violated. The doors left wide open, and the food inside allowed to defrost and spoil.

A quick tour of the house found the same story everywhere. Not a drawer, cupboard, or container had been missed. Someone had gone through the place like a hurricane. No finesse. Just a very rapid and very thorough search. I looked at the mess in my study and the broken monitor on the floor. Felt an overwhelming urge to kill someone.

Back downstairs I thought about the watcher I'd disturbed the night this all started. In hindsight I should have seen to the security of my property before haring off to Manchester. Though I wasn't sure it would have made a difference. This had to be connected to whoever it was turned over my office and killed Bianca.

I looked for the spare car keys. They were missing from the hook. I went to the garage and found it unlocked. Sitting inside was the Explorer: doors and tailgate open. Scattered across the floor were the contents of the glove compartment. Lying amongst them were the keys.

Putting everything back in the car I moved it out onto the drive. I was locking the garage doors when my phone sounded. It was Andy Morton.

'Yes Andy?'

'Nothing on any waterfront development, Terry' he told me. 'Not in this area. Looks like someone's feeding you false information!'

I thanked him for checking it out and rang off. His words had only confirmed what I had thought.

Securing the house as best I could, I set off for Weymouth. Thirty minutes later I approached the gate at the back of my office. It was sealed with crime scene tape. I peered over the gate. Standing outside his back door, smoking an e-cigarette, was the estate agency manager, David Ward.

'I hope you're not contaminating the crime scene,' I said, startling him.

'Jesus, Terry!' He came over to the gate and opened it up. When I hesitated he waved me through. 'It's alright, they've finished out here.'

Stepping over the tape I followed him across the yard.

'This is awful, Terry!' he said. 'Bloody awful! That poor girl. I can't believe she was lying up there, and we didn't even know.' He shook his head in genuine sadness. 'Bloody awful!' he repeated.

'What have the police said?'

'Nothing! Not to us. They had Betty Hughes in the back of a police car for an hour. Came in here asking questions, too, but there was nothing we could tell them. The first we knew something was wrong was when Betty ran in, screaming like a mad woman. What have they told you?'

'I've only spoken to them on the phone. They didn't say much. They want to talk to me, so I'd better go and present myself. Find out what's happened.'

The rear door to my office was also sealed with crime scene tape. David let me pass through the agency office and out his front door. A couple of police cars and a crime scene investigator's van were parked by the kerb. Standing guard outside my office door was an overweight police constable.

'I'm Terry Dutton,' I told him. 'This is my office. I need to speak to DCI Ryan.'

He blinked in surprise. 'He's not here!' he exclaimed. 'Hold on, I'll find out where he is.' Turning aside so I couldn't hear, he spoke quietly into his personal radio. Occasionally he glanced in my direction to make sure I was still there.

'The DCI's on his way back to the station,' he told me at last. 'I'll get someone to run you there.'

'Don't bother, I've got my car. I'll drive there.'

He looked vaguely worried. As though I might be about to do a runner.

'It's all right, constable, I know where it is!' I started to turn away then stopped. 'I don't suppose there's any chance of a look inside?'

He shook his head. Pointed at the SOCO van. 'Sorry! They're not finished in there yet.'

I returned to my car. Drove to Radipole lake and turned into Granby Way, heading for the station. Five minutes after arriving I was ushered into an interview room. Told to sit down at the table. Ten minutes after that, DCI Ryan entered the room with another officer.

21

Ryan had a tall, stooping, frame. He had a face like a bloodhound and reminded me of Clement Freud. I put him in his fifties, counting down to retirement.

'Sorry to keep you waiting Mr Dutton,' he offered.

'Terry will do,' I told him.

'I was with the parents. They were identifying the body.' He sat across the table. Indicated his colleague. 'This is DI Buckland.' The Inspector nodded then sat down. Stared at me with a bored expression.

Ryan looked at his watch. 'You soon got here?'

'Air taxi,' I explained.

His eyebrows went up. 'Business must be good?'

'Bianca was more than an employee. She was a friend. I wanted to get down here as soon as I could.'

He nodded. 'Well you're an ex-copper, so I'm sure you know how these things go. This is a formal interview and the tapes will be running. I am obliged to ask if you wish to have legal representation present?'

'Am I a suspect?'

He looked at me sadly. 'Right now everyone's a suspect. But since you appear to have been at the other end of the country when this happened, I don't think you have any reason to worry. Do you?'

'No lawyer,' I told him. He started up the recorder. Went through the formal introductions for the benefit of the tape. 'Who was the dead man?' I asked.

Ryan gave me a look. 'In case you've forgotten, Terry, it's my job to ask the questions and yours to answer them. I think you understand that, don't you? But I'm not altogether insensitive to your feelings. So when you have answered my questions, I'll try to answer some of yours. That alright with you?'

'Sorry,' I offered.

'Right,' he began. 'Let's start with Tuesday. Tell me what you did.'

'I went into the office, early, to clear the decks.'

'For your Manchester trip?'

'For my Manchester trip, yes.'

'Was everything as it should be in your office?'

'Everything was fine. Exactly as I'd left it.'

'Did you see miss White?'

'No. Bianca isn't - wasn't - an early starter. Nine to nine-thirty she usually arrived. I was gone by then.'

'On your way to Manchester?'

'To Swanage. I went to Swanage first.'

'Why?'

'To speak to someone about my current case. Then I left for Manchester.'

'Pursuing your current case?'

'Yes.'

'So you left Swanage at what time?'

'Around eleven.'

'And arrived in Manchester when?'

'About five o clock.'

'And then what did you do?'

'I booked into a hotel.'

'Called?'

'The Tipsy Fox.' I saw Buckland write this down. 'It's in Timperley, just outside Manchester,' I told him. He wrote this down, too.

'Then what did you do?' Went on Ryan.

'Had a beer or two with the landlord, he's an old friend, and then walked Lucy. After that I had dinner and went to bed.

'Lucy?'

'My dog.'

'Right! So what did you do Wednesday?'

'I went to the Arndale Shopping Centre.'

'In Timperley?'

'In Manchester. I spent the whole day there, looking for my missing person. Showing her picture. Asking people if they'd seen her.'

'So lots of people saw you.'

'They did.'

'And they would remember you?'

'Some will.'

He changed tack. 'When was the last time you had any contact with Miss White?'

'The last time I actually saw her was Monday. Late afternoon. But I called her, Tuesday night, to let her know where I was staying. I called again at lunchtime, Wednesday. She didn't answer. Now I know why!'

'What time did you call her on Tuesday?'

'Around eight-thirty.'

He gave me an odd look. 'That's well out of office hours?'

'She didn't mind. I often called her outside working hours if something came up. Or if I remembered something I should have mentioned during the day.'

'Did you call her at home?'

'I called her mobile. She was out on the raz.'

'Raz?'

'Sorry, Northern expression. She was out clubbing. I presume she was killed later that night?'

'What makes you think that?'

'When I spoke to her I asked her to call the Alarm Company. I wanted them to fit two dummy alarm boxes on my house. She said she'd do it first thing Wednesday morning. The call was never made.'

'Why?'

'She was probably dead.'

'No, why did you want the boxes fitting?'

'Someone was hanging around outside the house, Monday night.'

'Did you report this to the police?'

I shook my head. 'I wish I had. My house has been turned over, too.'

If this surprised him he was too experienced to show it. 'You've been home then?'

'From the helipad. To pick up my car.'

He asked for my address and a key. Passed them to his Inspector. 'Get the team up there,' he instructed. 'Forensics too. We'll treat this as a secondary site until we know otherwise.' Buckland hurried from the room.

Ryan reached over and stopped the tape. 'Back in a minute,' he said. Then he followed the Inspector out of the room.

22

Fallon:

Fallon sat in the car. Just up the road from the GMP headquarters. He watched Dutton's car being moved from the visitors car park to somewhere around the back of the building. It looked like the investigator planned on being inside for some time.

He grunted impatiently. With his low boredom threshold Fallon quickly became restless. He was hungry too, and considered going for something to eat. He could use the tracker to keep an eye on Dutton, remotely. But then if the device was discovered, and removed by police security, he'd lose his quarry for the rest of the day.

Pushing open the door he stepped out and lit up a cigarette. Leaned back against the car, enjoying the sunshine. Up ahead a police traffic car nosed out of the compound gate. It started to turn towards the exit road then stopped as the driver spotted him. It turned his way instead.

'Shit!' breathed Fallon. Casually he flicked away the cigarette and climbed back into the car. Dropped the ignition keys into his jacket pocket.

He rummaged around in the glove compartment until he found the other key fob. For a moment he considered taking out his gun then decided against it. Wouldn't be very clever to shoot a copper. Not right outside Police HQ. That's the sort of thing they'd take personally. He'd just have to rely on the old broken key trick.

The police car cruised past. Through the mirror he watched it turn around and pull in behind him. The traffic cop was speaking to someone on his radio. Probably doing and insurance check. At last he climbed out and approached the car. Fallon rolled down the window.

'Afternoon sir,' the officer began. 'Could I have your name?'

'Fallon. Joseph Fallon. Is something wrong?'

'Do you have any identification, Mr Fallon?'

Fallon pulled out his driving license and handed it over. The policeman checked it and handed it back.

'You're a long way from home Mr Fallon.'

'I'm up here on business.'

The policeman nodded. 'Are you aware that waiting here is limited to twenty minutes? You were here when I arrived an hour ago: and you're still here.'

'Sorry,' smiled Fallon.' I pulled off the road for a break, and to make a few calls. But when I went to start the engine the ignition key snapped off.' He held up the fob with a small, jagged, piece of metal showing where the key should be. 'I'm waiting for the tow truck.'

The traffic cop looked at the broken key then at Fallon. 'Never seen that before,' he commented. 'Well since you are, technically, broken down I won't issue a fixed penalty notice. But if you're still here when I get back, your vehicle will be impounded. Understand?'

'Shouldn't be too long now,' Fallon assured him.

The policeman wasn't finished. He slowly strolled around the car. Examined the tyres. Carefully peered through each window, studying the interior. 'Would you mind opening the tailgate, sir?'

Fallon sighed and released the catch. He heard the man rummaging around, and then the tailgate was shut down again. The officer came back to the window. Nodded towards the building up ahead.

'That's the police headquarters,' he pointed out. 'So it's a security issue. Best not to hang around too long or people less friendly than me might start pointing their guns at you.' With this warning the cop returned to his car and drove away.

'Nosey bastard!' breathed Fallon, waving him off with a friendly smile.

23

Dutton:

Ryan came back into the room with a female officer. Restarting the tape he introduced her as Detective Sergeant Mallory then continued the interview.

'Right Terry, let's get back to the main event. What I'm having difficulty with is why Bianca would be in your office at all. It looks like she went there straight from the club. Any thoughts on that?'

'Who was the man?' I asked again.

'He hasn't been identified yet.'

'Thirty-ish. Tall. Well built. Blond hair.' I touched the side of my neck. 'Red Devils tattoo here?'

He nodded. 'You know him?'

'I met him once. He's called Gary Lapworth. They have a sort of on-off thing going.'

'What do you call an on-off thing?'

'Exactly that! I don't think either of them saw their relationship as serious or long term. I know she didn't. Bianca had lots of men friends. But she and Gary moved in the same circles. The same clubs and pubs. Sometimes they'd spend the evening drinking and dancing. Then go back to the office for a bit of privacy.'

Ryan raised his eyebrows. 'You knew they were doing this?'

I shrugged. 'He's in lodgings somewhere. She lives at home with her parents. They needed somewhere to go. She never told me she was using the office, and it never came up in conversation. But I knew it was going on. I could tell when they'd been there. Sometimes they got a bit careless. Left things lying around.'

Ryan frowned disapprovingly but went on. 'These other men friends. Do you know any of them?'

'No. The only reason I know Gary is because I saw her out with him once and she introduced us. But I don't know anyone else she's friendly with. Generally she keeps her private life private. You'll have to ask her friends about any other men she knows. Or knew.'

'Can you think of any reason why someone would want to harm either of them?'

'I can give you a theory,' I offered.

'Go on!'

'Last year my wife died, in an accident at sea.'

'Yes I remember.'

'Well it now appears the accident was a sham. She faked her own death.' This did provoke a reaction. Ryan's sad eyes widened noticeably. 'She was sighted in Manchester on Monday. I was up there looking for her when you called.'

'Why would your wife fake her own death?'

'I'm still trying to work that out. The only thing that makes sense to me is that someone was out to cause her serious harm, so she decided to play dead. If I'm right, now that she has re-surfaced they'll be searching for her again. And if Bianca and Gary had the misfortune to get in their way - ?' I left the question hanging.

'How positive is the sighting of your wife?' he asked.

'Very positive.'

'And this person, or persons, you think might be after her, do you know who they are?'

'No.'

'Do you have any evidence they even exist?'

'No.'

Ryan folded his arms. Stared at me, thoughtfully. Then he nodded slightly. 'Well it's an interesting theory: and you can be sure I'll bear it in mind. But at the moment that's all it is. A theory. Full of ifs, buts, and maybes.

You've been on this side of the table, Terry. You know that most murder victims are killed by someone close to home. Or in some random, and often senseless, attack. So I think for now I'll stay with the book on this one, if that's okay.'

'It's your investigation.'

'At the moment we are looking at a robbery that escalated into something else. The dead man's wallet and mobile phone are missing. So are Miss White's handbag, phone, and purse.

The fact that your home was also ransacked might suggest an organised gang who knew you were away. Perhaps they decided that now would be a good time to target you. This may be what the victims walked into. Is there anything of value missing from your home?'

'I haven't had time to check.'

'Then when the crime scene officers have finished, perhaps you'll check both your home and office. Let us have a list of any missing items.'

I nodded.

'Well that's all for now,' he said, bringing the session to an end. 'Thank you for your cooperation Terry.' Ryan checked his watch. 'Interview terminated at seventeen-twenty.' He switched off the tapes.

'Okay,' he began, relaxing slightly, 'I'll tell you what I can. You are right about her being on a night out. She told her mother she was going to a club called the Twisted Rigging. Do you know it?'

I nodded. 'Five minutes from the office.'

'The next morning when she hadn't come home, the mother tried calling her. All she got was her messaging service. She called your office several times with the same result. By mid afternoon she was worried enough to call here and report her daughter missing.'

He spread his hands, apologetically. 'Not a lot was done I'm sorry to say. But I'm sure you know how it is? A twenty-five year old woman doesn't come home from a night out? It's not quite the same as a fifteen-year-old, is it? Add to that a known history of drug abuse, and you can see no one's going to start jumping through hoops.'

'How did she die?'

'We don't know, officially. Her friend was shot in the head. She was probably strangled. Not with a ligature, though. Manual strangulation I'd guess.'

'How many burglars do you know who carry guns?' I asked.

'Yes I know what you're saying. And I won't completely rule out your theory. But until we have something more substantial to support it I must work with what we have. Look Terry, I'm sure you were very close to your wife and thought you knew her well. But someone with your experience must know that people disappear all the time. For reasons not always obvious, or palatable, to those closest to them.'

He was right of course. In his shoes I would have said the same thing. We all think we know the person we live with. Yet all too often it turns out we don't. But I still believed Bianca's death was connected to Alex's re-appearance. Anything else was too much of a stretch.

'I have to tell you,' he said sombrely, 'Miss White was very badly beaten. She was also sexually assaulted, which brings yet another dimension to this.'

I felt sick. 'She'll have fought back you know,' I told him. 'Bianca was a tough little thing. She'd kicked the drug habit and was working hard to make something of her life. She didn't deserve this.'

'I agree with you. Now, what I just told you I did so purely as a professional courtesy. Superintendent Hale has vouched for you, so I'm sure I don't have to remind you to keep these details to yourself. I don't want to see them appearing in tomorrow's newspapers.'

He stood up. Dug into his pocket for a card and handed it to me. 'I can't let you go back home yet. Forensics and SOCO will be all over your house. Is there somewhere you can stay?'

'I'll book into a hotel. It's not a problem.'

'Good. Give me a call in the morning. Hopefully they'll be finished by then and you can check out what's missing from your home.'

24

Ballinger:

Almost midnight. Ballinger sat outside the Tipsy Fox. He picked up the phone and made the call he'd been putting off making. 'I've lost him,' he said, simply.

'Go on,' said Devine.

'I followed him to police headquarters and waited. He never came out. He must have left some other way. I'm at his hotel now. Been here for hours, but he hasn't come back.'

'And Fallon?'

'I don't know. He left around midday. He has a tracker on Dutton's car, so he's probably still with him.'

'Then you'd better start looking. What about your informant? Has she heard from Dutton?'

'She's not answering her phone.'

'Great! Then stop wasting your time talking to me. Get out there and find him.'

Dismissed, he closed the phone. He looked towards the rear of the small hotel. There was a light showing on the ground floor. He called up the hotel's phone number from enquiries and asked to be put through. The call was answered after four rings.

'Tipsy Fox,' announced a tired voice.

'Can I speak to Terry Dutton.'

'He's not here.'
'Do you know what time he'll be back?'
'He won't be back. Not for a day or two.'
'Do you know where I can contact him?'
'Do you have his home number?'
'Yes.'
'Try there!' The line went dead.

'Thanks,' murmured Ballinger. He called Dutton's home. The phone rang three times then went to answer. He hung up. Either Dutton didn't want to be disturbed, or he wasn't there. Yet his hotel seemed to think he had gone back to Dorset. Considering the importance of the man's mission here, he must have had a really good reason to do that.

He wondered where Fallon was. If he was still following his man? There was one way to find out. Switching on the sat nav he entered the address of the place where the Kozaks were staying. Then he made his way back to the A56 and drove out towards Cheshire.

Altrincham was practically deserted as he passed through the former market town. Soon he was heading south-west towards the M56 and M6 motorways, before turning off towards Ladymere.

Ballinger followed directions through the darkened village. He entered a narrow, winding lane that took him past several rural properties, and a farm. Then he turned off his lights and crept slowly forward.

He stopped before reaching the house. Backed the car into the wide entrance to a gated pasture. Killing the engine he opened the samples case. Took out the Glock, his shoulder holster, and a flashlight. He put on the holster and inserted the gun after checking it was fully loaded.

Locking the car he pulled on his gloves. Then walked along the road to the house, staying close to the hedgerow. The place was in darkness. He checked his watch. One a.m.

The modern, brick property was surrounded by a four foot high wall topped by a low, iron, railing. Between two brick pillars hung a pair of wrought-iron gates. These gave access into a wide courtyard, covered in shale chippings. To the left of the house stood a detached garage. Large enough to hold three or four cars. Between the garage and the side of the house ran a dark passageway about six feet wide.

Ballinger climbed the gates. Dropped lightly onto the ground where the chippings had been compressed by car tyres. Walking carefully along the flattened tracks he approached the garage doors. They were locked.

He walked all the way around the garage. The wall furthest from the house held a small window. He peered through the glass pane. It was too dark inside to see much of anything so he pulled out a small torch. Shone it through, into the interior. The narrow light beam picked out two vehicles. A silver-coloured Mercedes SUV, and Fallon's blue Honda Accord.

As he moved back from the window the torch slipped and hit the glass with a sudden, sharp, tap. Moments later an alarm began to wail. The house was bathed in light from flood lamps set around the eaves.

He looked around, anxiously. Behind him lay the side wall of the property. Gripping the iron rail he vaulted over. Into a dark meadow covered in long grass.

Keeping low he loped away, into the darkness. Then he turned and threw himself face down. Peering back at the garage he saw the figure of a man appear from around the front of the house. It looked like Fallon. The figure moved stealthily towards the garage and tried the doors. Finding them secure he came around to Ballinger's side of the building and carefully checked the window.

Another man now appeared. This one from around the back of the garage. Heavily built, Ballinger guessed this would be Petrovich. The Serbian bodyguard. Both men went to the front of the squat building and unlocked the doors. They went inside and the lights came on.

They weren't in there for long. A minute later the lights went out and they re-emerged. The Serb locked the doors and Fallon strolled over to the wall. He leaned against the rail and lit up a cigarette. Stood there looking out over the field in which Ballinger lay. Soon he was joined by the Serb who, half-heartedly, began sweeping the field with a beam of torchlight.

After a while the torch went out. Ballinger stayed put. Minutes later the alarm stopped and the security lights went out. Still he didn't move. He gave it a further ten minutes then cautiously lifted his head. Around the house everything was in darkness, with no sign of the two men.

Ignoring the road he took a circuitous route back to the car. Through two fields of stubble running parallel with the lane. Finally he climbed over the rusty gate where he'd left the Discovery. He peeled off the gloves, wiped his feet on the road surface, and climbed in.

Driving back to the hotel he tried to make sense of it all. He'd seen Fallon drive away from Central Park around lunchtime. Assumed the man had grown tired of waiting. With the advantage of the tracker it wasn't necessary for him to sit on Dutton's coat tails, anyway.

So why was Fallon still here? Was Dutton, too, still in Manchester? Pretending to go back to Dorset, to throw anyone who might be tailing him off the scent.

There was nothing he could do about it tonight. Tomorrow he would call his contact down there. Find out if Dutton really was back at home. Meanwhile he would spend some time watching the watchers. With any luck Fallon would lead him to Dutton.

25

SATURDAY

Ballinger:

Six o clock in the morning. Ballinger was back in Ladymere. Crouched behind a hedge he watched the house through binoculars. At seven o clock there was movement. It was Fallon. He opened up the garage doors and drove his car out onto the lane. Ballinger ran to the narrow farm track where he'd left his own car. When the blue Honda drove past he went after it.

They joined the A556. Turned towards Altrincham. Drove through the town then took the Timperley road. As they approached the Tipsy Fox, Ballinger dropped back and pulled in. He watched Fallon drive aimlessly up and down the road, looking for Dutton's Audi. Finally the Honda pulled onto the hotel's car park.

After a couple of phone calls Fallon left the car and entered the hotel. Minutes later he returned to his car and quickly drove off, heading back the way he'd come. Ballinger made a U-turn and followed him back to the house. It seemed that, despite having a tracker on the man's car, Fallon too had lost Dutton.

The morning passed slowly. Apart from the blue Honda standing out on the wide courtyard, there was nothing to show that the house was even occupied. At midday he called his contact in Weymouth. There was no reply. He tried Dutton's home number again. This time the call was answered.

'Mister Dutton?'

'It is!'

'Hello, mister Dutton. We are doing promotional work in Portland, and are looking for homeowners who might be interested in low-cost installation of our new energy saving windows to - '

' - no thank you!' interrupted Dutton, abruptly ending the call.

Having confirmed that Dutton was indeed back in Weymouth, Ballinger settled down again to watching the house.

Just after one o clock the front door opened. A man came out of the house. Big-boned and bullet-headed, with short blond hair. Ballinger recognised the huge figure from the previous night. It was Petrovich, the Serb. The man entered the garage, brought out the silver SUV, and waited by the front door.

Ballinger hurried to his car. Minutes later he saw the Mercedes pass down the lane. The Serb was at the wheel and two men sat in the back. When Fallon's Honda didn't appear behind them, he set off in pursuit.

They didn't go far. Just down to the Duke Hotel in the village. Lunchtime, guessed Ballinger. Driving on he tucked the car out of sight behind the village hall next door, and walked back to the hotel.

The place was busy. He pushed his way up to the bar and ordered a drink. Stood there observing the three men. When the waitress arrived, the Serb ordered food for all of them: three soups, followed by three eight ounce rib-eyes with chips and mushrooms.

He studied the Kozak brothers. Wondered which was Dauren and which Serik. Both were expensively dressed and wore identical, diamond, tie-pins. Both sported Cartier watches on their left wrists. One of the brothers wore a gold ear stud, and two gold chains on his right wrist. The men looked like caricatures of American *mafiosa*. Yet despite the penchant for style and bling, he knew he was looking at two very dangerous people.

When they spoke to each other the brothers used what he assumed was their native tongue. With their minder they adopted American-accented English.

Sipping his drink, Ballinger allowed his eyes to wander around the bar and dining area. In one corner of the room two tables had been pushed together for a group of young men. They were chattering animatedly as they studied the menu. Ballinger found himself smiling when the pack leader's unsuccessful attempt to chat up the waitress, was greeted with howls of derision from his friends.

The sound of raised voices brought his attention back to the Kozaks. Gold ear-stud was berating his sibling. The brother responded with something that, in any language, sounded like a whine. He was saved from a second tongue-lashing by the nonsensical warble of a ring tone.

Oblivious to the irritated glances of some diners, Gold ear-stud reached into his pocket and pulled out a phone. His expression became dour as he listened to what the caller had to say. When the call ended he angrily snapped the phone shut.

There then followed a low, but intense, discussion over lunch, with much gesticulating in evidence. He was sure they were speaking English. But their voices were too muted to be heard over the background noise. The talking stopped when the waitress came to take their dessert orders.

When they were done eating, Ballinger followed the men back to the house. He returned to his lookout position and watched Petrovich put the SUV back into the garage. There was no sign of Fallon, or his car.

After nightfall Ballinger moved in close to the house. Climbing into the meadow next door to the property, he crouched behind the side wall. Watched the front of the house through the railings.

Shortly after midnight the darkness was pierced by headlamps. A car came up the lane and stopped at the gate. Fallon was back. Locking his car in the garage the man headed, a little unsteadily, for the house. After several failed attempts to unlock the front door he thumbed the bell push. When the door was opened Fallon went inside.

Ballinger gripped the rails and pulled himself over the wall. Taking the passageway between the garage and the house, he stepped onto the rear patio.

There was a door and window to his right. A kitchen, going off the waste pipe coming out through the wall. Beyond these, built on to the rear of the house, stood a large sun porch. It was in darkness.

He peered through the porch window. Could just make out items of cane furniture, surrounding a low coffee table.

He heard the murmur of voices inside the house. Suddenly the sound rose up in volume. Ballinger put his ear to the window to hear what was going on. He couldn't make out the words being spoken. But there was no mistaking their loud and angry pitch.

The shouting didn't last long. Soon the voices tailed off. Minutes later the lights blinked out. Soundlessly Ballinger crept away. Made his way back to the car, wondering what that was all about.

26

Fallon:

Joey Fallon closed the gates. He opened the garage doors and put away the car. He was not happy. Fallon had long considered himself a man of very precise and useful talents. An expert in his own field. One of the best in the business. Yet here he was, reduced to the role of gofer. Having to drive halfway to Leeds on some fool's errand.

Predictably, the trip had been a waste of time. The farm was exactly what it said it would be in the brochure. But then it would be, wouldn't it. It was owned and run by professionals. People like himself, who knew what they were doing.

These Kozak brothers were not professionals. They thought they were! Strutted around like Al-fucking-Capone and Frank Nitti. But at heart they were nothing more than a pair of country bumpkins from some place no one could even pronounce, let alone spell.

'Go check the place out,' they said. 'Make sure it's what we need!' What was he now, a building inspector? Fallon knew exactly what they needed. He would like to be the one to give it them too, but he couldn't. Levkin had said to keep them sweet. So when they said *go,* off he went, whilst they sat feeding their ugly fat faces.

Until this week Fallon had never been any further north than Newmarket Racecourse. Now he knew why. If he thought Portland quiet, those bleak moors between Lancashire and Yorkshire were a whole lot worse. You can shove your Pennines, he thought. They weren't for him. Not so much the backbone of the country, he decided, as its backside.

On his way back he had discovered a decent pub. The food looked good, and the beer was halfway to being civilised, so he ordered a meal. When he'd eaten he decided to stay a while. Sink a few with the locals. Teach them how the game of pool should really be played.

In the end he stayed until closing time. Lost track of how much he'd had to drink. But he'd made it back here without being pulled. Now he couldn't unlock the door. One of those useless tossers had left his key in the lock.

He rang the bell. The door was opened by Petrovich. The big Serb regarded him with some amusement as he stepped into the hallway. Fallon ignored him. He'd met wood lice with more intelligence. Crossing to the staircase he headed up to bed. Petrovich let him climb halfway to the top before speaking.

'You are wanted. In the dining room.' Again the weird smile.

'Tomorrow,' Fallon told him. 'I'm knackered. It's been a long day.'

'Not tomorrow. Now. They are waiting for you.'

Something in the man's tone caused Fallon to stop. Muttering to himself he walked back down the stairs. Headed for the dining room, followed by the Serb. He found the brothers sitting at the heavy dining table, a vodka bottle and two glasses between them. Also lying on the table was Dauren's fancy gun. Serik looked pointedly at his watch.

'Where have you been until now?' he demanded.

'Christ, you sound like my old man,' grinned Fallon.

Serik wasn't amused. 'You left hours ago. With one place to go. One thing to do. So where have you been?'

'If you must know I stopped off for a bite to eat, like you did. Had a drink or two, like you did. Then had a few games of pool with the natives. Why? What have I missed?'

'We've been waiting for your report. We want it now! Today! Not sometime tomorrow. Or whenever you are sober enough to give one.' Serik turned to his brother. '*Faydasiz!*' he spat out, contemptuously. 'He is useless! We ask our friends in London for a soldier and we get a drunken fool.'

Fallon took a step forward. 'I am not drunk!' he said dangerously. 'And you had better watch who you are calling a fool, sonny. The last man to call me that had his tongue ripped out and shoved up his arse.'

Dauren stood up. He picked up the gun. Holding it loosely he came around the table. Fallon watched him approach. He didn't think the man would use the gun. That would be madness, even by their standards. These men were here for a purpose. They couldn't pull it off without his help and they knew it! He hoped.

Suddenly Dauren lashed out. Had Fallon been completely sober he would not have been caught out. But before he had the chance to move, the gun barrel struck him in the face and opened up a deep gash in his cheek. He staggered backwards. Was caught by the Serb, and propelled forward again.

The man with the gun leaned back against the table. Staring coldly. Fallon pulled out a handkerchief and pressed it against his cheek. Tried to stem the flow of blood from the wound. Serik came around the table to join his brother. 'How is the farm?' he asked.

'Good,' growled Fallon.

'Does it have a beamed cellar?' asked Dauren.

Fallon narrowed his eyes as he looked at the older sibling. 'It has a big cellar. Like you asked for. With beams.'

'Good,' smiled Dauren. 'I like a big cellar.'

'Where is Dutton?' asked Serik, casually.

'Back in Weymouth!' said Fallon. 'I told you.'

'Why are you not with him?'

'I told you that, too. The tracker's still transmitting from police headquarters. It's either been found, or it's fallen off. Or the car's there and he isn't. Your guess is as good as mine.'

'We don't have to guess,' said Dauren. He came at Fallon again, still holding the gun. 'We *know* Dutton is in Weymouth (he pronounced the word *Way Mouth*) and we know *why* he is there.'

'Good for you,' muttered Fallon.

'You want to know what he's doing there, hey?' Dauren jabbed Fallon in the chest with the gun. His voice rose angrily. 'I'll tell you what he's doing! He's talking to the cops is what he's doing. Talking about the two dead people some asshole left lying around in his office. Now which asshole would that be, do you think?'

Tiny droplets of spittle hit Fallon in the face as Kozak raged. He shrugged. Tried to front it out. 'I was looking for something that would lead us to the woman,' he said. 'Save us some time. The big feller decided to play the hero so I shot him. I couldn't leave her alive, could I? Anyway,' he asked truculently, 'what's it to you?'

Dauren spat out another oath in his own tongue. He jammed the barrel of the gun into the soft flesh beneath Fallon's chin. 'What it is to us, asshole, is that we are a mosquito's dick away from getting our hands on that bitch: someplace it has taken us years to get to. Now, thanks to you, the guy who was going to lead us right to her door is busy elsewhere. Talking to the cops.'

'You had one job to do,' Serik added. 'Watch the man, in case he contacted the woman. That's all you had to do. Not go off on some crazy treasure hunt, popping anybody who just happened to get in your way.'

'I just thought - '

Savagely Dauren rammed the gun upwards, choking off Fallon's reply. 'No asshole, you did not think. Because thinking requires a brain, and you so obviously do not have one of those. Maybe I should pop you, hey? Gift-wrap you, and send you off to the cops down there?'

'You won't do that,' croaked Fallon. 'Levkin wouldn't like it if you did that.'

'Levkin?' snorted Dauren, derisively. 'Do I look like someone who gives a rat's ass about what Levkin likes?'

Fallon turned his eyes on Serik. 'If he shoots me you're knackered. You don't know anyone here, and you don't know your way around. You can't do this on your own. And whatever he says, Levkin won't sent someone else up here to help you, because no one will come. Like it or not you're stuck with me.'

'He has a point,' Serik remarked to his brother.

Dauren regarded Fallon with contempt. 'Let's get something straight here, asshole. The only thing that counts right now is finding the woman. You got that? Do one more thing to put this at risk and I will kill you.' Again he lashed out. The gun struck Fallon in the mouth. He fell to the floor, spitting blood and teeth.

Without another word the Kozaks stepped around him and walked from the room. The Serb began to follow, then he paused and looked back. '*Now* you can go to bed. Asshole!' He flicked off the lights and was gone.

'Up yours, Slabhead!' growled Fallon.

27

SUNDAY

Dutton:

The telephone rescued me from a disturbing dream. It was a dark and stormy night. I was in the Sweet Ruthy with Alex, both of us in a state of panic. The yacht was rolling dangerously in heavy seas as we desperately tacked back and forth in a searching pattern. Lucy had been swept overboard, and we couldn't see her. We could hear her frantic barking. But the sound was growing fainter and fainter as she was carried away from us by the current.

From somewhere close by I heard the warble of a phone. Thinking the sound was coming from a nearby vessel I climbed onto the prow to take a look. Almost immediately a huge wave hit the yacht, sweeping me into the raging sea. I heard Alex cry out and then I was in the water, sinking like a stone.

The shock of plunging into the icy waves snatched me from sleep. The dream faded but the telephone continued to ring. Forcing myself awake I climbed out of bed.

I had spent much of Saturday putting the house back into some sort of order. Ryan had called, mid-morning. Told me the forensic people had completed their work, both at the office and my home. When I was finished at the house I drove over to Weymouth. Picked up a Kentucky Fried on the way, and ate it at my desk with the kitchen door firmly closed.

By midnight I had the place back to normal. Except for the kitchen. Unable to go in there, I decided to call in a cleaning contractor on Monday. Pay someone to do the job for me.

There was nothing missing from either property. Nothing obvious anyway. But then I hadn't expected there would be. I made my way home from Weymouth and fell into bed. It was just after two a.m. Now, as I lifted the phone at the bottom of the stairs, I checked my watch. It was eight-thirty.

'Hello?'

'Is that Mr Dutton, of Abacus Investigations?' The voice was local. Dorset.

'It is!'

'We need to speak to you Mr Dutton.' When I didn't say anything the man went on. 'It's about your wife.'

'What about her?' I asked, suddenly fully awake.

'Not on the phone Mr Dutton. This is something we need to tell you face to face. How about we meet in *The Sands,* off the Dorchester road? One o clock, say?'

'The Sands. One o clock.' I repeated.

'See you there then,' and the man rang off.

Making coffee I sat at the kitchen table. Wondered what I might be walking into. I had no choice but to go. I badly needed answers from somewhere, and I wasn't going to get them by doing nothing.

I took my time getting ready then drove into Weymouth. Had an all day breakfast on the promenade, and then set out along the Dorchester road. Shortly after twelve-thirty I walked into The Sands. Collecting a small dark beer from the bar I carried it to a table from where I could see the door.

Twenty minutes later I saw them come in. They looked like Father and son. The younger man was around thirty. He wore jeans, and a thin anorak over a roll-neck sweater. There was a duffel bag slung over his shoulder. The older man was well into his sixties. A more grizzled version of the first. They looked around the bar, spotted me, and headed for my table.

'Can we buy you a drink Mr Dutton?' asked the younger man. Good start, I thought. Civilised! Didn't sound like he was about to pull an Uzi from the bag and spread my brains across the bar. I lifted my almost empty glass.

'Dark,' I answered.

He went to the bar for the drinks. The older man sat down on a stool opposite me. 'Sam Adams,' he said, introducing himself. He nodded in the direction of the bar. 'My boy, Graham.' Adams senior was grey-haired, small and wiry, with a barrel chest. He had a deep and pleasant voice. The accent pure Dorset. The weathered face could only have come from years spent at sea.

'I won't offer you my hand, mister Dutton,' he said. 'You might regret shaking it when you hear what we did.'

'And what was that?' I asked.

'We'll wait on my lad if you don't mind,' he said simply. 'My story is his story too.'

Graham arrived with the drinks. 'Cheers!' saluted the older man. He took a sip of ale, looked at his son, then began.

'We run a trawler. Out of Poole. Used to do a bit of fishing, but there's no profit in that any more. Not like when my old dad had her. He made a good living from the sea. Now there's too much interference. Too many boats chasing the same fish.' Adams took another mouthful of ale.

'So we started hiring out to anglers. Just local fishing groups and tourists to begin with. Then we began advertising in the angling magazines. Now we have our own web site,' he nodded proudly towards his son. 'Graham's expertise, not mine.

Anyway, last September we got a phone call from this foreign chap. Said he wanted to hire our boat. It was pretty short notice - late in the season too - but I thought we could manage it. The next day he came to look her over. He was pretty pleased with what he saw. Said she was just what he wanted.

We're honest folk Mister Dutton, Graham and me. We might not always tell the taxman about everything we earn, but other than the Government we've never cheated anyone. Nor do we want to get involved in anything dodgy. So whenever we take on a hire, we like to know exactly what we're letting ourselves in for. When I asked this fellow that very question, his answer had us both truly gobsmacked.

I'll tell it to you the way he told us,' he said. 'Some of it you might find offensive. But these were his words, remember. Not mine.' I nodded, and he continued.

'He told us he had this sister. Married to some well-to-do Yacht Club type called Dutton. Reckoned she should never have married the bloke. That she had made a bad mistake. But being a stranger here, and a bit out of her depth, she had fallen for him big time.'

'I take it this sister is my wife?'

He nodded. 'According to this chap she was having a terrible time of it. Forced to keep her husband's business pals happy, if you know what I mean. Given a hiding from time to time too, to keep her in her place.

When I asked why she didn't just leave him, he said she was scared to death of him. Said that you - her husband that is - told her he would kill her if she tried to leave. That he still had lots of friends in the police force - him once having been a copper - and they would track her down and bring her back if she ran off.'

'He said that?'

'He did. Then he said he had this idea - from that film where Julia Roberts pretends to drown, so's her husband won't come looking for her. He'd worked out a similar plan. All he needed was someone with a boat to help them pull it off.'

'He was very convincing, Mister Dutton,' Graham interjected. 'Almost in tears he was, when he told us how she was being abused.'

Sam nodded confirming this. 'To be honest I wasn't all that sure I wanted any part in what he was planning. So I told him that whilst we had every sympathy with his sister, we couldn't afford to get involved in anything illegal. He just brushed my worries aside. Asked what was illegal about taking someone off a damaged yacht and carrying her back to Poole. Put that way there didn't seem much wrong with it at all.

He said he'd give us five thousand pounds, to do the job and then forget all about it. That's a lot of money for a couple of hours work. So in the end we shook his hand and said yes.'

Listening to Sam I felt unbelievably sad. The thought that Alex could paint such a bleak and distorted picture of me and our relationship was truly painful - and the bit about me once being in the police force could only have come from her

'This bloke,' I asked. 'What was his name?'

'Susnik, or something like,' answered Graham. 'Russian, I think. Said he was staying in an apartment in Swanage. Over a flower shop on Station road. Said the people in the shop would vouch for him.'

I'm sure they would, I thought. 'He'd be what, forty-ish? Ginger hair? Well built? Suit and tie man?' They looked at me like I'd produced a dove from my hankie. 'I've been looking into my wife's disappearance,' I told them. 'He keeps popping up.'

'Is he your wife's brother?'

'I doubt it. Her maiden name was Morel. She wasn't Russian, and if she did have a brother she never mentioned him to me. Having said that it looks like there's lots of things she didn't mention to me, doesn't it?'

There was an awkward silence. I pointed at their near-empty glasses.

'Another?' I asked.

28

I used the visit to the bar to get my head around what I'd just been told. Lots of emotions were running around in my head. Alex's impromptu television appearance was evidence enough that she was alive. Yet it still came as something of a shock to have this fact confirmed by those party to her disappearance. When I returned to the table I was ready to hear the rest of the story. Nervous too, about what else I might learn.

'You ok?' asked Sam Adams.

'I'll do,' I told him. 'Go on when you're ready. I've heard the worst, I hope. I might as well hear the rest.'

Sam nodded. 'He called us on the Wednesday. Said it was set for Friday. We were to rendezvous at nineteen hundred hours, in Mupe bay. Near Lulworth military ranges. He even gave us the GPS co-ordinate.'

Mupe Bay. I knew the place. It was a good spot. Susnik had done his homework. There was little chance of them being seen from land: and in the failing light, against those rocky escarpments, they'd be almost invisible to any passing ship.

'We arrived on time,' the older man went on. 'Sure enough the yacht was there, waiting for us. We dropped anchor and they came alongside and climbed aboard.'

'They?'

'Oh he was there, too. Him and your missus, both. We took them on board and that was it. Job done - or so we thought. But it weren't, were it Graham?'

The son shook his head. The older man continued. 'As we pulled away he asked me to go back and ram the yacht. Ram her, indeed! I can tell you mister Dutton, I didn't like that. Not at all! I told him so, too.

But he said they needed to make it look like a real accident. That it was her yacht anyway, and this was what she wanted. Well, by this time we were in too deep to argue. So I went back and hit her amidships, hoping just to cause some superficial damage. But I must have caught her too hard 'cause it cracked open her hull.'

He shook his head with genuine regret. 'We really are very sorry,' he said. 'We should never have listened to him.'

'What happened next?' I asked, impatient to hear the rest of his tale.

'That's about it! We took them back to Poole and dropped them ashore. He gave us the money, said thank you very much, and off they went in a car they had waiting. That was the last we saw of them.'

'Did she speak to you at all?'

'She said *thank you*. Twice. First time when she climbed on. Then again when she climbed off. Apart from that, never a word. He did the talking for both of them. She had an occasional word with him but we don't know what was said.. They spoke foreign.'

'How did she seem?'

'Not happy,' said Graham. 'Not like you'd expect

someone to be, escaping from a bullying husband. In fact she looked downright miserable. Like she'd been crying her eyes out all day. We put it down to nerves. But later we began to wonder.'

'We tied off then went to the pub,' Sam continued. 'To celebrate, I suppose. Except we didn't feel much like celebrating. Seemed like the more we talked about what we'd done, the more dodgy and dirty it began to appear. I think it was beginning to dawn on us that we'd put all our trust in the word of a total stranger. Never once knowing if he was telling the truth or not.' The old man shook his head. Still wondering at his own gullibility.

'Anyway, next day the word comes down about the sea-search going on for a missing woman. Got us real scared. All that time and money, and men putting their own lives at risk, searching for someone we knew wasn't even there. It began to dawn on us that when you do something as big as this, without knowing all the facts, then you really don't know how much damage you might have done. Or how much trouble you're in.' Sam looked at his son. 'Tell him the rest.' he sighed.

'We read about her in the papers,' said Graham. 'About her being this successful business woman. Running her own flower shop in Swanage. That set a few alarm bells ringing, I can tell you. Didn't sound to us like a woman under the thumb of some bullying husband. Convinced us even more, we'd been conned.

In the end we decided to go to the memorial service. See for ourselves what you were like. It just made things worse. When we saw you there with that little dog, and the look on your face, that was when we knew we'd done something really bad.'

'We watched you throw them flowers into the water like a man who wanted to throw himself after them,' put in Sam. 'Right there and then we both knew you weren't the man he'd made you out to be.'

'Dad was all for goin' to the police,' said Graham. 'I persuaded him not to. Said for all we knew we might be party to a crime, and us with an envelope full of money to prove it. I told him if he opened his mouth, he'd likely talk the both of us into prison. And for what? Trying to help someone? Where's the justice in that?'

'So we said nothing,' the older man said. He dipped into the duffel bag and brought out a large envelope. Laid it on the table. 'We never touched his money Mister Dutton. An' I know we can't undo what we did. But we want you to know that at the time we were acting with the best of intentions.'

He pushed the envelope towards me. 'Here, you take it. If anyone should have that, it's you. It won't buy you a new yacht. But it's all we have to give you. That, and our deepest apologies.'

I took the envelope. Looked inside. The money was in bundles, held together by elastic bands.

'Why now?' I asked.

Both looked uncomfortable. Graham spoke up. 'We saw in the paper yesterday about what happened to that office girl of yours, and her friend. It seems to us that you have more than enough trouble on your plate, without us sitting on this and adding to your misery.'

'Then there's the police,' added Sam. 'They're going to be all over everyone. Looking for whoever it was killed that young couple. God knows what stones they might turn over? So we decided to come clean. Tell them what we did before they find it out from someone else. We just needed to put things right with you first.'

'You're going to the police?' I was surprised. 'What's the point? They already know my wife faked her own death. They're not treating it as a crime. So they won't be interested in the people who helped her. In fact the Dorset police are not interested in her at all. She's hiding out, miles away from here.'

'But they'll find out about us?'

'Not from me they won't. Not from her either, if I know anything about her. I don't want your money Mr. Adams,' I told him. 'It's yours. You earned it. Take it.' They looked at me in amazement.

'We can't do that Mister Dutton. What we did wasn't right.'

'What you did probably saved her life,' I told them. 'She wasn't running from me. But she was running from someone. Probably the same someone who just killed my receptionist and her boyfriend. I think if you hadn't helped her disappear when you did, she'd be as dead as they are by now.'

'I don't know what to say,' said Sam Adams.

'If I was you I'd say nothing. To anyone. You really don't want these people coming after you. And they will, if they think you might know where she is. Keep the money. Spend it on yourselves. And if I ever need the use of a boat, I'll know who to call.'

Sam took a business card from his pocket and solemnly passed it to me. 'Anytime we can help, Mister Dutton, you just call us. Anytime at all, d'you hear?'

29

Ballinger:

Ballinger watched the Kozaks being driven to lunch by their minder. It seemed to be a regular daily event. He followed them onto the Duke Hotel car park, pulled into a gap, and watched them enter the hotel. There was no sign of Fallon. Clearly he was not considered a desirable lunch companion.

After a couple of minutes he followed them inside. The place was buzzing with friends and families out for Sunday lunch. He went to the bar and ordered a beer. Nursed it until he saw Petrovich order the food. Then he returned to his car and drove back to the house.

Hiding the car, he approached the place on foot. Fallon's Honda was nowhere to be seen so he pulled himself over the wall and took a quick look through the garage window. The place was empty. He went to the rear of the house and looked for an access point. The kitchen door was the easiest. Taking out his picks he had it open in two minutes. He waited. But the alarm didn't go off.

From the kitchen he passed through into a dining room, dominated by a large table with eight chairs. To his left, a set of patio doors gave access to the sun porch. On his right, a wide archway opened up into the main hallway of the house. On the polished floor tiles, between the table and the arch, was a large, dried, bloodstain.

He knelt down and examined the stain. Then followed the blood trail through the hall and up the wide staircase. It stopped before a closed door. Pushing it open he stepped into a bedroom.

The bed lay unmade. The pillow and sheets were heavily bloodstained. On the wall beside the bed were two large posters of Billie Piper. One of them showed the actress in her role as prostitute Hannah Baxter. The other as Doctor Who's companion, Rose Tyler.

This had to be Fallon's room. A quick glance into the bathroom confirmed this. The few toiletries he found were generic British products. The sort available in any supermarket. The sink, bathroom floor, and the towel hanging over the bath, were also stained with blood.

Ballenger didn't know how much time he had. Fallon might have simply slipped out to a local shop or filling station. Quickly as he could he checked out the other bedrooms.

There was little of interest. The clothes hanging in the wardrobes had Continental labels. Mostly German and Dutch. A laptop sat on the dressing table in one of the rooms but he made no attempt to open it. Lying in a drawer in the third bedroom was a wicked-looking 9mm SR1 Vektor pistol. He left the Russian-made gun where it was.

At the end of the landing was a heavier, more solid, door. It was locked. Using his picks he opened it up. Stepped into a large business study. There was a desk and a drawing board. Plus all the accoutrements of a well equipped working office. He took a quick look through the desk drawers then left the room, relocking the door behind him.

Back downstairs he moved from the hall into the main lounge at the front of the house. Lying on an occasional table was a deck of playing cards and three empty, unwashed glasses. A foreign-language paperback sat on the arm of a chair. On the settee, the TV remote lay next to an e-book reader.

Bored men, he thought. Waiting around. Boredom causes friction, which triggers fights. He remembered the raised voices from last night. Wondered who Fallon had been fighting with. Probably the Serb.

He left the house the way he came in. Returned to his car and went back to the Duke. When the Kozaks came out he followed them back to the house and took up watch again. He thought Fallon might be back but he wasn't. It was sometime around eight o clock in the evening when the blue Honda finally reappeared. Ballinger waited another hour, and then returned to his hotel.

30

MONDAY

Ballinger:

He had just stepped from the shower when his phone sounded. 'What's happening?' asked Lucas Devine.

'Nothing's happening. They sit in the house, waiting. Like me. Bored, probably, like me. They've had some sort of fight. There's blood all over the place. Most of it Fallon's, from what I could see.'

'You've been in there?'

'Just for a look round.'

'Don't push it,' warned Devine. 'You don't want to mix it with these people, you really don't. Right now Fallon's lucky the Kozaks haven't put a bullet in his head. Looks like he went on a killing spree before he left Weymouth.'

'Who'd he kill?'

'Your friend Bianca, for one.'

'Bianca? Bianca is dead?' Ballinger's face became grim.

'Well someone killed her - and her boyfriend - in Dutton's office. Sometime on Tuesday. Can you think who else might have done that? You said yourself Fallon was crazy, and we can't put him in Manchester until the day after the killing.'

'Why would he do something as stupid as that?'

'Like you said, the guy's a nut? My guess is, with Dutton out of town he decided to turn over his office. They must have walked in on him, so he killed them.'

'Well that explains Dutton's sudden recall to Weymouth!' Ballinger felt an immense anger. He didn't know Bianca well, but he had liked her. For months she had helped him keep an eye on Dutton. Now he felt ashamed and guilty for using her the way he had. He also regretted that he would never get the chance to explain his actions and apologise to her. He just hoped that some day he would have Fallon in his sights again. There'd be no hesitation a second time.

'Don't do anything stupid,' voiced Devine, reading his mind. 'Just stick to the job I'm paying you for.'

'How was she killed?'

'They haven't released the details. It's thought a gun was used.'

'Do the police know it was Fallon?'

'I doubt it. The cops will have talked to Dutton of course. But he won't be able to tell them much. He doesn't even know Fallon's on his tail.'

'I'll kill the bastard!'

'Pretty much how the Kozaks feel, I guess.'

'How would they know?'

'You tell me? Perhaps Fallon opened his mouth? Or maybe they saw it on TV and put two and two together, like I did.'

'Okay, well since you're so clued up about what's going on down there, when can we expect Dutton back?'

'Don't ask me! I just read the reports, is all. Dutton will be helping the police with their enquiries, as they say. So he'll be back when they let him come back. Meanwhile, lay off Fallon. And steer clear of that house. We don't need complications.' Devine rang off.

Ballinger finished dressing. Then went down to breakfast. As he ate, he thought about Fallon. The man was unpredictable and dangerous. At some point he would have to be taken out of the equation. But not yet. Not with things on hold. He didn't want the opposition to know there was another player in the game. Not until it became unavoidable.

Besides, the Kozaks might even do the job for him. Their idea would have been to come over here. Do what they had to do, quietly and discreetly. Then get back to Holland at the first opportunity. But with Fallon running around acting like Billy the Kid, everything could be thrown into jeopardy for them.

Something else was bothering Ballinger. On two separate occasions Fallon had been off the radar for the best part of a day. The man was up to something, somewhere, and he would like to know what it was.

Ignoring Devine's advice he began his day once again watching the house. There was no sign of movement during the morning but at twelve o clock a pizza delivery van arrived. The Serb took in the boxes.

By six o clock Ballinger was ready for calling it a day when Fallon suddenly appeared from around the back of the house. Even from a distance the man's face looked a mess. His right cheek was black and blue. It carried a deep cut, held together with sticking plaster. His mouth looked like someone had tried to force a brick into it. Sideways.

Fallon unlocked the garage and drove his car out into the courtyard. Ballinger hurried to his own car and waited. Minutes later the Honda drove past the end of the track. Once again he took up station behind it. When Fallon took the Altrincham road then cut off towards Timperley, he knew exactly where they were heading.

The Honda pulled onto the Tipsy Fox car park. Ballenger drove on by, glancing that way as he passed. Sitting in its usual spot was the familiar Audi. Dutton was back. The waiting was over. It was game on again.

31

Dutton:

Before leaving, Monday morning, I rang DCI Ryan. Told him I had found nothing missing, either from my home or office.

'Rules out burglary then!' He didn't sound happy. I asked if there was any progress. 'When there is I'll issue a press release.' Taking that as a no I asked if he needed to speak to me again. This brought a 'not at this present time,' so I told him I was returning to Manchester. He wished me a safe journey. Said he might call me back if the need arose, and that was that.

Leaving the Ford in my garage I took a taxi to Weymouth station. The first leg of my journey took me to London Waterloo. From there I rode the tube to Euston. I called Tony Hale and told him what time I was due in Manchester. He said he'd have someone meet me.

Sitting on the train I reflected upon the journey itself. It was a huge dog-leg of a trip, with train times that didn't mesh. I probably could have done it quicker by car, driving up through the west country. But I already had one car in Manchester. I didn't need another.

I was collected from Manchester's Piccadilly Station by a Community Support Officer. Driven to Central Park in a pool car. Tony met me in reception and handed over my car keys.

'How was it?'

'Not good!' We went to the canteen for a coffee. I filled him in on the details. Told him also about the mess in my house. I didn't mention Sam Adams and his son.

'Lucy's at home,' he said. 'I didn't know you were coming back until you called. I'll bring her in tomorrow. Leckonby wants to see you, too. He's got news for you.'

'I'll go down now.'

'He's not in today. But he'll be here in the morning.'

I thanked Tony for his help. Collecting my car, I drove to Timperley.

George greeted me with news. 'Had a couple of people asking after you while you were gone!'

'Oh?'

'One on the phone, Friday night. Said he needed to speak to you, urgently. I told him to call you at home.'

'Did he sound foreign?' George shook his head. 'And the other one?'

'Shifty little bugger. Called in Saturday morning. Claimed he was a courier with a special delivery for you. I told him he could leave it with us, but he wouldn't have that. Said you had to sign for it, personally. Darren told him he had a bloody long drive in front of him then, 'cause you were in Weymouth. Sorry, he shouldn't have told him that.'

'No problem!'

'We had Dorset police on, too,' he gave me a look. 'Wanted to know what time you arrived here Tuesday?'

I told him what had happened in my office.

'Jesus!' he exclaimed. 'What do the investigating officers think?'

'A robbery gone wrong,' I said.

'Is that what you think?'

'I don't know what to think? Perhaps they're right!'

'One thing you can rely on,' he stated knowingly. 'There'll be drugs involved somewhere along the line. It's always about drugs with these people. Stealing to feed their habit.'

32

TUESDAY

Dutton:

I was back at Central Park for ten o clock. Tony came down to the foyer with Lucy and I put her in the car. I found Leckonby in his office. He was wearing a suit. Looking strangely ill at ease out of uniform. There was a monitor screen set up on his desk.

'Had no luck following her from the cafe,' he told me. 'She jumped into a taxi that lost itself in all those back streets on the other side of Piccadilly. So we tried a different approach. We worked backwards from when she actually arrived at the cafe. Followed her all the way back to her starting point. She was on foot. Watch.'

He pressed start. Alex appeared on the screen. She was walking backwards into the Arndale centre, her figure highlighted so she was easy to follow. He speeded up the machine. The figure ran backwards through the Mall, pausing at the main enquiry desk before exiting onto Market Street.

She backed rapidly down Fountain street and into St Peter's Square. In and out of a stationery store and then along Oxford street, calling in three more shops. On Oxford road she spent some time in a small shopping precinct, close to what used to be the polytechnic. The sequence came to an end with her stepping backwards into the main entrance to the university.

'The University?' I asked.

'That's where she set out from.'

'What's she carrying?'

'Posters, we think. She's delivering them to various locations. Stationery stores. Book shops. Places like that.' He ran the sequence fast forward and the figure of Alex made the same journey in forward gear. When she arrived at the enquiry desk in the Arndale Centre he paused the sequence. 'This could be her final delivery.'

He set the viewing to normal speed. I watched Alex chat briefly to the woman behind the enquiry desk. She handed over a rolled up poster from the tube she carried. Seeing her there, smiling and interacting with the guide, caused a strange lurch within my stomach.

'So,' I said, forcing myself to concentrate, 'she sets out from the university handing out posters, and ends up in the Arndale Centre.'

'Then goes for a coffee.'

'What's on the posters?'

'I don't know? Let's go and find out, shall we!'

We went in a pool car. Passed through the city centre then headed out towards the University. As he drove, Leckonby explained why he wasn't in uniform.

'We have something of a softly-softly approach with the University. Try to keep uniforms out of there as much as we can. It's their idea, but we're happy enough to go along with it. Most of the time, at least. It's supposed to help with relations between police and the students.'

'Does it work?'

He shrugged, non-committedly.

Leaving the car illegally parked behind the Arndale Centre, we made our way inside. The woman we saw on the security video was on duty behind the desk. With her was the old man who thought he recognised Alex from the picture I showed him.

'Let me do the talking,' said Leckonby. He showed his warrant card then held up a still picture of Alex, standing there at the desk. 'Do you know this woman?'

'She's from the university,' the woman said at once. 'What has she done?'

'She hasn't done anything. But we need to speak to her. What was on the poster she left?'

She bent down to rummage under the counter. The old man leaned forward and looked at the picture.

'That's her!' he exclaimed, looking at me. 'The one you were looking for. If you'd brought that picture with you I'd have recognised her straight away.'

The woman pulled out a rolled up sheet of paper. Opened it out so we could both see. It was an advertisement for the next Umac Theatre production.

'Does she deliver these on a regular basis?' I asked.

The woman shook her head. 'They're usually delivered by students. But sometimes she brings them herself. They're her posters. She designs them.'

Here was another surprise. Apart from flower arranging I had never seen Alex display any kind of artistic talent. Again I was finding out just how little I knew about the woman I'd married.

'Thank you,' smiled Leckonby. 'You've been very helpful.'

Fifteen minutes later we were at the vehicle security gate, outside the Umac Theatre. The man waved us through when Leckonby showed his police ID. We left the car by the main entrance and entered the foyer.

The girl manning the reception desk directed us to the first floor. 'The offices are up there,' she informed us, picking up the telephone. 'I'll let them know you're on your way.'

We climbed the stairs. Found ourselves in a lounge area dotted with tables and chairs. After a three minute wait a door at the far end of the lounge opened. A tall, academic-looking, woman peered out.

'Are you the policemen?'

'Inspector Leckonby!' He showed his warrant card. She held open the door to let us through. Led us down a corridor to an office at the far end. The sign on the door read **Jean Harlowe. Production Director.** She ushered us inside. Pointed to two plastic seats, then sat down behind the desk.

'Jean Harlow?' Leckonby raised an enquiring eyebrow.

'It's spelt differently,' she pointed out. 'Mine has an 'e' on the end.' She studied us evenly. 'So, what can I do for you?'

The Inspector took the picture from his pocket and passed it across the desk. 'She one of your people?'

The woman glanced at the picture and passed it back. 'Katarina Skala. She's a Czech citizen and yes, I have seen her passport.' She regarded us with a faintly worried expression. 'Has something happened to her?'

'Not as far as we know. Why do you ask?'

She shrugged. 'I just wondered why you are asking about her?'

'Is she on your books?'

'She's freelance.'

'What does she do?' I put in.

'Set and poster design,' she told me. 'She's very good, too.'

'Is she here?' enquired the Inspector.

'No.'

'Do you have her address?'

'Is she in trouble?'

'No, she's not in any trouble.'

'Is that why there are two policemen looking for her? Because she's not in trouble?'

Leckonby kept his cool. 'Ms Harlowe - '

'Mrs - ' she interrupted.

'Mrs Harlowe, Katarina is not in trouble. Not in the way you are thinking, anyway. But we do need to speak to her, and your co-operation would be appreciated.'

With a theatrical sigh she picked up the phone. Punched in a single number. 'Lucy, will you bring in Kat's file please,' she instructed.

Two minutes later a young woman entered the office. Placed a slim buff file on the desk. She gave Leckonby and I a quick appraisal before leaving. Jean Harlowe, with an 'e', pushed the file across to the Inspector. He opened it up and studied the contract inside. It showed the name, address and phone number of Katarina Skala.

'Can I have a copy of this?' he asked.

She left the office for a minute or two. When she returned she placed the original document back in the folder and handed him a copy.

'Anything else I can do?'

Leckonby folded the paper. 'I must ask you not to contact her. Or warn her in any way that we are looking for her. You won't be doing her any favours if you do. But you could find yourself in serious trouble.'

For the first time since we arrived she smiled. 'I think you'll find it's a little late for that,' she told us. 'I've been trying to contact Katarina since last Tuesday. She hasn't been in work. Her phone is dead. Nor does she appear to be at home. Now, perhaps, I can see why? It looks like she saw you coming, Inspector: and unless I'm mistaken, I think you'll find your bird has flown.'

Back in the car Leckonby handed me the address. 'Want me to come with you?'

I shook my head. 'No! Take me back to Central Park. I'll go in my own car. If she is at this place I'd rather be alone when I get there. Getting her to open the door might need delicate handling. Having Lucy with me might just be my way in.'

'What if she's moved on, like the woman said?'

'Then it's back to square one,' I answered ruefully.

'Well don't forget, officially she's a wanted person. If you do find her, try not to let her disappear again before we have a word with her. And if there's anything else I can do, give me a call.'

'Thank's!' He dropped me back at police HQ. Wished me luck. 'Will you let Tony Hale know what we found,' I asked. 'Tell him I'll keep him posted. You too,' I promised.

I went to collect my car.

33

Susnik:

Inside the Russian embassy, Peter Susnik entered the office of Gregor Belkin, head of security in London. The room smelled of furniture polish and cigarette smoke.

The man sitting behind the desk waved him into a comfortable visitor's chair and continued talking on the phone. Susnik gazed at the plump figure of his superior. He was on a scrambled line, talking to the Director in Moscow. The conversation was about postage stamps.

Susnik knew nothing about stamps. He thought philately a pointless and infantile obsession. But as both Belkin and the Director were avid collectors, he would never dream of voicing his opinions. Not while he still enjoyed working for the Directorate.

When the conversation ended Belkin was smiling broadly. The smile faded when he looked at Susnik.

'How are you Pyotr?' he asked, using the Russian form of the name.

'I am well. You?'

Belkin raised a hand in a gesture that said *well enough*. He reached into his desk and pulled out a sheet of paper. Studied it for a few moments then looked across the table.

'Do you know why you are here?'

Susnik shook his head. Quickly searched his memory for anything he might have done wrong.

'It's about your transfer request.'

Now Susnik looked confused. 'Transfer!' he voiced. 'What transfer request?'

'Prague,' answered Belkin. 'Are you saying you did not apply for head of security in Prague?'

'But that was years ago. Before I came here. The position was given to Verasov.'

'Verasov is dead. Killed by a stroke. Too many Czech dumplings, no doubt.' Belkin's grave face melted into a smile. 'You have been appointed his successor Pyotr. As of today you are head of security in Prague. May I offer my congratulations.'

He climbed to his feet, reached forward, and shook Susnik's hand. Then he went over to a drinks bureau, poured a useful amount of vodka into each of two glasses, and passed one to Susnik. 'Tva-jó zda-ró-vye, Pyotr,' Belkin toasted his health. 'It is only what you deserve.'

'Bóo-deem zda-ró-vye,' returned Susnik, raising his own glass to toast both of their health. For a moment he was barely unable to contain his surprise and joy. Then he remembered Altyn. 'When am I due in Prague?'

'I was just talking to the director about that. Telling him you have some leave due. He has given you a week to tie up any loose ends here and brief your successor. Then you fly to Moscow for the formal hand-over. Afterwards you may have a few days off to visit your family before taking up your new position in Prague. I am very pleased for you, Pyotr. I am sure you will make an excellent chief of security.'

'Thank you. I've learned a lot from you during my time here. I'm very grateful for your support.

When they had finished their drinks the two men shook hands again. Susnik returned to the office he shared with two other attachés. When he walked through the door he was greeted by a rousing cheer. The room was full of embassy staff, all wishing to offer their congratulations.

Later, when the office had returned to normal, Susnik sat at his desk. Reflected on what this would mean to himself and, more importantly, to Altyn.

When he had applied for the Prague posting, he had not expected to get it. Lack of years and experience were against him. So he was not surprised when he was turned down. Instead, he was appointed number two in London, under Belkin: a position formerly held by Alexi Verasov. Since then he had put all thoughts of Prague out of his mind.

Now the job was his. Prague! A dream appointment. But the timing couldn't have been worse. It gave him less than a week to get Altyn to safety. He thought about this and shook his head. It couldn't be done.

He unlocked a desk drawer and took out a throw-away phone. Punched in a number. 'Justin,' he began when the call was answered. 'I have a question. How quickly would you be able to get a new passport and another set of papers for my friend?'

'Two weeks, earliest,' he was told. 'Probably longer with the passport office being in the state it's in. Do you want me to set the wheels in motion?'

'No no,' said Susnik. 'I'm just planning ahead, that's all. Thank you Justin. I'll get back to you.' He ended the call. Two weeks? Impossible. With a heavy heart he called Altyn. She picked up immediately. 'I'm afraid something has come up at the Embassy. I cannot be with you until tomorrow.'

'I feel like a prisoner in this place, Peter,' she told him. 'I need to get away from here soon, or I'll go mad.'

'Unfortunately there are things happening that will affect our plans. Things I cannot discuss on the phone. But I'll be with you as soon as I can. Then we will talk. Do not worry, I will make sure you are safe. You know this, don't you.'

'I do.'

'Good. So now I must go. I have many things to do.'

He closed the phone. Sat back, deep in thought. Finally he took out the telephone directory and looked up a number. Re-opening the phone he tapped this in. After four rings the call was answered.

'United States Embassy,' announced the switchboard girl.

'Lucas Devine, please,' he requested.

34

Ballinger:

At one o clock Ballinger caught sight of Dutton's car coming down Gateway. Some way behind him was the ever faithful Blue Honda. He watched the cars turn towards the City then followed on behind. Today, Fallon was not alone. With him was Petrovich.

He stayed close as the two cars worked their way across the city. Soon they were on a wide thoroughfare with university campuses on one side, car show-rooms on the other.

They passed the Royal Infirmary, and Children's Hospital. A short time later they turned off. Entered an area of student accommodation. Finally they turned into a narrow avenue, fronted with apartment blocks.

Both sides of the avenue were lined with parked cars. Up ahead Dutton reversed the Audi into a rare gap. Fallon pulled into the only other available slot.

Ballinger was forced to drive on to the next junction. He took a left turn into an almost identical street and found a space. Slipping the Glock into its holster he left the car. Walked back the way he'd come. By the time he got back to where the two cars were, both stood empty.

He approached the Honda. Pulled a small module from his pocket and attached it, magnetically, to the underside of the car. Moving on to Dutton's car he groped around underneath until he found Fallon's tracker. Removing it, he dropped it down a nearby drain. Heard it hit bottom with a splash.

Crossing the road he took up a position in a gravelled fore-court in front of one of the apartment blocks. He had a good view of both cars. Unless his quarry was in the building right behind him, he should remain undetected.

He waited patiently. If this was where the woman lived, then the opposition had got there first. Which was not good for the private detective, and even worse for his wife. It was not good for himself either. But at least it was a recoverable situation.

Sooner or later Fallon and his partner had to return to their car. If they came out with the woman he would have to take her from them. But not here.

The lane leading down to the house was an ideal place for an ambush. Being so close to their base would leave them relaxed. Off-guard. It should give him an edge. Hopefully, though, it wouldn't come to that.

In the event, it didn't. Minutes later he spotted movement across the street. The double doors of a squat apartment block opened and Petrovich came out, followed by Fallon. The two men walked quickly to their car. Climbed in, and pulled away. They did not look happy. Once they were out of sight Ballinger left cover and strolled across the avenue.

He entered the block. Found himself in a wide entrance hall. Directly facing him was a stairway. It was flanked by two passageways that ran back into the main body of the building. Two ends of a continuous passageway, he guessed.

Taking the entrance on his left he walked past three apartments before, as expected, the corridor turned sharply to the right. Three more apartments were situated along this stretch. The door into the last one stood partially open.

Drawing the Glock he stood beside the door with his back to the wall. He reached back and pushed the door inward until it was fully open. When this brought no response he risked a quick glance inside. Then took a longer look.

He was peering into a short hallway. The door on his right was open and showed a bedroom. On his left was a bathroom. Facing him was a door leading into the lounge. There, lying on the floor in the open doorway, was Dutton.

Ballinger went inside. Closed the outer door. He knelt beside the investigator and checked his breathing and pulse. The man was alive. His face was a mess and he was bleeding from a scalp wound, but apart from these he could find no other injuries.

Leaving Dutton where he was, he checked out the rest of the apartment. There was little left, in the way of personal possessions. Just a couple of coats hanging in the wardrobe, and a few scraps of clothing in the drawers. If this was where the woman had been living, she was long gone.

Back in the kitchen he found a clean tea towel. Turning on the tap he soaked the towel in cold water and carried it over to where Dutton lay.

35

Dutton:

I climbed from the car in the narrow street. Checked the names on the buildings. The block I was looking for was the next one along. A flat-roofed, ugly, cement-rendered, piece of architecture. Very nineteen-sixties.

As I walked along the pavement a slow-moving black Discovery drove slowly down the street. The sudden appearance of the dark SUV set alarm bells ringing. I slowed my pace. Let the car turn out of sight then hurried on, hoping to get off the street before it came back.

The door into the building was not locked. I stepped into the entrance hall and looked around. There were corridors off either side of a central staircase. Ignoring the stairs I entered the corridor on the right. Followed it down then round, to apartment number four. Alex's apartment.

I stood before the door, breathing deeply to slow my racing heartbeat. Then I placed my index finger on the bell push and pressed. Inside I heard the hollow sound of a musical chime. Thirty seconds passed and no one answered. I rang the bell again. Still no response.

Taking a thin, plastic, card from my wallet I inserted it into the gap between door and frame. Worked it forwards with a series of rocking motions until it pushed aside the tongue of the lock. Nudging open the door I stepped into the hallway.

'Hello? Alex?' My voice echoed around the rooms, creating a sense of emptiness. A scattering of envelopes and leaflets on the hallway floor told their own story. I gathered them up and stacked them together on the radiator shelf.

Pushing through the nearest door I entered a bedroom. The wardrobe was almost empty, the dresser drawers too. An abandoned pair of slacks lay on the bed. I picked them up. Touched them to my cheek hoping to get a sense of Alex. I felt nothing.

Leaving the bedroom I entered the lounge. The room was bright and modern. Fitted out with Alex's favourite furniture from Ikea. Apart from this there was nothing to suggest she had ever been there.

In the kitchen I found units stocked with dried food. There was crockery, pans, and other kitchen wares and utensils. I opened the refrigerator door to find it empty. The freezer too had been cleared out.

I heard a noise in the hallway. Heard the front door close. Someone had entered the apartment. I quickly crossed the lounge and opened the door. Expecting to find Alex standing there.

It wasn't Alex. It was a man. Two men, in fact. The one with a short baseball bat in his hand rushed straight at me. I had a momentary glimpse of a face that was familiar, yet strangely out of context. Then without even breaking stride, he head-butted me in the face.

The blow was as savage as it was unexpected. I went down like a bowling pin. The man leapt over me and burst into the lounge, followed by his companion. Dazed, I began to climb to my feet but didn't make it. Without warning the bat was slammed against the side of my head, robbing me of consciousness.

Awareness returned. I opened my eyes but couldn't see anything. I had a momentary panic, thinking I was blind. Then I realised there was something being held over my face. Someone was trying to suffocate me. I raised my hands to fight off my attacker. Kicked out with my feet.

'Easy,' said a calm voice. 'I'm on your side.'

The object was lifted. Light hit my eyes triggering a sudden, and savage, pain inside my head.

'Christ almighty!' I moaned, covering my eyes with my arm.

'Close your eyes,' said the voice. 'Then open them more gradually. Let them get used to the light.'

I did as he said and the pain eased. Looking up I saw a man kneeling over me. He was holding a wet, and bloodied, tea towel.

'Help me up,' I said.

The stranger stood up. Reached down a hand and pulled me slowly to my feet. He guided me into the lounge and sat me down at the table. I rested both elbows on the table-top. Cradled my sore head in my hands.

He wandered off. I heard him moving about in the kitchen. Then he was back. with two mugs of coffee. He placed one in front of me then sat down with the other, in the chair opposite .

I picked up the mug. Drank the coffee slowly. Any sudden movement of my head sent sledge hammers flying around inside my skull. As I slowly got my head together I studied the man sitting before me.

Late thirties with light, ginger, hair. His clear green eyes gazed at me across the table with a glint of amusement. The leather jacket over his black tee-shirt looked expensive. It concealed neither his muscular torso, nor the gun he carried. When he spoke there was more than a hint of Ulster in his voice.

'Private Investigator, eh? Can't say I'm impressed.'

'Me neither!' I acknowledged, drily.

'Who hit you? Was it Fallon?'

'Who's Fallon?'

'You know him. He's been watching you for months. He followed you here from Weymouth.'

I had a sudden recollection. Saw the familiar face coming towards me in the hallway.

'The yob!' I exclaimed. 'With the pit-bull!'

'That's him.'

'I don't understand?'

'He was hoping you'd lead him to your wife. Which you almost did.' He waved a hand, casually. 'This where she's been living?'

I nodded. Wished I hadn't when my head started to spin. 'Does he drive a black Discovery?' I asked.

'No, that's me. When did you clock me?'

'I didn't. It was a friend of mine.'

'Hale?' He grinned. 'I thought he'd sussed me. Him being a policeman and a trained observer, and all that.'

'Okay,' I growled. 'So you know all about me! Who are you? And why are you following me?'

'Name's Ballinger. I'm here for the same reason as Fallon. To find your wife. Except he's doing it for the people who want to kill her. I'm doing it for those who want to keep her alive.'

'But then you would say that, wouldn't you?'

He simply shrugged and glanced casually around the room. 'They said you were good. They weren't wrong, were they. How did you find this place?'

I ignored the question. 'How long have you been following me?'

'Months.'

'*Months?*'

'It's a long story,' he shrugged

'I'm not going anywhere!'

A faint pinging sound came from Ballinger's pocket. He took out his phone and studied the screen. 'I think you are,' he said, quickly putting away the phone and climbing to his feet. 'Unless you want another run-in with your friends. Looks like they're coming back. You okay to drive?'

I nodded optimistically, and followed him from the apartment.

36

Fallon:

In the blue Honda the Serb was reporting their failure to Dauren Kozak. He had the phone on speaker.

Kozak wasn't happy. 'What d'you mean she ain't there? Where is she? At the goddammed Walmart?'

'No, I mean she is not there, period: and from what she took with her, she's not coming back.'

There was a short pause while Dauren related this information to his brother.

'Where's Dutton?'

'In the apartment. Out cold. We had to subdue him.'

'Oh great! So where are you?'

'On our way back.'

'On your way back? On your way back to where?'

'To the house.'

Kozak exploded. 'What? Are you crazy? What if the guy went there for a meet? Did anybody think about that? Christ, she could be there right now while you two assholes are driving around with your freakin' brains switched off?'

Much to Fallon's delight the Serb's face grew red. 'Sorry,' he mumbled. 'We did not think.'

'Get back to that apartment Janko. Right now! Stay there until something happens. And do not come back here until you have something good to tell me. You got that?'

'Got it?'

Dauren broke the connection.

'You heard him,' said the Serb.

'Heard him?' grinned Fallon. 'I'll bet they heard him down in Pimlico. Stamping his little foot, was he?'

'Just drive Fallon. You're not funny.'

Fallon turned the car around. Drove in silence. Still smiling at his passenger's discomfort.

'Will this thing not go any faster?' complained the Serb.

Fallon looked at Petrovich in disbelief. 'Oh, right? So now you want to get us pulled for speeding, with a shooter in your pocket?' He shook his head. 'Why don't you do something useful. Check the tracker. See if he's still there?'

The Serb switched on the tracker screen. 'No signal!' he stated.

'Great! He's dumped the tracker. Which means he'll be long gone, with no chance of picking him up.'

'This is your doing,' pointed out the Serb. 'Rushing in as you did. Always the hot head. You are *npenpeka* - a liability.'

'And you just missed a golden opportunity, my old son. We should have done what I said. Brought Dutton out with us. Find out what he knows. I'd soon have him telling us where she is.'

'I don't think he knows where she is. If he did, he would have gone to her days ago.'

'He knows where she *was* though, doesn't he? I have a tenner says that's not all he knows.'

Arriving back on the quiet street there was no sign of Dutton's car. Inside the building they found the door to the apartment locked shut. Angrily Fallon kicked it open.

The place was much as they'd left it, though not quite. There was no sign of Dutton. But on the dining table sat two, half-empty, coffee mugs. Fallon picked one up. It was still warm. 'Well someone's been having a cosy chat?' He put down the mug and took out his phone. Offered it to the Serb. 'Here! You're in charge today. I'll let you do the honours.'

Petrovich called the number. He gave Dauren the news then braced himself for the expected tirade. Strangely, it didn't come. 'Okay,' said Kozak. 'Forget Dutton. Just get your asses back here. We've got things to do.'

37

Dutton:

I drove behind Ballinger to the Copthorne Hotel. Sat on a comfortable chair in his room. He asked if I wanted another coffee. When I said no, he began making one for himself.

'What do you know about your wife's past?' he asked.

'A lot less than I thought,' I admitted. 'Which wasn't much to begin with.'

'What was she calling herself when you met?'

'Alexana Morel.'

'That's not her real name.'

Somehow I wasn't surprised. 'Okay,' I said.

'That's the name she was given by the US Marshals Office. When she went into their witness protection program.'

'She's American?'

'Sort of.'

'So her Latvian passport is a fake?'

'Everything about her is a fake.'

'Why is she in witness protection?' I asked.

'She's on a hit list.'

'Why? What has she done?'

He shrugged 'I don't know?'

I shook my head. 'I don't get it! Why would someone in witness protection move from the States to somewhere like Swanage? I mean, if you want to lose yourself then you don't choose to live in a small rural community do you? A densely populated area is your best bet. Somewhere like London!'

'Or Manchester,' he said pointedly. 'Look, I don't know why she's on a hit list. Nor why she chose to live in Swanage. These are things you'll have to ask her yourself - if you ever find her. I only know what I've been told.'

'So tell me,' I demanded

He nodded. Picked up the coffee and sat on the edge of the bed. 'There are two brothers,' he began. 'Dauren and Serik Kozak. Eastern Europeans, possibly Russians but I can't be certain. They've put up a million dollars for anyone who can track down your wife for them. Seems they want her dead.

Last September they almost had her. But before they could close the net she had her 'sailing accident' and vanished. All this happened before I came on the scene, by the way, so my knowledge of events is a bit second hand. What I do know, is that the drowning stunt she pulled was a complete waste of time. First of all it fooled nobody: and secondly it wasn't necessary.

There are contingences in place for when someone in witness protection finds themself in danger. In your wife's case, all she needed to do was call a guy named Lucas Devine at the US Embassy. He was her contact with the Marshalls office. Had she done this, and let him know she was in trouble, she would have received all the help she needed.'

'Did she know this?'

'She knew it. Everyone on witness protection is given a contact number to call. For some reason she decided not to make that call. She chose to disappear instead leaving everyone, including Devine himself, thinking she was dead.

Devine reported her death to the Office of Marshalls in Washington. Because the circumstances of her death looked suspiciously like a hit, they asked US field agents in Europe to look into the matter.

They learned that the Kozaks, or more specifically their agents in the UK, had been within a whisker of finding her at the time of the 'fatal' accident. They also discovered that the brothers did not believe she was dead. That they were still actively searching for her. Since this meant she was still in danger, they told Devine that he had better find her first. Which is when he hired me to watch you.'

'Why me?'

'He thought that if anyone had the motive and skill to organise a fake death, without a body turning up, it would be you. You not only had a personal stake in your wife's welfare, but when it comes to the business of vanishing into thin air, you deal with people who do that all the time.

Devine's thinking was that with the Kozaks closing in on your wife, you arranged the 'accident' yourself and spirited her away. He reasoned that after a suitable time - a year or so perhaps if you were a cautious man - you and she would get back together again. Perhaps in some other part of the world.'

'And you'd be there to blow the whistle on us.'

'My job is to put her in contact with Devine. That's all. So he can offer any help that's available, if she wants it.'

'She seems to have managed well enough without his help, so far,' I pointed out.

'Until she was careless enough to step in front of the cameras,' he reminded me.

'I'll have that drink now,' I said. 'Have you anything stronger than coffee.'

He pulled a miniature whiskey from the dumb waiter. I sipped the whiskey slowly from the bottle. The fiery liquid spread a feeling of well-being through my body. Revived my spirit. 'So where does Fallon fit into all this?' I asked.

'The Kozak brothers operate out of Holland. They run illegal immigrants, guns, and drugs, into the UK. This end of their operation is run by a local Bratva boss called Dooby Levkin. Fallon is Levkin's enforcer.'

'Bratva? The Russian mafia?'

'That's right! It was almost certainly Levkin's people who were on your wife's trail last year. When they lost her Levkin must have used the same logic as Devine. He put Fallon onto you, hoping you'd lead him to her.'

'Who else am I up against here, besides this Fallon?'

'There's Janko Petrovich. He's the guy with Fallon today. Then there's the Kozak brothers themselves.'

'They're here?'

'Arrived two days after Alex made her television debut. They know she's here somewhere: and they know you're here. They must have got pretty excited when you made a bee-line for that apartment. Right now I don't know who'll be feeling most disappointed, them, me, or you?'

'Me,' I claimed. Then I shook my head ruefully. 'I almost blew it, didn't I? I've been so single-minded about finding her, I've been walking around with my eyes shut. I could have got her killed.'

'You were lucky not to get yourself killed. Fallon doesn't usually leave witnesses. We saw that from what happened with Bianca.'

'What do you know about that?' I asked, sharply.

He ignored the question. 'The only reason he didn't kill you today is because they need you alive. You are the only key they have to finding your wife.'

'What you know about Bianca?' I repeated.

He shrugged. 'Only what everyone knows. That she and a friend were killed in your office. When did it happen?'

'Tuesday night.'

'It figures. We've put it down to Fallon. He didn't arrive here until Wednesday. Must have decided to search your office.'

'And my house.'

'Really? I didn't know that. Fallon's problem is that he's not a very good team player. Words like patience, and restraint, were never a part of his vocabulary. Direct action, that's Fallon: and if anyone gets in his way then it's their funeral. Literally.'

There was a silence between us. I was thinking about Bianca. If I'd stopped her entertaining her boyfriend in the office, she'd be alive today. I felt guilty about that, even though I'd turned a blind eye for the best of reasons.

Ballinger knocked back his coffee. Placed the cup on the bedside cupboard. 'Still, you almost found her,' he said. 'Too bad she was one step ahead of you. She's one clever lady that wife of yours. Resourceful, too.'

I didn't tell him about the help she'd received. I still didn't fully trust him. Everything he'd told me sounded plausible enough. But he could just as easily be working against Alex as for her.

'Alright,' I said, 'you've told me what the Kozaks will do if they get their hands on her. What happens if you and your posse of Marshalls find her first.'

'Nothing bad, that's for sure. She'll go back into protective custody. *Reprogrammed*, is the expression they use. Given another identity. Somewhere back in the States most likely.'

'So I'll lose her again?'

'I think you lost her some time ago,' he said, not unsympathetically. 'But at least you'd know she was alive and well, somewhere.'

'And that's supposed to make me feel better is it?'

38

'Right then!' Ballinger looked at me expectantly. 'You're the expert. Where would she go?'

I eyed him suspiciously. 'I'm not sure I'd tell you if I knew.'

'What, you think I'm making all of this up?'

'Not all of it, no! But you might have other reasons for wanting to find her. A million dollars-worth of them, maybe?'

Ballinger acknowledged my problem with a small nod. 'Okay! So check me out. You've got a phone in your pocket. Use it. Call the American Embassy in London and ask for Lucas Devine. He'll back me up.'

'Is this the Yank who called me? Told me to watch the news.'

'He wanted to make sure you saw her. Wanted you to go after her. Just call him,' he urged. 'If you want your wife to have the best chance of coming through this alive, we should work together. Which means it's important you trust me. So go on, make the call.'

Reluctantly I took out my phone. Asked for the number of the American Embassy. When asked if I wished to be put through I said yes.

'Nice to speak to you again Mister Devine,' I began when I was put through. 'It's Terry Dutton.'

'Where did you get my name?'

'Your man Ballinger.' Devine's silence confirmed Ballinger's claim. 'He tells me you work for the Office of US Marshalls. That you're my wife's handler?'

'Wrong on both counts, Dutton. I liaise with the Office of US Marshalls, and I am not Alex's handler. I never met your wife. I knew she was here somewhere, that's all. I was her contact in the event of her cover being blown.'

'So why didn't she call you last year when these people were closing in on her?'

'You'd have to ask her that. She obviously didn't want our help.'

'Perhaps she doesn't trust you,' I suggested. 'I'm not sure I would. People like you play games with other people's lives.'

'How do you figure that?'

'Spying on me,' I said. 'Hoping I'd lead you to my wife. Letting me believe she was dead, when you had information that suggested she was not. Have you any idea how cruel that is? If you had come to me with your suspicions I could have helped you find her. Instead you've wasted months, during which time she could have been brought to safety.'

He came back sharply. 'First off, Dutton, we didn't tell you anything because we don't know you. In our business we don't trust people we do not know. And we do not work with people we don't trust. For all we knew you could have engineered that whole accidental death thing yourself. In which case, any approach to you would have meant her disappearing even further into the trees before we had a chance to speak with her.'

The anger in his voice melted away. 'As for her being safe? I'm not sure she'll ever be safe here. This is a small country. Those who want her dead will keep looking until they find her. They have resources, and money, and it will only be a matter of time before they succeed - like they almost did last year. I promise you she'll be much safer back in the States.'

'Maybe she'd rather stay here?'

'Then she will die, Mister Dutton: and if you are anywhere near her when she does, you will die too. Now put Ballinger on will you!'

I passed over the phone. The conversation was brief, but forceful. Devine was clearly unhappy about my being brought on board. Ballinger insisted that either he handle things his way or he wouldn't handle them at all. In the end the American had little option but to agree.

'So that's how you talk to your boss?' I remarked when he passed back the phone. 'I'm impressed.'

'He's not my boss. I'm my boss. Devine only pays for my services. And right now he needs me more than I need him.'

'And you need me more than I need you.'

'Don't be too sure, Dutton. Just about now Fallon and his pals will be having a crisis meeting. I suspect you'll be very much on the agenda. They might even decide to come after you.'

'Why would they? They must know by now that I don't know where she is?'

'Nothing to stop them using you as bait, though. To flush her out. Wouldn't be the first time that's been tried. What do you think? Would she give herself up to save you?'

There was a time I'd have known the answer to that question. Now I wasn't sure. I sidestepped it. 'So you think we should work together, do you? My brains and your muscle?'

'However you see it!'

'I want everything up front,' I told him. 'Anything you know, I know. That's the deal.'

'That goes both ways,' he reminded me. 'I've already told you most of what I know.'

'One more thing,' I warned him. 'You stay a million miles away from my friends in Central Park! Especially with that thing under your jacket!' I pointed at the gun.

'Deal,' he smiled, offering a handshake which I took. 'So tell me, how did you find the apartment?'

'Good police work. Street surveillance showed us where she worked. So we went along to Umac and got her address.'

'Umac?'

'The university theatre.'

'When did you go there?'

'This morning.'

He looked puzzled. 'You can't have! I was watching all morning and you didn't - ' sudden comprehension dawned. 'A cop car!' he exclaimed. 'You went in a cop car! I wasn't looking at cop cars.' More understanding flickered across his face. 'And Friday! When you went back to Weymouth? You used a cop car then, didn't you? Left your car behind?'

'How did you know I was in Weymouth?'

'I called your hotel. They said I'd catch you at home.'

'Right! And how's the energy-saving window game?'

'Sorry!' he grinned. 'Just checking you were there. So what is she calling herself now?'

'Katarina Skala,' I told him. 'She had papers in that name, and a Czech passport.'

'Christ, how would she get those?'

'She's not acting alone.'

'What do you mean?'

'I don't know who he is, or what their relationship is. All I have is a name, Susnik. Which might not even be his real name. He's the one who arranged the 'fatal' yachting accident. Probably fixed her up with a new identity too.'

'Susnik? Sounds Russian.'

'Those who've met him think he's Russian.'

'Those who've met him?'

'Jenny, Alex's shop assistant, and the two trawler men who took him and her off my yacht before wrecking it.'

'My word, you have been busy haven't you? This Susnik character. Could he be someone from her past? A relative? Old flame, perhaps?'

'I've no idea? She never mentioned the name to me. Apparently he moved into the apartment above the shop, just before she disappeared. Whoever he is, he turned up again last Wednesday. Nosing around the flower shop in Swanage. Asking if anyone had been making enquiries about Alex. From what Bianca told me, I think he called my office too.'

'Damage limitation?' he suggested. 'He saw the news broadcast and is covering her back?'

'Probably,' I agreed.

'Anything else?'

I shook my head. 'What about you?'

'I've told you most of what I know. What you probably don't know is that you've been driving around with a tracker on your car. Our friend Fallon again, no doubt.'

'The cheeky bastard,' I bristled. Ballinger sat back on the bed. Looked pleased with himself. 'What?' I asked.

'I took it off. Put one on his car while he was inside the apartment, smacking you on the nose.'

'So we can see what he's up to, right?'

'It'll give us an edge, at least.'

Ballinger suddenly grew serious. 'There's something else I need to tell you,' he said. 'It's about Bianca.'

'What about her?'

'I knew her. She was working for me. Keeping me informed of your movements.'

'No way!' I protested. 'She wouldn't do that! Why would she do that?'

'I lied to her,' he explained. 'Said I was with Special Branch. Told her someone you put in prison was coming after you. That we were keeping a protective watch on you. I asked her to help us by letting me know where you'd gone, each time you left the area.'

'I don't believe you! She would have told me.'

'No she wouldn't. I asked her not to. I said if you knew about the threat, the first thing you'd do is go looking for the man yourself. Which would put you in even greater danger.'

'And she swallowed that?' Even as I asked the question I knew the answer. Bianca would have been too concerned about my safety to even question it.

'I'm sorry,' he said. 'She wasn't being disloyal. In her own way she was trying to protect you.'

'You know she was beaten don't you,' I told him. 'For information she didn't have.'

'No I didn't. I was told she'd been shot.'

'Her boyfriend was shot. She was beaten, sexually assaulted, then strangled.'

'Sounds about right for Fallon,' he said grimly.

'You know him?'

'I've met him. He's an animal. Needs putting down.'

'People talk under torture,' I reminded him. 'She might have told him about you?'

'She might have. But even if she did, I doubt he'd tell anyone. He's in enough trouble already, because of the killings. If the Kozaks hear Bianca was involved with Special Branch, they'll kill him for sure.'

There was a long silence between us.

'Anyway,' he offered, 'I just wanted to clear the air about Bianca. Put you in the picture. Tell you how sorry I am about what happened to her.'

'Okay,' I said, finally. 'So now you have.'

39

Ballinger studied his phone screen. 'What are you doing?' I asked.

'Checking where they are. Look!' The screen showed a map of the south Altrincham area. Heading along the A556 was a moving green dot.

'Shows green when the target's moving away. Red when it's coming towards you. When it gets to within a kilometre of you, it sends out a series of warning bleeps that grow more urgent the closer they come.'

I studied the map. 'Altrincham?'

'They have a rented house. In a village, just the other side.'

'You've seen it?'

'I have.' He adjusted the map. Pointed to a country lane that appeared to go nowhere. 'It's there. At the end of this lane. Not very clever to pick a property with only one way out.' He closed the phone and turned to me. 'Okay, so you're the professional. Where do we go from here?'

'How long does it take to create a new identity?'

He thought about this. 'Long enough. Two to three weeks at the very least. Longer still if the passport office is busy. What are you thinking?'

'People are predictable,' I told him. 'The last time she was in this situation Susnik took control. He didn't panic. Just got everything organised then stayed close by, right up to the day she disappeared. I think he'll do the same again. And if that's how long it takes to create a new identity, then she won't be going anywhere yet.'

'You think she's still here? In Manchester?'

'I'm sure she is. This is the only place she knows apart from Dorset. She won't go back there, that's a given.' I opened my phone and called Leckonby. Told him I'd found the apartment but missed Alex. 'Can you do a PNC check for me,' I asked. 'See if there's a car or driving license, registered to a Katarina Skala at that address?'

'I've already put the name through the system. No car, no license, no insurance. No anything in that name. Just a bank account into which her pay cheques are paid.'

'She'll be drawing on that,' I stated. 'We can use it to find her.'

'No you can't. It was cleared out last week.'

'Where was it drawn?'

'Various machines, in and around Manchester.'

'When was the last withdrawal?'

'Thursday, p.m.'

Again she was ahead of us. 'Could you chase up taxi and private hire firms in the area. Find out if any of them picked her up from the apartment, anytime last week: and if they did, where they dropped her.'

'That's a big ask! I'll give it a try, but don't hold your breath. Most taxi operators are too busy to spend time wading through back records, just to help the police.

Half of them don't even keep records. And if she just flagged down a passing taxi, it could have come from anywhere. It's a bit of a long shot, don't you think?'

'I know. But it's the best I can come up with.'

'Ok, leave it with me. I'll do what I can.'

'Thanks. Did you get anywhere with the profile search?'

'No. The only Alexana Morel born in Limbazi in 1981 died of leukaemia at the age of nine.'

No surprise there. 'Could I ask one more favour,' I enquired.

'Go on!'

'There's a man called Susnik. Probably Russian. He's in this somewhere. Can you run a PNC check. See if he's in the system?'

'Susnik? Possibly Russian? That the best you can do?'

'Sorry, that's all I've got.'

'Is Susnik his first name, or surname?'

'Surname. I think.'

He sighed, audibly. 'I assume he is here. In the UK? Not back in mother Russia with the other twenty million members of the Susnik clan?'

'He was here last week, if that's any help?'

'Alright I'll give it a go. But if Susnik is the Russian equivalent of Smith, we're struggling.' He rang off.

'Taxis?' queried Ballinger.

'According to DVLA she doesn't have a car. Since she seems to have left the apartment with most of her clothes, I assume she used a taxi. Possibly more than one if she made several trips. It's not much, but it's a starting point.

There's something else we now know for certain,' I said. 'She was still in Manchester last Thursday. She used her bank card to clear out her account. This supports my theory that she's still around somewhere. So now all we need to do is find her, before our friend Susnik whisks her away for good.' I hoped I sounded more optimistic than I felt.

40

WEDNESDAY

Altyn:

Susnik arrived five minutes after her flatmate left for work. She let him in and they sat at the small kitchen table. He drank his coffee, she ignored hers. Instead she anxiously smoked a cigarette in rapid, jerky, motions.

'I thought you'd given those up?'

She shrugged. Gave him a thin, tired smile. 'Don't tell me they'll kill me, Peter. I should be so lucky to live so long.'

'I called at your apartment. Someone has been there.' He didn't mention the blood on the floor.

'How would they find me so soon?'

'Your husband, I expect!'

'Terry? Terry is here?'

'Looking for you, I'm sure. His office girl told me he'd driven north on business.'

'I should have stayed in the apartment. Let him find me.'

'It would have got you killed. They'll be watching him, for sure.'

'I need to see him Peter, to ask his forgiveness. He's a good man. He didn't deserve what I did to him.'

'And you did not deserve what was done to you,' he reminded her sharply. 'Life is not always about what we deserve. It's about what we get. And we all have little choice in that.'

She sighed. 'All I want is for things to be the way they used to be.'

'You can't go back, you know that. They'll find you. Kill you both. Is that what you want? You've seen how cruel they can be.'

'So, what are my options?'

He regarded her sadly. Spread his hands, helplessly. 'There are no options. Things are happening that are beyond my control. My time here is over. They are moving me to Prague and cannot refuse to go. I am not going to be able to help you like before. This time, I'm afraid, we'll have to put our trust in the Americans.'

'Peter I can't go through all that again. Even if they help me - which they might not - they'll send me back to America. I may never be allowed to leave again. I'd be a prisoner there.'

'Better life in an open prison than death at the hands of those people. You must have courage, Altyn. The world changes all the time. There will come a day when all that is hanging over you will pass. Then you will be free to live as you wish. But for now there is no choice. You have to move on, and the Americans are your only hope.'

For a long moment she sat there staring at the untouched coffee. Then she took a long pull on the cigarette, inhaled deeply, and blew out a long stream of smoke. 'You're right of course. You were right the last time, and I should have listened to you. This time I have no choice. So tell me, what I have to do?'

'There is nothing for you to do. I have spoken to your Lucas Devine. Told him what has happened. He too has been greatly concerned for your safety. You are his responsibility and he will help you.'

'They didn't want me to come to England, you know. Perhaps I should have listened to them.'

'Perhaps you should. But regrets are a waste of emotion. Now you must use your time and energy on securing your future.'

'What about us Peter?' she asked. 'You are all I have now. Promise me that whatever happens we'll stay in touch?'

'When you are settled in your new life call me at the embassy in Prague. Use a throw-away phone and give the name Kursarov.'

'Kursarov? That was your wife's maiden name, wasn't it?'

'It was. So anyone listening will think one of my in-laws called.'

She put her arms around him. Hugged him strongly. Kissed him on the cheek.

'Thank you Peter. For all you have done for me.'

'You don't need to thank me. We are family. It is what we do. I only wish I could do more, but I cannot.'

'I wish I knew where Terry was,' she sighed. 'I'd love to see him one more time. If only from a distance.'

He shook his head firmly. 'Forget him Altyn. That part of your life is over. It is time to move on.' He took out his phone. Looked at her expectantly. 'Shall I call the American? Make the arrangements.'

For one more moment she hesitated. Unnerved by the implications of what he was about to do. Then she nodded.

He tapped in the number and was put through at once. 'Mr Devine? Peter Susnik here. It is decided. She is coming in. But I cannot be seen approaching the US Embassy. Nor will I leave her side until she is in your care. You will have to collect her from here.'

'No problem Mister Susnik. Tell me where you are and I'll have Alex picked up tomorrow and put on a plane out of there.'

Susnik gave him the address. 'What time can we expect you?'

'Not me. I'll send one of my team, Scott Devlin. He should be with you around midday. He's armed, very experienced, and he'll stay with her until she reaches a place of safety.'

'Thank you. We'll be waiting.'

'She's doing the right thing, Peter. She'll be much safer back in the States. I can guarantee that.'

'I hope you can, mister Devine. I hope you can.' Susnik closed the phone. He nodded to Altyn. 'It is done. Tomorrow they will take you away from here. Then you will be safe.'

41

Ballinger:

Ballinger finished his second coffee. He left the breakfast table, crossed the lobby, and went up to his room. Inside he opened his laptop and switched it on. When it came to life he brought up the tracker map.

Fallon was on the move. The screen showed his car climbing up the trans-Pennine motorway. Heading into Yorkshire, just east of Rochdale. Idly he tracked the car. There was no point chasing after Fallon. Wherever he was going, he'd be there and back before Ballinger caught up.

The phone in his pocket vibrated. Devine. 'So, how's it going?' The man sounded particularly upbeat.

'Dutton thinks the woman has a guardian angel. Some guy called Susnik. Seems he helped her relocate the last time. Fixed her up with new identity papers, plus whatever else she needed. He also believes she's still in Manchester. Waiting for this guy to provide a new escape route. Oh, and he's got the police trying to find the taxi that collected her from the apartment when she moved out.'

'Will they do that?'

'They'll try. The cop he spoke to wasn't optimistic. But we live in hopes. Can you check out this Susnik character? It might help to know something about him.'

'That'll be Peter Susnik. The Russian Intelligence officer.'

'You know him?' This time it was Ballinger's turn to be surprised.

'He just called me. From the woman's hidey-hole. Dutton's right, she is in Manchester. But not for long. He's persuaded her to come back into the program.'

'Well that's good, isn't it? So where do I pick her up?'

'You don't. I'm sending an official car to collect her. I have another job for you.'

'Go on?'

'Stay with Dutton. Don't let him out of your sight. It's important he doesn't find her. The last thing we need is for him to start messing with her head, just when she's finally agreed to come in. Think you can handle that?'

'I can try. But Dutton's a man on a mission. If something breaks he'll be off like a bat out of hell, and no one will stop him.'

'Look, by mid afternoon tomorrow she'll be out of here for good. So just do whatever it takes, Ballinger. Tie him to his goddamned bed if you have to, but don't let him find her.'

'I hear you.'

'Good. Now, what are the opposition doing?'

'I'm just on my way to find out.'

'Take Dutton with you. It'll keep him occupied.'

'I was going to.'

Ballinger shut down the phone. Returned to his laptop. Fallon had left the M62 and was on the A640 moorland road, heading east towards Huddersfield. Ten minutes later he changed course again. Veered off towards Brighouse. Soon the car left the road altogether and struck out across the moors. He watched its winding progress along some unmarked track until finally it stopped, somewhere in the middle of nowhere.

He checked the map for a ground reference point. There was nothing. Was Fallon playing some game of his own here, he wondered? Or was he on an errand for the brothers Grim. It might be useful to go out there sometime. See what Fallon found so interesting. He made a note of the GPS co-ordinate, just in case.

Now that the search was over his job was done. There was still a score to be settled for Bianca, but that could wait until the woman was safely out of the way. Right now he would follow instructions and stay with Dutton. Do his best to keep the investigator from finding his wife before she was spirited away by Devine. The task left him feeling conflicted.

The phone buzzed. Coincidentally it was Dutton.

'So how's breakfast at the Copthorne?' asked the private investigator.

'Very good. There are plenty of rooms here. You don't have to rough it in some run down, rural, pub.'

'The Fox is not run down, and the landlord is an old friend. An ex-copper, like me.'

'That figures. What do you want?'

'What are you doing?'

'Tracking Fallon. He's up and about already.'

'Where?'

'On the moors. Somewhere between Denshaw and Brighouse.'

'What's he doing there?'

'I'll call him and ask him, shall I? Is that why you called? To find out what Fallon is doing?'

'Leckonby's been in touch.'

'That was quick. Has he found the taxi?'

'Not yet. He put Susnik's name into a Special Branch database and it threw up a result. There is a Pyotr - or Peter - Susnik working out of the Russian embassy in London. He's listed as a cultural attaché.'

'A spook?'

'Probably FSB?'

'That explains a few things. A man like that would have access to lots of resources.'

'Including fake passports and other false identity documents?'

'Okay, so assuming this is your man Susnik, what's his connection to your wife? Why is he helping her?'

'I don't know? But if we can find him, we'll probably find her.'

'You might just find a bullet in the head, too. These people don't take kindly to being 'found.' You know you're clutching at straws here, don't you Dutton?'

Dutton sighed. 'Just juggling ideas around, that's all. I have to do something! I've got Leckonby trawling through hours of video footage, looking for taxis. Trying to narrow it down to just a few. But that could take forever. Meanwhile I'm slowly going mad.'

'Tell you what, I'll come over there and pick you up. Take you out to lunch.'

'Why?'

'There's someone I want you to meet: and what else have you got to do?'

42

Ballinger waited on the Fox's car park for Dutton to show. When the investigator arrived he had his dog with him.

'Put her in the back. If she makes a mess you'll clean it up.'

'Where are we going?' asked Dutton as the car headed out.

'Nice little place I know. Near Ladymere.'

'Ladymere? Isn't that where -?'

'That's right! We're having lunch with the Kozaks.'

The Duke Hotel was busy enough for a weekday. They occupied a table in the bar area some distance from the Kozaks. Dutton sat with his back to the trio.

'They come here every day,' said Ballinger. 'Usually for lunch. Always have rib-eye, chips, and mushrooms. You might think they'd get bored with the same food in the same place, but they love it?'

They ordered their own food.

'Who's who?' asked Dutton.

'I think I've worked it out. The one with the gold ear stud seems to be the boss. So he must be Dauren. The other one will be Serik, the younger brother.'

'And the gorilla?'

'Janko Petrovich. Their minder. He's seen you, don't forget, so don't let him catch sight of you.'

'He looks useful.'

'Very!'

'Tell me something Ballinger, what do you do when you're not snooping on people?'

'I rebuild cars.'

'What kind of cars?'

'Classics. Right now I'm working on a Railton Drop Head coupe.'

'I've heard of Railton. They once held the land speed record, didn't they?'

'That was the Railton Special. Built by Reid Railton for John Cobb. What a piece of engineering that was. But the saloons and coupes were not built by Reid. They were made by Fairmile Engineering, using the Railton name as a marketing tool. Production ended when the second world war began. Probably started turning out spitfires instead.'

'So what do you do with these cars when you've built them?'

'Run them for a while. Take them to shows and rallies. Then sell them, and move on to another project. I've got an old Brough Superior ready to start on when I've finished the Railton.'

'Interesting hobby.'

'More obsession than hobby. But it keps me busy. What about you? How do you fill your spare time?'

'You should know!' Dutton chided him. 'You've been watching me long enough. Up until last year I used to sail a lot. Play golf. Now I just eat, sleep, and get pissed.'

They settled for a main course only. Left the hotel when the Kozaks ordered their desserts. Back in the car Ballinger did a quick check on Fallon. His car was still firmly anchored out on the moors.

'Come on, I'll take you to the house. You can see how the other half lives.'

Five minutes later they pulled into the farm track. Leaving the car in its usual spot he steered Dutton across the field to the gap he had made in the hawthorn hedge.

'Straight ahead,' he said, indicating the house.

Dutton took a long look. 'Very nice! And they say crime doesn't pay.'

'No one believes that anymore. People like the Kozaks do very nicely from its proceeds. But they don't actually own this place. It's rented. Probably through some agency controlled by one of the mobs. The guy who lives here works abroad.'

'How do you know?'

'About the agency? Devine told me. The man knows everything about everybody. Or so he says. As for the guy who lives there, I went in and searched his office. He's an engineering consultant, working in Dubai. I don't know what the Arabs are paying him, but looking at this place he doesn't come cheap. I don't think he'd be too happy about the kind of people using his house, right now.'

Dutton turned and looked along the lane. 'Car coming!'

Ballinger moved in to peer through the gap. An ancient Mondeo was approaching the house. It stopped before the gates and a man climbed out. Medium height and slim he was wearing grey jeans, with a light hoodie over a black tee-shirt.

'Looks like he uses the same clothing store as you,' commented Dutton.

The driver of the Ford tried the gates. Finding them unlocked he entered the courtyard. Cutting diagonally across the shale chippings to the front door he rang the doorbell. When no one answered he hammered on the door. When this didn't work he returned to his car. He made no attempt to drive off. Just sat there, waiting.

'Know him?' asked Ballinger.

Dutton shook his head. 'Did you get the registration number?'

'No I didn't! Did you?'

'Yes.'

'Well that's your police training for you. So now you'll be able to call your Inspector friend and find out who he is.'

Half an hour later the Kozaks returned. The waiting visitor was obviously expected. When Petrovich opened the gates he was waved though. Both cars were then locked away in the garage, and the four men entered the house.

43

Dutton:

We were in the bar of the Tipsy Fox, waiting to hear from Leckonby. I'd asked him to run the number of the Mondeo and he said he'd get back to me. Now we sat at a table, staring at Ballinger's phone screen. Watching the moving dot that was Fallon, on his way back from Yorkshire.

'Whatever he's doing up there, nothing good will come from it,' voiced Ballinger. He was probably right. But I wasn't really concerned with what Fallon was doing. Just as long as it didn't interfere with my efforts to find Alex.

I was beginning to despair. Any day now she would be moved on by the mysterious Susnik. I had a feeling that once this happened Alex would be lost to me forever. Ballinger seemed to read my mind.

'What will you do if you don't find her?'

I shrugged. 'Go back to being a widower, I suppose. I'm more unsure about what happens if I do find her. We had a good marriage until all this began. It would be nice to think we could take up where we left off, but I really can't see that happening.'

My phone rang. It was Tony Hale.

'How's it going?' he asked.

'I found the apartment, but missed Alex.'

'I know. Leckonby told me. He's looking at taxis seen in the area from Tuesday onwards. But it's not very promising. I think you should start considering the possibility that she'll be long gone by the time he finds anything useful: if he finds anything at all.'

'I know what you're saying,' I told him. 'But I'm convinced she's still somewhere nearby. Planning her next move.'

'I admire your optimism mate, and we'll keep at it from our end. I'm just reminding you that time's running out, that's all. Now, this car you were asking about. Where does that come into things?'

'I think it's following me,' I lied. 'It was behind me today when I left the Fox. Stayed with me into the city centre until I lost it in traffic. I'm pretty sure I saw the same car yesterday, close to Alex's apartment.'

'You could be right! It's registered to a dope-head called Douglas McAndrew. Douggie has spent sixteen of his forty-two years inside. For drugs, armed robbery, and assault.'

'Sounds a real charmer. Is he local?'

'Salford lad. Works for a trafficker called Cezar Barbu - and there's another East European connection for you. Barbu is someone we have a special interest in, but we don't want to rattle his cage just yet. If McAndrew becomes a major problem, call me. I'll put Traffic onto him. I'm sure they'll find some excuse to pull him over. Get him off your back for a while.'

'Thanks.' I felt uncomfortable lying to Tony after all the help he'd given me.

'And don't forget that Discovery!' he added. 'They

might be working as a team.'

He broke the connection. I told Ballinger about McAndrew.

'Recruiting locally? Why would they do that, I wonder?'

'A replacement for Fallon? They must know I saw his face.' I changed tack. 'Ballinger, you do know that at some point I'm going to have to put Tony Hale in the picture, don't you?'

'Yes! But not yet. Concentrate on finding your wife. Once you've found her you can tell him what you like. Right now, what he doesn't know won't hurt him.'

He had a point. I didn't need further complications just now. But it didn't make me feel any happier. Ballinger went back to studying the phone-screen.

'You could be right about the new guy,' he went on. 'You certainly seem to have lost Fallon's attention. But who's watching you right now, that's what I can't figure. Don't they care what you're doing any more? Or where you go?'

George came over, collecting empty glasses. I introduced Ballinger.

'What happened to him?' George pointed at my still-swollen face.

'Ask him,' grinned Ballinger.

'I did. He said he walked into a low-flying lamp-post.'

When Ballinger had gone I took Lucy for a walk, hoping to put in some serious thinking time. I felt nervous. Twitchy. My chances of finding Alex were slipping away and I hadn't a clue what to do next.

The search had hit a brick wall. I was waiting around for a single piece of information which, with any luck, might soon be uncovered by Leckonby. But it wasn't enough to rely on luck. What I really needed was some inspirational thinking. Oddly enough, when it came, it came from George.

Back in my room I fed Lucy, had a shower, and went down for a snack dinner. George was in the bar, reading the Evening News. He put the paper aside and pulled me a pint.

'I was just reading about this couple,' he chatted. 'Took their kids to McDonalds for burgers and chips. Five minutes after they left the house it was blown apart by an explosion. Completely destroyed. If they hadn't gone out when they did, they'd have been blown up with it. Who says fast food's bad for you?'

'Gas leak?' I asked.

'That's what they reckon. Poor buggers! They've lost everything. Had to move in with her parents.'

'At least they're alive.'

'God knows what we'd do in their place?' he went on. 'We might have to come down to Weymouth, and free-load on you!'

I was about to make some appropriate jocular response then froze, as the significance of what he'd said hit home. 'Here, don't worry lad,' he said quickly, seeing my expression change. 'I'm only joking.'

'Tell you what George,' I assured him, 'you can come and visit anytime. Stay as long as you like. You've earned it. You just hit on something I should have thought of days ago.'

'Happy to be of service,' he grinned.

I finished my drink, thinking about George's throwaway remark. Most people who suddenly lose their home have no option but to move in with some relative, or friend. Short term at least. Eventually they would have to find fresh accommodation. No one can freeload forever. But then Alex wasn't going to be around forever, was she? And although she had no relatives to call on, she might very well have friends.

44

Ballinger:

Ballinger left the Fox. He drove towards Manchester for half a mile then did a U-turn and doubled back. Pulling into the layby a hundred yards from Dutton's hotel he settled down to watch the place. He didn't think the investigator would be going anywhere. But at this stage in the game he wanted to be sure.

Minutes later Dutton set off with his dog. He was gone for twenty minutes before returning to the hotel. Sitting there, keeping watch, Ballinger's mind drifted back to Fallon, and his mysterious trips out to the moors. He recalled his first encounter with the killer.

It was two years ago. In London. Ballinger was riding shotgun for an American hostage negotiator called Steve Carpenter. Carpenter was working for a Kurdish businessman whose daughter had been kidnapped by one of the Russian gangs.

A price had been agreed. The release arranged. He and the negotiator arrived at the meeting place. An abandoned canal dock in Uxbridge, behind an empty flour mill.

They arrived early. Carpenter liked to play it that way. He said it gave him a chance to work out an escape route in case things went belly up. Patiently they waited. The time set for the exchange came and went with no sign of the kidnappers. Carpenter leaned casually against the side of the car. Ballinger hovered behind it.

At last a car came around from the front of the mill. It followed the canal-side road and turned onto the dock. The passenger door opened. A man climbed out. He wore a badly creased light suit, over a dark red shirt and yellow tie. He had cruel features. The face of a professional thug, topped by closely cropped hair.

'You're late,' announced Carpenter.

'So, sue me,' offered the man.

Carpenter reached into the car and removed a bag. He placed it on the floor and nudged it forward with his foot. 'You can check it if you want. When we've seen the girl.'

The man nodded. He opened the back door of the SUV, reached inside, and pulled out a slim, hooded, figure in a grey tracksuit. Unable to see where she was going, and with her hands tied behind her back, the girl lost her footing as she stepped down. She fell heavily onto the hard, concrete, surface. Her captor laughed.

'Enough of that,' barked Carpenter. 'We don't pay for damaged goods.'

'A bit late for that, Yank,' retorted the man, with a leery grin. Pulling the girl to her feet he brought her to within ten feet of the negotiator and lifted the hood, exposing her face for a moment. Then he approached the bag, crouched down, and checked the contents. 'Looks about right,' he grunted.

The kidnapper snapped the bag shut. He gripped it with his left hand and climbed to his feet, smoothly pulling a Berretta from his pocket as he rose. With the gun pointed at Carpenter's head the man's grin widened. 'Tell you what, Yank. How about I take the money, *and* keep the bit of skirt?'

Behind the car Ballinger racked a round into the Remington hunting rifle he had sighted on the chest of the man with the gun. The sound echoed loudly around the empty dock.

'You can try, Limey,' smiled Carpenter.

The kidnapper gave Ballinger a long, hard look. Then he relaxed. Lowered the gun and slipped it back into his pocket. 'Just kidding,' he smiled, coldly. He turned on his heel and headed for his car. 'Bye, sweetie,' he said to the girl as he passed her.

The two men watched him climb into the SUV. It did a reverse three point turn and drove quickly away. When it had disappeared, Ballinger put away the weapon and moved into the driving seat.

Carpenter went to the hostage. He cut her bonds and removed the hood completely. The dark-haired girl was seventeen, maybe eighteen years old. Leading her to the car he helped her inside and onto the back seat. She regarded the two men fearfully.

'You're safe now,' Carpenter assured her. 'Your father sent me to bring you home.'

Her face filled with relief. She slumped forward and began to sob. The American reached in to comfort her and she shrank away violently.

'Hey, it's ok,' he said. The girl shank back even further. Pressed herself into the far corner of the seat. Carpenter looked at Ballinger then back to the girl. 'He hurt you, didn't he?' She nodded. 'Did he rape you?'

She lowered her eyes. Gave an imperceptible nod and sobbed even more.

The men stared helplessly, not knowing how to comfort her. When at last the tears died away the girl looked at her rescuers. 'Please,' she begged. 'You must tell no one. This is a big disgrace amongst my people. If it becomes known that I have been used, I will never find a husband. And my family will be ashamed of me.'

Carpenter shrugged. 'It's your life, young lady. They'll hear nothing from us. Right Sandy?'

Ballinger nodded. The girl relaxed. 'Please take me home,' she said, tiredly.

The negotiator climbed in beside Ballinger. 'Evil Bastard,' he breathed as the car pulled away.

'You know him?'

'Joey Fallon. Works for Dooby Levkin. They call him Loon. He's a psycho.'

'Nice people you work with,' commented Ballinger.

By midnight the Tipsy Fox was in darkness. Ballinger went back to his own hotel. In his room he lay on the bed, nursing a whiskey nightcap and a problem. Well two problems, really.

The first was of his own making, which didn't make it any less of a problem. He had come to like Dutton. Even feel sorry for him. The man had been the victim of a cruel deception and was desperate to be reunited with his wife. Yet here was he, pretending to help him find her, whilst all the time conspiring with others to make sure this never happened. The whole thing left a bad taste in his mouth.

The other problem concerned the opposition. The reason for the sudden appearance of McAndrew was an unknown. He disliked unknowns. Also, he was less than happy about Fallon's frequent trips out to the moors. The place looked too much like the perfect killing ground for his liking.

It seemed to him that the Kozaks were preparing for some kind of end game. They'd lost interest in Dutton: and the only inference he could draw from this was that they no longer needed him. In which case they held some other key to the woman's whereabouts.

Ballinger could not believe they had stumbled upon her by accident. She had proved herself far too smart to allow that to happen. Nor would she have been careless enough to leave some clue lying around her apartment. Yet since the confrontation there between Dutton and Fallon, the game seemed to have changed.

So now he had a decision to make. The choices simple. He could follow orders. Keep Dutton too busy to run interference until after the pick-up, then go home and collect his money. Or he could stick his nose in where it didn't belong. Do his best to ensure that the woman did not fall into the wrong hands.

It was a no-brainer.

He called Devine. The call went to voicemail. He tried again. Then again. On the fourth attempt the man picked up.

'Jeez, you know what the time is?'

'Why is she coming in?'

'What?'

'The woman. Why has she suddenly decided to come in? I was thinking about it, and it doesn't make sense?'

'Makes perfect sense,' said the American. 'Susnik's been posted. He can't help her this time. So she's coming in.'

'Posted?'

'Out of the country. To some other Embassy, in some other part of the world. You happy now?'

'Yes. I just wondered, that's all.'

'Well now you know. Go to bed. And keep Dutton out of the way tomorrow.' The call ended.

Ballinger opened his lap top. Googled up some information. When he found what he wanted he checked the time then picked up the phone. Made a second call. Twenty minutes later, grim-faced and pensive, he finished the whiskey and went to bed.

45

THURSDAY

Ballinger:

Six-forty-five a.m. Ballinger was in his car. This was not going to be an easy day. He needed to be in two places at once, watching two men and hoping against hope that they didn't come into contact with each other.

Fortunately he had an edge. He could watch one of them remotely whilst he sent the other off in the wrong direction. But he had to be careful. Dutton was now on his guard, and he was nobody's fool.

He glanced down at the map on the phone screen. The stationary green light indicated that Fallon's car was at the house in Ladymere. While it stayed there things should be manageable. Flipping his indicator he once more turned off the A56 towards Timperley. Hopefully for the last time.

A few minutes later he arrived at the Tipsy Fox. He glanced into the car park, then looked again. The private detective's Audi was not there. He checked the time. Not yet seven o clock, and already his day was going down the pan. Dutton had given him the slip: and god only knew what he was up to.

46

Dutton:

I was up early. On the road for six, with Lucy walked and fed. There was little traffic around, which was the reason for the early start. It isn't easy to follow someone along empty roads without being spotted.

An hour later I was having breakfast in a cafe in the city centre. My phone rang. I checked the number. Ballinger.

'Where are you?' he asked.

'Manchester. Eating my breakfast.'

'You're out early?'

'I'm going to Central Park. Try and speed things up a little. I wanted to make sure I wasn't followed so I set off whilst there was no traffic on the road.'

'You will let me know if you find anything?' he asked.

'Of course I will. I'm probably wasting my time, but I can't just sit around doing nothing. It's driving me crazy.'

'I can understand that.'

'So, what are you doing? Besides watching an empty car park.' I couldn't keep the smugness out of my voice.

'I was going to ride shotgun with you. Keep anyone from knocking you on the head again. But I suppose you'll be safe enough in a building full of coppers. I might take a run out to Ladymere. Keep my eye on things there. See if I can find out what they're up to.'

'Don't get caught!' I closed the phone and turned it off. Taking my time over breakfast I sat at the table until the place began to fill with market traders. Then I collected a newspaper and walked back to the car.

I drove through the city centre. Headed out along Oxford road, past the University, and approached the Umac theatre. There was restricted parking around the building so I turned into the grounds of the nearby Royal Infirmary. In the visitors' car park I pulled into an empty space and sat reading the newspaper.

At nine-thirty I put a ticket on the car and walked the short distance to Oxford road. Dodging through traffic I crossed to the theatre and went inside. Students are not famous for rising early and the place was almost deserted. The same receptionist was behind the desk.

'Hello,' I said. 'Remember me?'

'You're one of the policemen from the other day,' she smiled.

'Do you know why we were here?'

'Looking for Katarina, they said. Did you find her?'

I shook my head. 'Her apartment's empty. We have no idea where she is, and we're becoming concerned for her safety. Her ex is looking for her. He's a head case, so we're trying to get to her before he does.'

'Will he hurt her?'

'He's threatened to: and she obviously thinks he will or she wouldn't have done a runner. I wondered if there was someone here she was particularly close to? Someone she might have confided in?'

'She worked with Christopher,' she confided. 'Thick as thieves him and her. If she confided with anyone it'd be him'

'Christopher?'

'Chris Heenan. One of our production managers.'

'Where do I find him?'

'I'll call him.' She tapped in a number on the keyboard. 'Chris, there's a policeman in reception asking to see you. Yes, I did say a policeman. He wants to talk to you about Kat.' She replaced the receiver. 'He'll be out in a minute.'

I moved away from the desk. Tried to make myself invisible in case the formidable Mrs Harlowe walked in. Minutes passed. Then the auditorium doors swung open and a man stepped through.

Heenan was about fifty. Bearded and prematurely grey. His body was lithe and muscular, his voice and demeanour overtly gay.

'Hello there,' he greeted me nervously.

'Is there somewhere we can talk?' I asked.

'Upstairs!' He led the way up to the empty lounge. Waved vaguely, inviting me to sit anywhere. I chose a table well away from the office door and sat down with my back to it. He slid into the seat opposite, steepled his fingers, and tried hard to avoid direct eye contact.

Most people, with the exception of career criminals, are nervous about being questioned by the police. It's a natural reaction, and one that an experienced officer will exploit. The man seated before me was an octave up from nervous, before I'd even opened my mouth.

I gave him the silent treatment for a while. Allowed him to squirm. Then I spoke, using my hard but fair policeman's tone.

'You and Katarina Skala work closely together, I believe.'

'Yes,' he nodded, still avoiding eye contact. 'We do.'

'Did you know the police are looking for her?'

'Yes,' the word came out in a dry whisper.

'Do you know why they're looking for her?'

He shook his head. But his worried face displayed a hint of curiosity. I leaned in closer, as though relating a confidence.

'Katarina once had a partner. A drunken, violent, man who used to beat and bully her. Do everything he could to make her life a misery. Trouble was, like so many women in that position she was too scared to do anything about it. She simply accepted whatever abuse she was subjected to.

But last year he was arrested on drugs-related charges. Jailed for eighteen months. This gave Katarina the chance to get away, and she took it. She moved here, to Manchester, and began building a new life for herself. She was doing pretty well, too.

Then a month ago he was released from prison. We have information that suggests he is now here, in Manchester, looking for her. I doubt he wants to kiss and make up.'

I paused to let this sink in. 'In recent years there have been several high-profile cases of women being seriously injured - killed even - by violent ex-partners. Police forces are under great pressure to make sure it doesn't happen again. This is why we need to find her before he does. The man is a serious threat. Not just to her but to anyone sheltering her, too.'

I didn't have to say anything else. His eyes widened with consternation and words came tumbling from his mouth.

'She told me she needed somewhere to stay for a few days,' he said quickly. 'Said someone was looking for her. That she'd been caught on camera by the BBC news - which I knew because I'd seen her on the telly - and she was worried he might have seen her.. She didn't tell me who it was, or what it was about. Dear god, that poor girl! No wonder she's afraid to set foot outside the door.'

'Christopher?' I asked, gently. 'Where is she?'

'Am I in trouble?'

I shook my head. 'No you're not. You were helping a friend. It's what friends do.'

'She's in my apartment. In Didsbury.'

An almost overwhelming feeling of relief and triumph flooded through me. I could barely keep my voice even. 'Will you take me to her?'

'I can't!' He looked wretched. 'I couldn't face her. She'll think I've betrayed her. Besides, we have a dress rehearsal today. I need to be here.' He produced a key from his pocket and handed it over. 'Here. When you're done leave it on the kitchen table. I have another I can use.'

I took the key. Reached for my pen. 'Address?' He gave me the address. I wrote it down then climbed to my feet, outwardly calm but inwardly quaking with jubilation and excitement.

'Will she be alright?' he asked.

'She'll be given protection. He's in breach of his parole, so he'll be going back inside when we catch him.'

'Is he likely to come here?' he asked nervously

'I doubt it. But we have someone keeping an eye on the place, just in case. Don't tell anyone about this, Christopher. You wouldn't want him to find out you've been hiding her.' With a brief nod I walked away, heading for the stairs.

'Will you tell her I'm sorry?' he called after me.

'I'll tell her.' I left the theatre and made my way back to the car. I gave my un-expired parking ticket to a young woman who had just arrived, then drove from the hospital grounds, heading south.

Didsbury sits just outside the city. Now a part of the Greater Manchester conurbation, the village straddles a major route heading south towards Wilmslow and the airport. The road there is lined with busy shops, pavement cafes, and quirky pubs.

After passing through the centre, the sat nav took me off the main highway and down a narrow side road. Following directions I turned into a long avenue lined with trees and apartment buildings. Several cars and a large white van were parked alongside the kerb. I pulled into the next available parking slot and turned off the engine.

As I reached into my pocket for Heenan's address the white van roared up alongside. It screeched to a halt, so close I couldn't open my door. Then with a dull thud, the passenger window shattered, showering me with glass. I turned to see Petrovich pointing a gun at my head.

'Climb out this side,' he instructed. 'Very slowly. Any sudden move and I will shoot you!'

Carefully I climbed across the centre console, and stepped down onto the pavement. Outwardly calm, inside I was raging at my own stupidity for walking blindly into their hands. 'Move to the back of the van,' I was ordered. 'Try anything else and I will kill you.'

I did as he said. The van's rear doors were open and Fallon stood there. He was carrying the baseball bat he had used on me before.

'Taken your gun off you, have they?' I asked.

His face darkened. 'Inside hero, and kneel down.' I did as he said. He climbed in and frisked me. 'Hands behind your back,' he ordered. I took this as a good sign. If they were about to kill me they wouldn't waste time tying my hands. Would they?

With my wrists and ankles bound with cable ties, a sack was pulled over my head. Then, without a word, Fallon brought the club down onto my skull and the world shattered into a million fragments.

47

Fallon:

Fallon sat behind the wheel. On the bench seat next to him was McAndrew. Beyond him, sitting beside the passenger door, was Petrovich. The Serb was on the phone, talking to Dauren Kozak.

'We need to bring this forward,' he was saying. 'Dutton is here again. We think he is alone, but we cannot be certain. The police could arrive any time.'

Kozak swore in vexation. 'Okay, here's what you do. At the first sign of police interference you go in there and kill the woman and anyone with her. You got that?'

'Got it!'

'What have you done with Dutton?'

'He's in the back of the van.'

'Keep him with you. If all goes well he can watch his wife dance for us. But if you have to abort, kill him too. Do not let us down Janko. Whatever else happens this day, the woman dies. Do you understand?'

'I understand.'

'Good. Now I'll call our man. See how quickly he can get there, and then call you back.' The phone went dead.

'What's happening?' asked Fallon.

'They're calling him. Telling him to hurry.'

Fallon snorted. 'They couldn't organise a crap in a karsie. Tell you what, why don't we just go up there, kick in the door, and blow the bitch's head off.'

Petrovich gave him a hard stare but said nothing. They sat in silence for a while.

'So, how long have you worked for the Chuckle Brothers?' asked Fallon, giving McAndrew a wink.

'Chuckle?' Petrovich looked puzzled.

'The Kozaks.'

'Many years. First in New York. Then in Holland. They are good people to work for.'

'Well, rather you than me, pal. The sooner they're back on that plane and out of here the better, as far as I'm concerned. Especially that Dauren?'

'Dauren has much responsibility: and he does not tolerate fools. But then you have discovered that for yourself, have you not?'

The phone sounded. The Serb lifted it to his ear. He listened, then shut it down. 'Thirty minutes,' he told his companions. 'He'll be here in thirty minutes.'

'Thirty minutes?' voiced Fallon with dismay. 'A fucking lot can happen in thirty minutes.'

'Then you'd better make sure it doesn't,' advised the Serb. 'Because if we miss her again you are a dead man.'

'*I'm* a dead man? You're the one in charge of this little operation, kiddo.'

'They will not kill me,' smiled the Serb. 'But you are of no consequence.'

'You think, pal!' muttered Fallon under his breath.

They waited. Thirty minutes passed, with still no sign of the pick-up car. Fallon played nervously with the steering wheel. He fully expected the street to be filled with armed police at any moment. Again he checked his watch. 'Bloody long thirty minutes, this!' he complained. 'I think we should move in now. What do you reckon, Doug?'

McAndrew looked at Fallon. Then at the Serb. He had no wish to become drawn into the bad blood that so obviously existed between the two. 'Don't ask me pal,' he declared neutrally. 'Kozak's the boss. If he says wait, then I wait.'

Fallon gave him a despairing look. 'And if he said jump under a bus you'd do that too, I suppose!'

48

Altyn:

The doorbell rang. Altyn started nervously. 'It can't be him? It's too early!'

Susnik walked to the door, gun in hand. 'Yes?' He stood beside the door, his back against the wall.

'Scott Devlin, Mister Susnik.'

'Let me see your authority?' An envelope was pushed through the letterbox. Inside, on headed Embassy paper, was a written authority. It named Scott Devlin as a bone fide representative of the US State Department. It was signed by Devine. Cautiously the Russian opened the door. He waved the man inside with the gun. 'You're early. I don't like surprises.'

'Made good time,' explained Devlin. 'The word is, Dutton's getting close to finding this place. So we need to get her away, before he comes knocking on the door.'

'Show me your ID?'

Devlin pulled out his State Department ID card. Susnik checked the man against the photograph then carefully examined the card. He'd seen enough forgeries in his time to know this one was genuine. Satisfied, he handed it back.

'She's ready to go. But don't say anything about Dutton. I don't want her to change her mind.'

'Amen to that,' voiced the American.

In the small lounge Altyn climbed to her feet as the two men entered. The American smiled and shook her hand. 'Scott Devlin ma-am.' He picked up the two suitcases. 'I'll take these down to the car while you say your goodbyes.'

When he was gone Altyn threw her arms around Susnik. 'Thank you for everything, Peter.'

'I would have done more if I could, you know that. But there's so little time: and I must go where I am ordered to go.'

'Will I see you again?'

'Perhaps,' he said. 'Sometime in the future when you are no longer under threat. But for now stay safe. Try not to repeat past mistakes.' They embraced again, then followed Devlin from the apartment

In the street they found the American waiting beside a black limousine carrying US Embassy plates.

'Up front or in the back?'

'I'll sit in the front, if that's alright,' she told him.

'No problem, lady,' he opened up the passenger door and guided her in. Then he climbed into the driver's side and started the car. She gave a final wave to Susnik then he was lost from sight as they left the avenue and worked their way back to the main road.

They turned south. Devlin drove in silence. 'What time is the flight?' she asked.

He checked his watch. 'Three hours. Lots of time. You're booked on a Delta flight to Atlanta. Then on to Washington.'

'Atlanta? I thought we were going to London! I have no passport. No papers.'

'All taken care of, lady. You're travelling with me. On diplomatic papers.'

She settled back in the seat, overwhelmed by a sense of loss and sadness. In just a few hours she'd be back in America. But instead of feeling relieved, she wanted to cry. Somewhere in the city, falling away behind, was Terry. How she would have loved to see him one more time, if only from a distance.

Her reverie was broken as they approached a set of traffic lights. The driver flipped the indicator and moved into a right turn lane. When the lights changed he swung the wheel and turned into a business park.

'Where are we going?' she demanded, sharply. 'The airport's straight ahead. Where are you taking me?'

'Relax,' smiled the driver. 'Just following procedure. Making sure we're not being followed.'

He drove along the perimeter road then turned onto a service lane. Followed it around to the rear of an empty unit. Waiting there was a silver SUV. Devlin pulled up alongside the empty car and switched off the engine. Altyn looked around nervously.

'What's going on? Why have you stopped?'

'We're switching cars,' he told her, matter-of-factly. But he didn't move. Suddenly a white van appeared, heading straight for them. She went for the door, but Devlin was too quick for her. He grabbed her by the hair, pulled her backwards and wrapped an arm around her throat. Then the van was alongside. Blocking off any chance of escape.

The American kept hold of her but she made no further attempt to resist. She just slumped against him, as if resigned to what was about to happen. 'Good girl,' he told her. 'Now you're being sensible.'

Three men climbed from the van. The passenger door was pulled open. 'We'd just about given up on you,' grinned Fallon. 'Thought we'd have to do the job ourselves.' He looked at Altyn and the grin widened. 'Hello sweetie. Isn't life a bitch?'

She gave him a dismissive look, then her face blanched as the Serb peered in through the door.

'Yes Altyn, it is me. Janko! Here to take you to Dauren and Serik. They are waiting anxiously to see you again.'

They pulled her from the car. Took her to the back of the van. When the door was pulled open she saw the body of a man, lying face down on the floor. His wrists and ankles were bound and a sack had been tied over his head.

'Inside, and kneel down!' She was ordered.

She knelt on the floor just inside the van. Fallon secured her hands and feet. Placed a sack over her head, then pushed her down on her face.

'Any noise from you and you'll get a knock on the head - like your old man there. You got that?'

'What - ?' she began, but the words were cut off by the slamming of the doors. Fallon turned the lock and joined the other three men.

'Take them to the farm,' instructed Petrovich. 'I'll collect the others and bring them there.'

'Am I done here?' asked the American.

'Yes. Thank you for your help.'

'Don't thank me buddy!' he told the Serb, throwing a contemptuous glance at Fallon. 'You think I had a choice?' Then without another word he returned to his car and drove off.

Petrovich climbed into the SUV. Wound down the window. 'See you at the farm,' he called. Then he too drove away.

Fallon watched them go. Turning to his companion he grinned. 'How do you fancy a bit of fun then?'

'What d'you mean?'

'The skirt in the back! How do you fancy a piece of that?'

'No way,' said McAndrew, forcefully. 'They'll have our guts for garters.' Fallon sighed. Shook his head in disappointment.

They climbed into the van. McAndrew studied the driver closely as they moved off. 'They told me I'd have to watch you!' he voiced. 'Said you were a mad bastard. I see what they mean now.'

'You don't know shit, sonny!' observed Fallon.

'I know the Kozaks aren't the kind of people I'd want to upset.'

'You're scared of them?'

'Too right I am. So should you be, if you had any sense.'

'I'm not scared of anyone. Least of all a pair of clowns like those two. You want to know how tough these Kozaks really are? I'll tell you. Where d'you think they are right now?'

'Back at the house?'

Fallon shook his head. 'Wrong my son. Not at the house. Right now they're sitting inside the airport, bags packed, passports clutched in their sweaty little hands, and crapping themselves in case it all goes pear-shaped.

And if something had gone wrong with this little operation, and the old bill had jumped all over us, they'd have been out of here on the first plane to anywhere. Leaving you, me, and old slab-head, to carry the can.' With a snort of disgust he turned the wheel, pulled out onto the highway, and headed for the ring road.

In the back of the van Alex heard the muffled voices up front. She ignored them. She was trying to make sense of the man's throwaway comment just before he closed the door on her.

When the van settled to a steady pace she wriggled her body up against that of her travelling companion. Using her chin to find the man's shoulder, she placed her face close to his. Inhaled deeply.

Her nasal senses were almost overwhelmed by the odour of hessian. But behind the strong smell of the coarse fabric she detected the unmistakable scent of Armani Code. The aftershave and body spray that she herself had encouraged Terry to use. Pressing her body against his she began to cry.

49

Ballinger:

Ballinger checked his watch. Ten o clock. He had driven up to the police headquarters building and there was no sign of Dutton, or his car. Now he sat in his usual observation spot opposite the Gateway. He was thinking he'd been had.

There was always the possibility that the Audi was behind the building in the main parking compound. But he wasn't optimistic. He checked the tracker. Fallon's car was still at Ladymere, which was no guarantee he was there. But he didn't expect any movement from there just yet.

He gripped the steering wheel in frustration. Today was crunch day. Things were happening, and he was stuck here, out of it. It wouldn't do. Flipping open his phone he hit the speed dial number for Dutton. After three ring tones, the number again went to voice mail.

'Shit!' he swore aloud. He waited several seconds then tried again. Just in case. Again he went through to the investigator's voice mail. 'Call me!' he snapped. 'Now! It's important.' He broke the connection then called directory. Asked to be put through to Police headquarters.

'DI Leckonby please,' he told the switchboard.

'Who's calling?'

'DS Bolton, Dorset CID.'

'What can I do for you, DS Bolton?' enquired Leckonby when he came on.

'Good morning sir. I'm trying to contact Mr Dutton about the break-in at his home. But I just keep getting his voice mail. The landlord of his hotel thought he was on his way in to see you this morning. Is he there by any chance.'

'Not with me. Hold on, I'll check with reception. He might be with the Super.' Moments later Leckonby was back on. 'Sorry, no one's seen him this morning. Shall I ask him to call you if he comes in?'

'If you don't mind, sir. Thank you.' Ballinger closed the phone. Dropped it onto the empty passenger seat. Wondered again just what game Dutton was playing.

His sense of unease deepened. If what he thought was about to happen did happen, and Dutton showed up, then something more than a smack on the head might be coming his way. The man needed to be found. Soon. Time was running out.

50

Dutton:

When I opened my eyes I was in a cellar. The hood had been removed and I was tied to a heavy chair.

Facing me was another chair, a twin to the one I occupied. Looped over a beam above it was a noose, made of climbing rope. The other end of the rope was tied to the side of an open staircase, over by the wall. The sight of the noose brought a stab of fear.

The room was about eight yards square. The stone walls coated in white emulsion. Overhead, strong wooden beams supported the floor above. Except for the rope and chair, the only feature I could see was the staircase. It led upwards to a small landing with a door. Above the door was a bulkhead light that threw weak illumination down into the cellar.

I couldn't see what lay behind me. My hands had been pulled through the back spindles of the chair and my wrists bound together, locking my shoulders. It was impossible for me to turn around. My feet were strapped to the front chair legs, and my head was hurting from the blow I'd received earlier. But at least I was conscious, and able to think rationally.

One thing was clear. Fallon and the Serb had not followed me to Didsbury. They were there on the street when I arrived. Which could only mean they were there for Alex. But how had they found her? Had they discovered something in her apartment that told them where she was? In the end it didn't matter. They had found her. Which meant she had almost certainly been taken.

A chill was beginning to creep into my bones. The cellar was dry, but cool. Time passed. I had no idea how long I'd been there and I couldn't see my watch. When the door at the top of the stairs opened, a man stepped through.

It was Dauren. The older Kozak brother. He came down the steps. Stood before me. 'Mister Dutton,' he smiled, 'the bad penny. Well, since you are here you might as well make yourself comfortable. Sit back and enjoy the show, as they say.'

'Where's Alex?' I asked.

He frowned. 'Alex? Oh, you mean Altyn, the star of our show? Right now she is upstairs, entertaining mister Fallon. He asked for the pleasure of her company, and who am I to deny a man his last request.'

I exploded with rage. Fought furiously against my bonds. Had I been able to break free I would have killed him with my bare hands. But the ties and the heavy chair held fast. In the end I simply slumped back, breathing heavily, forced to accept defeat.

Dauren moved over to the empty chair. He climbed onto it and gripped the noose. Swung on it, testing its strength.

'What are you going to do?'

He dropped to the floor. 'What do you think? Altyn is a traitor. To her husband and her family. She will be punished. It is the custom, is it not, to hang traitors? Even here?'

Reaching into his pocket he took out a phone. Held it up. 'I will film the execution. Send it to my brother Arman. It will give him some small comfort and pleasure as he passes his days inside the American prison where Altyn put him.'

'And me?'

The man ignored the question. Stepping behind my chair he threw a switch. At once the cellar was flooded with light from a spotlight mounted somewhere overhead. He returned to my side and checked the view-screen again. Satisfied, he put away the phone.

'What about me?' I repeated.

'You are nothing to us,' he said, simply. 'You can watch her die. A punishment for defiling my brother's wife. Then you too will die.' He climbed the stairs and left me alone in the cellar.

51

Ballinger:

Ballinger drove into the city centre. Joined the inner ring road. Exiting at the Chester road he headed for Timperley.

Arriving at the *Tipsy Fox* he pulled onto the car park and walked in through the back door. A young man was stacking glasses behind the bar. He stared curiously at Ballinger.

'We're not open yet!'

'Is the landlord in?'

'And you are?'

'John Ballinger. I'm a friend of Terry Dutton's.'

George came through from the kitchen. 'Hello there!' he said, pleasantly. 'Terry's not here.'

'Have you any idea where he is?'

The landlord shook his head. 'Have you tried calling him?'

'He's not answering his phone.'

'Well I'm sorry, but I can't help you. He was away from here at the crack of dawn this morning. Didn't even have breakfast. I asked where he was going at that time, but he just made some joke about going to the theatre.'

'The theatre?'

'It's what he said.' George looked enquiringly at Ballinger. 'So tell me, what did happen to him the other day? He came back looking like he'd just done three rounds with Mike Tyson?'

'He found someone who didn't want to be found,' said Ballinger. 'It happens.'

George winced. 'Well I'll tell him you're looking for him when he comes back. Sorry I can't be any help.'

'I think you have been George, thanks!' Ballinger turned to leave.

Back in his car he opened his phone. He called enquiries and got the address of the Umac Theatre. Setting the post code into his sat nav he headed back into the city.

Thirty minutes later he pushed through the theatre door and walked up to reception. Flashed his fake Special Branch identity card. 'I'm looking for a colleague of mine. He was coming here this morning to make enquiries about Katarina Skala?'

'You've missed him,' the girl stated.

'When did he leave?'

She checked her watch. 'An hour ago. Longer, probably?'

'Shit,' he muttered.

'Have you tried calling him?'

'I can't get through. Either his phone's off, or there's something wrong with it. Who did he speak to?'

'Chris Heenan.'

'Is he still here?'

The girl nodded and reached for the phone. 'Do you want to speak to him?'

'I certainly do!'

Ten minutes later Ballinger entered Heenan's post code into the sat nav then set off for Didsbury. He marvelled at the tenacity of the private investigator. One day Dutton would get himself killed - if he hadn't already. He checked his watch. Eleven-forty. Lots of time before the pick-up. But if Dutton was already with the woman then things were going to get complicated.

Traffic was slow, and heavy. He drove impatiently down a major arterial road that headed out towards the airport. The road narrowed in places as it passed through busy shopping areas. Here, parked cars and delivery vehicles had traffic crawling, in both directions.

At last he arrived in the quiet street where the woman currently shared an apartment with Heenan. Spotting Dutton's car he pulled in behind it. There was no sign of the investigator. He approached the Audi on foot and tried the driver's door. It swung open causing the dog to bark furiously at him, from behind the wire guard.

Glass beads from the shattered passenger window covered the seats and floor. The keys hung from the ignition. Dutton's phone sat mutely on the centre console. Taking the keys and phone he headed down the street to the apartment block. Inside he made his way to number fifteen and rang the bell. There was no answer. He tried the bell again. Still no one came.

Ballinger took out his picks and went to work. A minute later the lock unlatched with a soft click. He had no idea what pick-up arrangements had been made by Devine and the last thing he wanted was to get his head blown off by the woman's Russian helper. Cautiously he pushed the door open.

'Hello! Anyone home?' There was no response.

With a keen sense of déjà vu he stepped into the hallway, his hands in plain sight to show he wasn't a threat. When he didn't find Dutton lying senseless on the floor he wasn't sure whether to feel relief, or concern. He checked every room in the apartment. The place was empty. The woman was gone: Susnik was gone: and so too was Dutton.

Back in the car he checked the tracker again. Fallon's car still sat on the edge of the village. This meant nothing now since it was unlikely that Fallon would be there. But he needed to be sure.

He was about to drive off when he spotted Dutton's dog. It was looking at him through the rear windscreen of the Audi. It wagged its tail cautiously. Ballinger looked at the sky. The clouds were breaking up. The sun was out. It was going to get hot in there.

With a sigh he returned to the Audi. He threw open the tailgate and grabbed the dog before it had a chance to jump out. Tucking it under his arm he placed the animal on the back seat of his own car. 'Don't make any noise. Don't cause any trouble. And don't crap in there,' he warned. As the car moved off the dog jumped onto the floor and urinated on the carpet.

It was one o clock when he reached Ladymere. He drove straight up to the front gates of the house. Found them unlocked. He approached the garage and looked through the window. The blue Honda and McAndrew's Ford were inside the building. There was no sign of the silver Mercedes.

Gun in hand he slipped round to the back of the

house. Let himself in through the kitchen and stepped into the dining room. Three minutes later he was satisfied the house was abandoned. Apart from the two cars in the garage, all traces of the temporary occupants had been removed.

He found keys lying in an ash-tray, on an ornamental stand in the hallway. He carried them to the garage. One of them opened the doors and he went inside and searched both cars. There was something odd-looking about the glove compartment in Fallon's Honda. Probing with his fingers he soon discovered the drop down section holding the Berretta.

Leaving the gun where it was, he relocked the garage and returned to his own car. There was only one other place they could be. If he was wrong it was a long way to go for nothing. But that was a chance he'd have to take: and quickly. They were anything up to a couple of hours ahead of him.

On his lap top he looked up the GPS co-ordinate he had noted. Feeding this into his sat nav he headed out through the village. Ten minutes later he was heading north-east towards the M62 trans-Pennine motorway. On a journey to the middle of nowhere.

52

Dutton:

More time passed. The door at the top of the stairs opened again. Fallon appeared with McAndrew. Between them was Alex. Naked, battered, and bruised, she was pulled backwards down the stairs, kicking struggling and swearing magnificently. They dragged her across the cellar floor and forced her down onto the chair below the noose. When her eyes fell on me she stopped yelling. A series of emotions flitted across her face and she lowered her eyes.

'Bastards!' I screamed at the two men as they tied her to the chair.

Fallon looked at me and grinned. 'Tell you what Dutton, she's a bit of a goer this old woman of yours.'

Again I tried to break free, and again all I did was inflict more damage upon my wrists. Once the two men had Alex secured McAndrew headed for the stairs. Fallon remained behind Alex's chair. He made sure I was watching, then began pawing her.

'Fallon!' The sharp voice came from the top of the stairs. Petrovich stood there, glaring down. 'Enough!' he snapped. 'We have things to do.' Fallon patted Alex on the head like a child. Then with a wide grin, he crossed to the stairs and followed his companions from the cellar. Alex spat after him as he left.

I looked at the woman I had thought dead. Her body and face were bruised. One of her eyes was already beginning to discolour. I could only begin to imagine what she had been through.

'Hello Alex,' I said, unable to keep the emotion out of my voice.

She looked up. Smiled wanly. 'Hello Terry. I'm so glad you are still alive. I thought they might have killed you already. It's so good to see you, but I am sorry you are here. The last thing I wanted was get you involved with these animals.'

'It was my choice! I didn't have to come looking for you. But you wouldn't expect me not to would you, once I found out you were still alive.'

'Terry, I am so sorry for what I have put you through.'

'You have nothing to be sorry about.' I told her. 'You did what you had to do to stay alive. I know that now.'

'No Terry, I did it to keep us both alive. If these madmen had found me you would have tried to stop them: and they would have killed you. I couldn't allow that to happen so I pretended to be dead. Hoped they would stop looking for me. It was the hardest thing I have ever done in my life. It broke my heart.'

'Even though I abused you?' I said. 'Beat you, and forced you to have sex with my business associates?' The words came out unbidden, revealing the enormity of the hurt these accusations had caused. Her eyes went wide with shock.

'I don't understand?' she said. 'Why are you saying these things.'

'That's what your friend Susnik told the trawler men who picked you up from the yacht.'

She shook her head fiercely.

'Terry I know nothing of this. You must believe me! If this is what he said then I am very, very sorry. I would never say such things about you: and had I known he was saying this I would have stopped him.!'

'It doesn't matter!'

'But it does!' she exclaimed. 'I cannot bear for you to think I would do such a thing. I would never betray you in that way, whatever the circumstances. I love you too much to do that.'

I found myself believing her. I certainly wanted to believe her. After all, it was Susnik who had made the arrangements. It was he who had to sell his plan to Sam Adams and his son.

'Quite a character your mister Susnik,' I smiled. 'In his shoes I'd have done the same, I suppose. Told whatever lies it took to keep you safe. I would have done it because you're my wife, and I love you. I don't know what his motive was?'

'He is my brother. This is why he helped me.'

'You have a brother? Now there's something else you failed to mention.'

'Terry, how could I tell you who I was? I was warned never to tell anyone about my previous life. Not even those closest to me. Relationships break down, they said. Lovers become strangers. Enemies, even? So tell no one. Or someday you may find your life in the hands of someone who no longer cares about you.'

She smiled, sadly. 'There was another reason why I told you nothing of my past. A more selfish reason. I was afraid you would see me as damaged goods and want nothing more to do with me. I couldn't risk losing you like that.'

'You wouldn't have lost me Alex - or should I call you Altyn? I presume that's your real name?'

'Please do not call me by that name. Altyn died a long time ago. I am your Alex. It is all I ever wanted to be.'

I shook my head, sadly. 'I don't think I know who you are anymore?'

'Then I will tell you,' she said. 'Because before I die I need your forgiveness.'

53

Fallon:

The farmhouse stood half a mile back from the road, hidden from traffic by the sweeping moorland hills. It was surrounded by a dry-stone wall and looked down into a narrow valley that fell away, eastwards, running parallel with the motorway further to the north.

From the outside the place looked like it had seen better days. But this was a facade. Inside, behind grimy windows and dirty net curtains, the building was pristine. Filled with modern fittings and furnishings.

In the kitchen stood a heavy oak table. Around it were four chairs, with two more down in the cellar where they had been taken for the 'guests.' On the table top sat a plastic tray holding a bottle of vodka and five glasses. Three of the glasses were to toast the successful culmination of a five-year long hunt. The other two were for show. Only three men would be celebrating here today.

Modern units were fitted against the wall. They supported a stainless steel sink, a microwave, the compulsory kettle, and a range of mugs and crockery. The room had an oven with hob. It had a refrigerator and freezer, both of which had been stocked up by Fallon when he came to set up the noose and spotlight, in the cellar.

Next to the kitchen was a low-ceilinged lounge. It held a comfortable leather suite and a forty-two inch television, connected to a satellite dish. On a book shelf next to the television lay a selection of DVDs. An open staircase climbed from the lounge to an upper floor with three bedrooms and a shared bathroom.

The farm was rented, from the same agency as the house in Cheshire. There were many such properties dotted around the country. They were used as bolt holes. Staging posts for human trafficking. Drug cultivation, and storage. This particular place, with its extreme remoteness, was ideally suited for use as a place of torture and execution.

Behind the farm a faint track wound down into the valley. Moving slowly along this uneven surface was the Kozaks' rented SUV. Petrovich was driving. Fallon sat beside him.

'When do I get my money?' asked McAndrew from the back seat.

'When I get mine,' Fallon told him. 'When the job's done.'

'Where are we going now?'

'Not far. Half a mile or so.'

'Then what?'

'Then we dig a fucking big hole and drop you in it,' grinned Fallon.

'Enough!' Petrovich snapped angrily. 'Too much talk!'

Fallon winked at McAndrew. The man frowned, worriedly.

They drove on between peat covered hills until Fallon told the driver to stop. The three men climbed out. Petrovich went round to the back of the car and opened the tailgate. He removed two spades, handed one to McAndrew and offered the other to Fallon.

'Get stuffed!' growled Fallon. 'I've done my bit. He can dig this one.'

Petrovich pulled his gun. Threw the spade at Fallon. 'You dig! It will be quicker.'

'Bastard!' voiced Fallon, picking up the spade. 'Come on my son,' he told McAndrew with mock cheerfulness. 'We have a grave to dig.'

'Who's grave?'

'Dutton's, of course!'

The three men climbed up a steep bank. At the top was a plateau covered with peat and heather. Twenty yards in they came upon an open grave, excavated by Fallon the previous day.

Taking off their jackets Fallon and McAndrew jumped down. They began to enlarge the grave, making it wide enough to take a second body. The Serb stood over them with the gun. After ten minutes Fallon stopped. 'That'll do,' he decided.

'Wider!' ordered Petrovich. 'Much wider.'

McAndrew sat down on the edge of the grave. Panting with exertion and kneading his sore hands, he looked far from happy. This was not what he had signed on for. He glared at the Serb. 'Tell you what pal, you want it wider then dig it yourself. If I wanted to dig graves for a living I'd go and work in a cemetery.'

Petrovich raised the gun and pulled the trigger. The bullet hit McAndrew in the throat and he went over backwards making a strange, gurgling sound. Petrovich fired again and the sound ceased. He turned the gun on Fallon and smiled.

'Now, you dig. Make it wider. Wide enough for four,' he grinned.

Cursing under his breath Fallon started to dig. He took his time. Conserved his energy. Gave himself time to think.

The original plan had been to kill the woman and bury her out here on the moor. Since the only creatures known to walk these isolated slopes were sheep, the chances of her body ever being found were almost non-existent.

Things had gone a bit pear-shaped with the husband turning up. But that just meant having two bodies to bury instead of the one. Now it was four graves. McAndrew was dead and here was he, digging what must surely be his own grave.

The Kozaks were tidying up. Which could only mean his employer had given them permission to off him. Probably because he'd killed that bitch and her boyfriend, which wouldn't have happened if the stupid git hadn't tried to be so macho.

As he worked Fallon considered his options. They were pretty thin on the ground. His gun was in the car back in Ladymere, where they'd made him leave it. All he had were his knife and the spade, neither of which would be much use against a man with a gun. But you never know. The Serb might grow careless.

His chance came minutes later. With a thunderous roar, two fighter-bombers suddenly appeared from nowhere and swooped overhead, barely a hundred feet above the ground. They were followed by two more in close formation, hedgehopping across the moorlands on a low-flying training exercise.

The sudden explosion of sound took the Serb by surprise. Startled, he glanced upwards, and in that moment Fallon struck. Swinging the spade savagely against the man's shin. The edge of the blade sliced through the thin layer of flesh and shattered the bone beneath it. With a howl of pain the Serb went down. Rolling and gasping in agony as he clutched at his leg.

Fallon leapt from the grave. He raised the spade and brought it down like an axe on the man's throat, almost taking off his head. Blood sprayed over the ground. The body convulsed for several long seconds then finally fell still.

Throwing down the spade Fallon picked up the dead man's gun. He checked the number of rounds in the magazine then went through the Serb's pockets. He found the car keys, and a wallet containing Stirling and Euro notes. Pocketing the money he threw the wallet into the grave, then rolled its dead owner in after it.

He moved around to the other side of the grave and searched McAndrew. The pockets yielded up a small amount of cash before his body, too, was pushed down into the hole.

Slowly making his way down to the valley floor, Fallon climbed into the SUV. He turned it around and, humming softly to himself, started back up towards the farm.

54

Dutton:

Alex's story was both remarkable and moving. She was born Altyn Nabiev, in the village of Tarasan, Kazakhstan. Her parents were Yana and Dagyan Nabiev. She had a half brother called Peter, eight years her senior.

Peter was the product of her mother's earlier marriage to a Russian power line engineer called Mikhail Susnik. This marriage didn't last long. Soon after the birth of his son, Susnik returned to Russia. There he divorced his Kazakh peasant wife and moved to Moscow.

For six years Yana struggled to raise the boy alone. Then she married local farm hand Dagyan Nabiev, and within a year Altyn was born. Tarasan was a poor rural community. The only work to be found was farm labouring, most of it seasonal and poorly paid. When Altyn was three years old, her father joined the Russian army to earn enough money to support his family. Posted to Afghanistan, he was killed just weeks later by the Mujahedeen.

At the age of sixteen Peter was invited to Moscow to live with his father. The widow Nabiev, who could barely afford to feed her children, was happy to let him go. Altyn remained in Tarasan with her mother. She was educated at the local school where she was found to have a natural talent for drawing. Encouraged by her teacher, she hoped to become a book illustrator, or commercial artist. Her ambitions were never realised.

Shortly after her seventeenth birthday Altyn was kidnapped by a family from another village and forced to marry Arman, their eldest son. There was nothing she could do. The practice of bride kidnapping was not uncommon in some of the more remote regions of the former Soviet empire. It went largely unreported, and unpunished.

The Kozak family, to whom Altyn now belonged, had five sons. Well known for their criminal brutality, the Kozaks were much feared throughout the district. They terrorised local communities. Stealing and killing with impunity. What passed for the law in that remote region was unable to touch them. No one was prepared to speak out against the family for fear of becoming their next victim.

Arman Kozak was a clever young man. He had ambitions that went far beyond running a gang of local thugs in somel rural backwater. Deciding that provincial Kazakhstan was no place for him he moved to America. With him went his wife, and two of his brothers, Dauren and Serik.

The Kozaks quickly established themselves in New York. They set up a pipeline bringing illegal immigrants and drugs from Eastern Europe into Canada. Then smuggled them across the border into the USA. Their activities quickly grew into prostitution and drug distribution, in and around the city.

Altyn knew nothing of the businesses they ran. She was never encouraged, nor allowed, to enquire. But she was no fool. Knowing the kind of family she had married into, she had no doubt that whatever the brothers were involved in would be illegal.

At first she loved New York. After life in a remote village, miles from anywhere, the big city seemed an amazing place to live. Of course, she was expected to stay home like a good Kazakh housewife. Cook meals, clean house, and help entertain her husband's dubious friends.

As the business grew Arman spent more and more time travelling around. Less time at home. So Altyn began to build a life for herself outside her marriage. She signed on for an arts course at the School of Visual Arts. Told her husband she was attending cookery classes. She spent eighteen months at the SVA and loved every moment of it. Then one day he discovered where she was really spending her time.

When he confronted her she demanded the right to a life of her own. Arman flew into a rage. He beat her so badly he was forced to take her to the hospital where he told the doctors she had fallen down the stairs. She backed up his story. Too afraid of what he might do to her if she didn't.

After that day things changed dramatically for Altyn. New York became a prison. She was forbidden to go out of the house alone. Only ever with her husband, or one of his brothers. As further punishment, all her artworks and painting materials were thrown out of the house. Unable to replace them, she couldn't even pursue her artistic talents in her own home.

The only outside entertainment she was allowed was the Opera. Arman had developed a love of musical theatre. He didn't really understand it, but he thought being an opera buff would make him appear more cultured amongst his associates. He became a member of the operatic set,. Taking his wife along with him to performances.

On their way home from the Met one night, Arman detoured to a junk yard owned by himself and his brothers. There Altyn witnessed the savage killing of an undercover FBI agent called Franklin Markov. When she attempted to intervene she was, herself, viciously assaulted by her husband.

For Altyn it was the final straw. The next day when her husband left the house she packed a suitcase and called a taxi, determined to leave for good. When the driver asked where she was going, she didn't know what to say. There was nowhere in New York she could run to. Everyone she knew were either friends or associates of the Kozaks. Feeling unbelievably wretched, and at a complete loss about what to do, she just burst into tears.

The taxi driver turned to look at her. He saw the black eyes, and the bruised and swollen face. Without being asked he drove her to the nearest police precinct house. 'Do yourself a favour lady,' he told her. 'Just go in there and show them what he did to you.' Then he drove off, refusing to take her money.

Altyn did just that - and more. She told the police what she had witnessed in the junk yard, the night before.

She was immediately passed on to the FBI, to whom she repeated her story. In exchange for testifying against her husband, Altyn was offered US citizenship and a new identity. It was a heaven-sent opportunity to turn her back on the whole Kozak clan and she immediately agreed. Arman was arrested, and put on trial.

The one good thing to come out of all this was the re-appearance of her half brother Peter Susnik. Learning about the trial on the internet he flew to New York, to support his sister. The two hadn't seen each other since the day he'd left Kazakhstan, and she was overjoyed to see him. It was he who suggested that, after the trial, she should move back to Europe. An ocean's width away from New York.

Arman was convicted. He was sentenced to forty years for racketeering, and ninety-nine years, without parole, for the murder of FBI agent Markov. The Bureau then turned its sights on his brothers Dauren and Serik. But they had already fled across the border into Canada, from where they made their way back to Europe.

After the trial Altyn divorced her husband. Her lawyer, Mary Dalton, was an Englishwoman. Married to a former US Air force pilot. When Altyn asked her what England was like, the lawyer told her about Swanage where she had grown up. Her stories made the county of Dorset sound such a safe and peaceful place. So she decided to settle there as Alexana Morel, the name she had been given.

'Then I met you,' she said wistfully. 'And everything became perfect.'

'So what happened?' I asked. 'How did they find you?'

Her expression turned bleak. 'I did something so stupid. Something I will never forgive myself for. I was so happy: and I wanted to share this happiness with my mother. I knew she'd be worried about me, wondering where I was and how I was doing.

So I sent her a letter, telling her all about my new life. About the wonderful man I had married, and how happy and content I was. Of course, I didn't tell her where I was living. Or mention any names. I even took the precaution of driving to Salisbury to post the letter. I know I shouldn't have done it. They'd warned me many times, never to contact anyone from my old life. But I was so worried about her I allowed myself to break the rules. I killed my mother, Terry' she said, sadly. 'The Kozaks stole the letter, and then murdered her so she couldn't warn me.'

She stopped talking, overcome with emotion. I wanted so badly to comfort her. But all I could offer were platitudes. 'You couldn't have known, Alex,' I tried. 'You mustn't blame yourself.'

'I will always blame myself,' she said bitterly. 'Sending that letter not only condemned my mother to death, it also set in motion things that would destroy everything we had together. I am the world's biggest fool.'

She was silent for a few moments. Then she pulled herself together and continued her tale.

'Three weeks after I sent the letter, Peter turned up at the shop. He'd been told by the Authorities back home that our mother had been killed. He called a friend of the family, back in Tarasan. She told him about the letter. It seems my poor mother was so proud of me, she had shown it to everyone in the village.'

'Peter told me I could not stay in Dorset. That if he could find me, simply from being told the contents of the letter, then the Kozaks most certainly would. He suggested I ask the Americans to take me back into protective custody.'

She shook her head. 'I couldn't do that. I knew they would have insisted I went back to America. Far away from you and everything I loved. So in the end he agreed to help me himself. He set up a new identity for me, and a home here in the north. Then he arranged my 'accidental death.' I think in the back of my mind I still clung to the hope that someday you and I would be together again.' She gazed sadly around the white walls of the cellar. 'I never imagined it would be like this.'

'I saw you on television,' I tried, cheerfully. 'You looked great! Though I prefer your hair the way you used to have it.'

'I couldn't believe fate could do that to me.' she sighed. 'It was unbelievable bad luck. But the thing that hurt most of all was the thought of you seeing me there, and what it would do to you. I am so very sorry for what I did, Terry. I really am.'

All the anger was gone. The past year with all its pain, and everything that had happened in the last ten days, were suddenly unimportant. The only thing that mattered now, for both of us, was staying alive. I refused to believe that we were going to die in this place.

'Alex, stop apologising. I thought I'd lost you and now I've found you again. I'm grateful for that.'

'We have so little time,' she sighed.

'We're not dead yet,' I said, wrenching uselessly at my bonds. 'God, I wish I could touch you.'

'How is my dear little Lucy?' she asked, a smile coming to her face. 'I missed her almost as much as I missed you.'

'Lucy's fine. She's waiting for you in the car. When we get out of here the three of us are going home to Portland.'

'We'll go for a walk on the beach,' she said. 'Call at the cafe for tea and scones - '

The door at the top of the stairs opened. Dauren Kozak stepped into the cellar. He came down the staircase and approached Alex. Cut her arms loose from the chair and secured her wrists behind her back. Then he cut her legs free and pulled her to her feet.

'Up on the chair!' he ordered. She turned around, and for the first time saw the noose. Her face blanched. She threw me a frightened, helpless, look, then gave a stubborn little shake of the head.

'On the chair!' insisted Dauren, 'or I will put him up there first, and you can watch him swing.'

'Don't do it!' I called to her but she ignored me. Resigned, she climbed awkwardly onto the chair, her face a frozen mask. Kozak climbed on beside her. He placed the noose around her neck, tightened it, then jumped back down to the floor.

He moved out of sight. I heard him rummaging about somewhere behind me then he came and pressed the gun into my right cheek.

'Open your mouth wide,' he ordered, 'or I will blow you a new one in the side of your face.' I did as he said. He stuffed a wad of hessian into my mouth and wound packing tape around my lower face to keep it in place. As he worked he looked at Alex. 'Don't think to cheat us by jumping off before we are ready,' he warned her. 'Or your man here will suffer for it.'

He moved over to the stairs. Untying the rope from where it was anchored to the stringer he pulled it taut, and then re-tied it. Alex cried out. She teetered on the chair as the noose cut into her neck. Lifted her onto the balls of her feet.

Dauren ignored her. Looking up the stairs he called out something in his own tongue. I caught the name Serik. He was calling for his brother.

He came back. Stood beside me as he had done earlier. Pulling out his phone he began taking movie shots. First of me. Then of Alex.

'Today I am Steven Spielberg,' he voiced, smiling happily. 'My brother is to be the executioner.'

I looked up to see Alex's desperate eyes staring into mine.

55

Ballinger:

Ballinger drove up the hill. Along what was little more than a cart track. Following the same route Fallon had used when he left the road and struck out across country. According to the sat nav he had almost reached the GPS co-ordinate he had entered.

Just below the summit he stopped the car. He switched off the engine, climbed out, and crawled to the top of the hill. He looked down. A hundred yards below, at the head of a narrow valley, stood an old farmhouse. The place looked run down. Derelict, almost. The only signs of life were the white van sitting out front, and the sound of a generator coming from somewhere nearby.

He checked the terrain. Searched for the best way down. A side-on approach was probably his safest bet. Cover was sparse, but there were no windows in the side of the building.

Distant movement caught his eye. Coming along the floor of the valley, towards the farm, was a car. As it came closer he recognised the Mercedes used by the Kozaks. He watched the silver SUV all the way, until it entered the farmyard. Sunlight, reflecting from the windscreen, prevented him make out who was driving.

When the car disappeared behind the house he stood up. Then set off running, taking a wide swinging curve to his right. Crouching low he took long loping strides down the hillside over spongy heather and wild bracken, avoiding treacherous patches of sheep dung. The going was difficult, the ground steep. Several times he almost lost his footing. But at last he reached the flat ground, beside the farm.

He moved to the dry stone wall that surrounded the place and crouched low: Pulled out the Glock and checked it was ready for use. Taking a deep breath, he climbed to his feet and quickly pulled himself over the low, stone barrier.

Sprinting across the yard he reached the side wall of the farmhouse. Carefully he edged his way towards the rear of the building. He peeked around the corner and studied the back of the house. There was no one in sight.

On the other side of the farmyard was a small barn, from where came the hum of the generator. The back door of the farmhouse was covered by a small porch. The SUV stood close by, a soft ticking coming from the engine as it cooled. The driver's door had been left open.

Carefully Ballinger ducked underneath a window and approached the car. Reaching inside he removed the keys from the ignition. He dropped them into his pocket and made for the back door.

56

Fallon:

Fallon left the SUV behind the farm. Carrying the Serb's gun he climbed out, went through the porch, and into the kitchen. The cellar door was open. Bright light shone from down below, up onto the kitchen ceiling. He hoped he hadn't missed all the fun.

'Serik!' The loud cry came from the cellar, followed by a stream of words that Fallon couldn't understand. From somewhere upstairs came a muttered reply. Then the flushing of a toilet. Moments later footsteps told him someone was descending into the lounge.

Silently he crossed the kitchen and tucked his body behind the open lounge door. He put away the gun, pulled his knife, and waited. The footsteps headed his way. Then Serik stepped into the kitchen, making for the cellar.

Fallon pounced. His left arm went around the man's throat, cutting off any sound he might make. The knife went in behind the right ear, forced upwards into the brain with tremendous ferocity. Serik's body went into a series of diminishing spasms then slumped, lifelessly, against him. Carefully he lowered his victim to the floor.

Removing the knife he wiped it on the dead man's jacket then stood beside the cellar door. He pulled the gun and waited. It didn't take long. He heard a muted curse, then heavy footsteps began to climb the cellar steps. Dauren was coming for his brother. Fallon counted five steps then swung quickly through the door, onto the small landing.

The man stopped dead when he saw Fallon. He was holding something in his right hand and Fallon didn't wait to find out if it was a gun. He fired twice, both bullets hitting his target in the stomach. With a grunt Dauren went down onto his knees. The phone dropped from his fingers and his hands clutched at his wounds. Slowly he fell face down on the stairs, softly moaning.

Fallon stepped around him. Descending the stairs he grabbed Kozak by the feet and pulled him down onto the cellar floor. Rolled him onto his back. The man stared up. Eyes wide with shock.

'Hey *asshole*' voiced Fallon, aping the man's accent. 'Remember me?' He lifted the gun and fired again. Then he turned and walked slowly into the cellar.

'Now here's an interesting scenario' he observed conversationally. 'Sorry I'm late folks, but I've been doing a spot of grave digging. Boris there,' he pointed at the dead man, 'decided to have me buried in the valley back there. Nice thought, but I'm not quite ready to settle down yet. So I gave my plot to his ugly Serbian friend.'

'How did you find me?' asked Alex. 'How did you track me down?'

'We didn't, sweetie. We traded you.' He moved around behind her. Rested his hands on the back of the chair. 'Take a tip from me, my love,' he advised. 'Never trust a foreigner. They'll always let you down.'

He suddenly rocked the chair violently. With a small cry of alarm Alex swayed perilously. Fallon stopped. He peered around the woman at Dutton. Winked, then grinned insanely. 'Had you going there kiddo, didn't I?' Then in one swift movement he bent down, grabbed the back legs of the chair, and pulled it from under her.

57

Ballinger:

As he entered the porch two gunshots rang out. Ballinger instinctively flinched. Seconds later came a third shot, clearly from somewhere inside the house. He cursed himself silently. The shooting had begun. He was too late.

Less cautiously now, he pushed on into the kitchen. Skirting around the table he discovered the body of Serik Kozak. It lay on the floor, near the entrance to a cellar. There was a light on down there.

After a cursory glance into the empty lounge he inched his way through the cellar door. Stepped lightly onto a small wooden landing. A set of open stairs led down into the brightly lit basement. The air was filled with the acrid odour of firearms discharge. He looked down.

Lying at the bottom of the stairs was the body of the other Kozak brother. Tied to a chair in the centre of the cellar was Dutton. Standing on a second chair, with a rope around her neck, was the woman. Even as his eyes fell upon her, the chair was snatched from under her feet.

He saw her body swing forward. Then a grinning Fallon stepped around her, moving in on Dutton with a gun in his hand.

'You're on next kiddo!' the killer said cheerfully.

'Fallon!' called Ballinger. The man reacted instantly. His head snapped around, followed a microsecond later by the hand holding the gun. Fast as he was, he was not fast enough. A glint of recognition came into the killer's eyes as Ballinger squeezed off three rapid shots.

The heavy bullets knocked Fallon off his feet. He hit the floor and stayed there, arms spread in supplication, dead eyes staring at the beamed ceiling above. In one fluid movement Ballinger drew his knife and sawed through the rope attached to the stairs. The rope parted and the woman fell heavily to the floor.

He leapt down the rest of the way and ran to her side. Quickly removing the noose, he cut her wrists free. Checked that she was breathing. Her pulse was strong and racing so he laid her in the recovery position and covered her with his coat. Only then did he give a nod of reassurance to a wide-eyed, frantic, Dutton.

The woman began shaking. Coughing. Her breath coming out in short, rasping, gasps. He knelt beside her until the reaction passed and her breathing returned to something close to normal.

'You alright now?'

She nodded. Pointed at Dutton. 'Help him!' she croaked.

'In a minute.' He picked up the fallen chair. Helped her into his coat and sat her down. Only when he was sure she was okay did he go to Dutton and cut him free.

Dutton leapt to his feet. He immediately fell on his face as pins and needles raged through his lower limbs.

Ignoring the pain he crawled across to his wife. Took both of her hands in his.

'Where are your clothes?' asked Ballinger.

'One of the bedrooms,' she told him.

He went upstairs and checked each room carefully. The house was empty. Collecting the woman's clothes he carried them down to the cellar and handed them to Dutton.

'Serik's in the kitchen. He's dead. But there are still two unaccounted for.'

Dutton shook his head. 'Petrovich is dead. Fallon killed him - or so he said. I don't know about McAndrew?'

'I'll go and find him.' Ballinger picked up the gun Fallon had used. Handed it to the private investigator. 'You ever shot anyone?'

Dutton shook his head.

'It's easy. Just point it and pull the trigger. If anyone but me comes through that door, that's what you do. Shoot them. You're not a cop now, so don't think you have to call out a warning. Just shoot them. That way you'll both stay alive.' He started up the stairway.

'Ballinger!' He stopped. Dutton nodded to him. 'Thank you. It's all I can say right now, but it's nowhere near enough.' Ballinger waved a hand dismissively and stepped out of the cellar.

Leaving the house he checked the barn. He looked inside the empty van then examined the surrounding land. The whole place appeared deserted. He climbed into the Mercedes and set off down the track. Retraced the route he had seen the SUV take on its approach to the farm. He drove slowly, scanning both sides of the valley. Half a mile along he spotted the spade Fallon had stuck into the hillside as a marker.

He stopped the car and jumped out. Carrying his Glock he climbed up the steep incline onto the flat apron of land. The two missing men lay together in a wide grave. Ballinger checked the bodies then, using the spade, levered them closer together to make room for two more.

Looking around, he wondered how many more bodies were lying in this remote valley. More than a few, he suspected. He brushed his gloved hands together to wipe off the dirt, stuck the spade back in the ground, and returned to the car.

58

They sat in the kitchen drinking coffee they had found in one of the cupboards. Alex was effusive in her gratitude towards Ballinger who, in turn, appeared almost embarrassed. He quickly changed the subject.

'Have you told Alex about Bianca?' he asked Dutton.

'Yes I have.'

'It's very sad,' said Alex. 'She was a nice girl, and certainly didn't deserve what that animal did to her.'

'You're right, she didn't!' agreed Ballinger. 'Tell me, Alex, have you any idea how they found you.'

'I asked Fallon. He said they'd traded me. I'm not sure what he meant. My brother arranged for me to be picked up by someone called Scott Devlin, from the US Embassy. When he arrived he had all the right credentials so I went with him. He drove straight onto a business park and just let them take me.'

'What was he like, this Devlin?'

'Tall, slim, late forties to early fifties with grey, slicked back hair: and an American accent, of course.'

Ballinger smiled ruefully, shaking his head.

'You know him?' asked Dutton.

'She just described Lucas Devine.'

'Devine? You mean Devine sold Alex out? But he's with the Marshall's office. How could he do that?'

'He was working for the Kozaks.'

'You knew this?'

'Not until last night. I was bothered by the way things were going,' he explained. 'McAndrew's arrival. Fallon's trips out here. It seemed like the Kozaks were getting ready to make some kind of play. Coupled with their sudden loss of interest in you, it all pointed to them having a new lead on Alex.

But only Susnik and Devine knew where Alex was, and I couldn't see Susnik betraying her. Not after all he'd done to keep her safe. So I decided any threat had to come from Devine. Or someone in his department.

Last night I put a call through to the Office of US Marshalls in Washington. When I dropped the name Alexana Morel I found myself having a good long talk, with a senior protection officer.

It seems they never received any indication that Alex was in danger. Not now. Not last year. They knew nothing about the sailing accident. Nor that she had gone missing. When I told the guy I was working for Lucas Devine to try and find her, he told me I couldn't be. Because Lucas Devine does not exist.

'But I was given Lucas Devine as my contact,' protested Alex. 'I was told to call the Embassy and ask for him if ever I was in trouble?'

'The name's a trigger,' he told her. 'A codeword. Anyone asking for Lucas Devine would be put through to a designated senior communications officer.

His job is to offer what immediate assistance he can, then call the Marshalls office and let them know there's a problem. They will then decide what further action should be taken. The officer currently responsible for taking these calls, in the UK, is called Scott Devlin.'

'But why would this Devlin - Devine, or whoever, betray me?'

'I don't know? But you can be sure I'll find out. Money's always a good bet.'

'Why did he hire you?' asked Dutton.

'He was convinced you knew where Alex was. My job was to stay with you until you made contact with her. Then let him know where she was. When Alex blew her cover on television, he thought it was all about to happen. He tipped you off, expecting you to rush up here and make immediate contact. Probably called the Kozaks too. Told them it was all set to go down, and to get themselves over here.

Devlin must have been really pissed when it began to look like you didn't know where Alex was after all. Fortunately for him the Kozaks were too distracted by Fallon's killing spree, to be on his back. Then when Susnik called him and said Alex was coming in, he must have thought it was his birthday.'

Ballinger turned to Alex. 'He came to Manchester himself, to pick you up. Handed you straight over to the Kozaks. It was brilliant. Who would know? Most people thought you were dead, anyway. Only Terry, myself, and Susnik, knew otherwise: and we would be told you'd gone off to start a new life somewhere.

The only way I could stop what was about to happen was to follow Fallon to the pick-up, and intervene. But I didn't know what time the pick up was scheduled. Devine hinted it was around mid-afternoon.'

He looked at Dutton reproachfully. 'But before I went after Fallon, I needed to know where you were going to be. You're like that terrier of yours. You get your teeth into something and you won't let go: and the last thing I needed was you walking into the line of fire while everything was going down. But you managed to do that, anyway.'

'How did you find us?'

'Well I missed Fallon, so I played detective, like you did. I spoke to Chris Heenan. He told me where you'd gone. When you weren't at the apartment but your car was, I went to the house. I thought you might have been taken there but the place had been cleaned out. The only other place they could have brought you was here.'

'So what happens now?' asked Alex.

'Well, the Kozaks are dead: and Petrovich: and McAndrew. I don't know why Fallon killed them. My guess is the Kozaks were not about to leave any loose ends, and he was a loose end. Somehow he must have turned the tables on them.'

He regarded Dutton. 'Most of the work's been done. We might as well take advantage of it. There's enough room in the grave for the two brothers, so I suggest we put them in there. They'll never be found: and the world will be a much better place without them.'

Just for a moment it looked like the policeman in Dutton was going to object. Then he looked at the rope burns around his wife's neck and the bruises on her face. He nodded. 'Fallon too?' he asked.

'No,' smiled Ballinger, grimly. 'I have other plans for him.'

59

Ballinger brought his car down to the farm. He opened the door and to Alex's great joy, and Dutton's obvious relief, out leapt Lucy. She made a fuss of the private investigator then sniffed suspiciously at her mistress.

'She's fallen out with me,' laughed Alex.

'She'll get over it,' smiled Dutton. 'A gravy biscuit always works for me.'

The two men returned to the house. They wrapped the Kozak brothers in bed sheets and placed them in the back of the Mercedes. Then drove them down to the burial site. Alex went with them. She didn't leave the car. Just sat holding Lucy while the brothers were buried alongside their bodyguard and Doug McAndrew.

'What about the farm?' asked Dutton as they drove back up the hill. 'There's evidence all over it!'

'I'll sort it,' said Ballinger.

Back at the farmhouse Ballinger transferred his things from the Discovery to the Mercedes. With Dutton's help he carried out Fallon's body and lowered it into the back of the Kozacs' SUV. He handed his own keys to the investigator.

'Take my car. Follow the track until you come to the road then turn left. You'll come to the A640, with signposts for Huddersfield and Oldham.'

'I know it,' Dutton told him. 'I lived in this area as a boy.'

'Really? Then make your way to the motorway and head back to Manchester. You'll find your phone and car keys in the glove compartment. Call your friend George so he knows you're alright, but don't go back to the Fox tonight. He'll ask too many questions. Take a room in the Copthorne instead. Unwind and catch up. Think up a good cover story.'

'Where are you going?'

'I've got some things to finish here then I'm taking Fallon home. I'll be back sometime tomorrow.'

Dutton nodded. Held out a hand. 'Thanks again, Ballinger.'

'My friends call me Sandy,' said Ballinger, gripping the hand and shaking it.

'Thank you, Sandy,' called Alex from the passenger seat.

Ballinger watched the Discovery climb the hill. When it had disappeared over the crest he went back into the farmhouse and began a thorough search of the place, starting with the cellar.

Picking up the rope, and the gun that Fallon had used, he dropped them into a sack with Dauren's phone, then added the bindings used to tie up the prisoners. He carried the sack, and the two chairs, up to the kitchen.

Seated at the table he carefully wiped the gun, removed the bullets, and dropped it into his coat pocket. Deleting the pictures of Dutton and Alex from Kozak's phone, he trashed the sim-card then smashed the instrument into pieces. He left these on the table, next to the bindings and the plastic mugs they had used to drink their coffee.

Upstairs he pulled the covers and pillow off the bed where Alex had been beaten and abused. Bundling them together he returned to the kitchen and added them to the table. Satisfied that anything carrying the DNA of Dutton and Alex was gathered together, he went out to the car.

He opened the tailgate: reached in, and turned out Fallon's pockets. When he found the wallet he carefully went through it, ignoring the cash he found. Tucked into one of the slots he discovered a folded paper bearing a flight number and a time - the Kozaks arrival details, he guessed. Taking out his pen he scrawled something on the reverse side of the paper, slipped it back into the wallet, and returned it to the dead man's pocket.

Closing the tailgate he climbed behind the wheel and drove once more down into the valley. There he buried the gun far away from the bodies, and scattered the bullets. Arriving back at the farm, he sat in the kitchen and waited for nightfall.

When darkness came he siphoned petrol from the van. He splashed it around the lounge, cellar, and kitchen, paying particular attention to the chairs, the table, and the items on it. Then he fired both the farmhouse and the van.

Driving to the top of the hill he sat and watched his handiwork. The flames spread rapidly through the building, racing along the stairway to the upper floor.

Out in the yard the van suddenly erupted in flames as the petrol tank exploded. Window panes began to shatter around the building. Flames leapt through, devouring the ancient wooden frames. When he saw tongues of flame emerging from beneath the heavy roofing slates, he drove away.

60

Ninety minutes later he was back in Ladymere. He backed the SUV into the garage then shut and locked the doors from the inside. Quickly he transferred Fallon's body from the back of the SUV to the trunk of the Honda.

Soon he was in Fallon's car, heading south-east towards the M6. Picking up the motorway he drove to Birmingham then joined the London-bound M40. Traffic was light. Driving at a steady speed, he made good time,

At around three a.m. he pulled into the Beaconsfield services. Sat there, dozing in his seat. He had time to kill. Driving along empty urban roads in pre-dawn hours, with a dead man in the trunk, was not a recipe for a long and happy life. Not with all those bored traffic cops sitting around in their cars, waiting for someone to pull.

It was seven o clock when he set off on the last leg of his journey. Leaving the motorway he joined the early rush-hour traffic on the Oxford road. He passed through Bakers Wood to Denham, then headed south towards Uxbridge. Once there he made his way to the old flour mill down by the canal. The place he had first encountered Fallon.

The mill was still derelict. The heavy gates of the property padlocked to keep out kids and vandals. Ballinger smiled at this. Locked gates would never have kept him out when he was a youngster. He doubted they would today's kids. He picked open the lock and drove through into the mill grounds. Closing the gate behind him, he hung the open lock on the hasp so the place looked secure.

He took the service road around to the back of the mill. Stayed with it, driving between the canal and the derelict silos where the distribution trucks used to load with flour. At the end of the main building he turned onto an old stone wharf, once used for loading flour sacks onto barges.

Climbing out he checked there was no one around. The place was as deserted now as it had been the time he was here with Steve Carpenter. Not for the first time he thought about the kidnapped girl they had collected that day. Wondered if she was still living happily in the bosom of her family. He hoped so.

This was a fitting place for Fallon to end up, he decided. A no-place. He hoped the killer appreciated the gesture. Leaving the car unlocked he threw the keys far out into the canal, tucked the gloves into his pocket, and walked away.

Forty minutes later he was on the tube heading for Kings Cross, and from there on to Euston. By lunchtime he was on the Pendolino, racing north. He called Dutton. 'I'll be in Manchester for two-thirty. Can you pick me up?'

They were waiting for him when he came through the ticket barrier. 'You collected your car then?' he observed as they led him to the Audi.

Dutton nodded. 'This morning. There's *residents only* parking around there after four o clock, so it had been clamped. Cost me seventy quid to get it released, and another hundred or more for a new window.'

'You can afford it. Have you decided what you're going to do?'

'We're going home,' said Alex. 'Try to pick up where we left off. If people will let us.'

'What about your friends at Central Park?'

'It's sorted,' Dutton told him. 'We'll give Tony Hale a version of the truth. Tell him Alex was on witness protection from the States and her cover was blown, so she played dead to keep us both alive. I'll say the problem's been taken care of by Alex's brother and his friends at the FSB. I won't mention you, of course. Nor Fallon. Nor what happened at the farm.'

Ballinger looked at Alex. 'Did you call your brother?'

'I did. He said he's going to kill Devlin. He might do, too,' she added worriedly.

'Call him back. I'll speak to him. Tell him not to bother. Devlin's finished. He just doesn't know it yet.'

'We owe you our lives,' she told him. 'We can never repay you, and nothing we can say will ever express our gratitude. But when we are back home, I hope you'll visit us. Come to dinner.'

'I'll look forward to it,' smiled Ballinger. 'I'm told you make a mean lasagne.'

61

THREE DAYS LATER

Scott Devlin entered the Starbucks. He wore the dark grey suit he always had on to work. He spotted Ballinger in the corner and joined him at the table.

'Coffee?' offered Ballinger.

The man calling himself Lucas Devine shook his head. He produced an envelope and passed it over.

'Cheers!' Ballinger pocketed the money.

'You aren't going to check it?'

'It'll be right!' He drank his coffee. Regarded the American. 'So, how's the woman? Nicely settled into her new life?'

'I guess,' grunted Devlin. 'I just shipped her out of here, that's all. After that it's over to the Marshalls.'

Ballinger nodded. 'That'll be Marshall Petrovich, right? With his deputies Fallon and McAndrew. In their white Transit van?'

For a brief moment the American's face betrayed shock and surprise. Then quickly he regained his composure. He gave Ballinger a tight smile.

'How did you find out?'.

'I was there,' lied Ballinger. 'I watched you pick her up and take her to the business park. Then hand her over to Kozak's men.'

'You shouldn't have been there. You were supposed to be keeping Dutton busy?'

'I know. You wanted us both out of the way. So you had me playing nurse-maid to Dutton. Unluckily for you he gave me the slip. By the time I caught up with him he'd been taken by your friends.' He looked evenly at the man opposite. 'I suppose they're both dead?'

Devlin shrugged. 'I didn't ask. As far as I'm concerned she's gone to start a new life somewhere. I guess Dutton went with her.'

'I hope they paid you well?'

'They didn't pay me at all,' snorted Devlin. 'But they did pay you. Where do you think your money came from?' He gave a small shrug. 'It was never about money, Ballinger. It was about survival. About doing what I had to do, because I was given no choice.'

'You're saying they blackmailed you? Who was it, Levkin's people? Fallon?'

Again the shrug. 'It's what they do, these people. They offer you something you want. Then, when you take it, they use it against you. But I should have known that, I guess. Anyway, it's over. They've got what they wanted, so I'm off the hook.'

'You think?'

'Yeah, well right now the Kozaks aren't my problem. You're my problem: and whatever you intend to do?'

Ballinger spread his hands. 'Me? I'm not going to do anything. It's not my concern. I've got my money so I'm finished here.'

'You're not going to come on to me for more?'

'You spend too much time with the wrong kind of people, Devine,' advised Ballinger. 'We're not all on the make. Just don't call me with any more assignments, okay. I'm not sure I like you very much: and I don't do business with people I don't like.'

Devlin climbed to his feet. 'I'll be on my way, then!' When Ballinger ignored the outstretched hand, he turned and walked out the door.

Outside, in the Autumn sunshine, the man in the grey suit headed for Grosvenor square, and the Embassy. He'd walked barely twenty yards when two burly men closed in from behind and gripped his arms tightly. A car came alongside and he was quickly and professionally bundled onto the back seat. One of the men climbed in beside him. The other shut the car door. He turned around and strolled into Starbucks.

'You get all that?' asked Ballinger when the burly man came to his table.

'We did,' said the man from the Marshall's office.

Ballinger reached into his coat. He removed the transmitter and handed it over. 'What'll happen to him?'

'He'll go to jail. For a very long time.'

'We can't testify! You know that, don't you.'

The man smiled. Held up the transmitter. 'Don't worry, we've got him cold. He'll be talking from here until Christmas, just to cut a deal. So you go ahead and keep your secrets Ballinger, and we'll keep ours. Now good day to you sir, and thank you for letting us deal with this ourselves.' This time Ballinger accepted the handshake. Then with an affable nod, the US Marshall turned and walked out.

62

SEVEN DAYS LATER

Tarasan: Kazakhstan.

The old Zis truck rumbled purposefully along the big road. In the cab Danyar Kozak and his two younger sons were on a mission. A Mercedes had broken down five kilometres north of Tarasan. They were on their way to the scene.

A Mercedes meant people with money, which meant a good ransom. His contact at the auto-repair shop reported that the driver had his family with him. A wealthy man would pay a lot to protect his family. Even more to get them back. The old man smiled. There could be rich pickings from this one.

Five minutes later they spotted the broken-down car up ahead. The hood was up. The man stood looking down at the engine as if he expected it to talk. Danyar pulled in. The man turned and saw them. Relief washed over his round face. Smiling broadly he came towards them.

'Looks like a soft one to me,' voiced the old man. He placed the pistol on his lap and wound down the window. Put on his 'friendly' face as their intended victim came up to the truck.

The first bullet hit Danyar between the eyes. The next two shots took out the sons. Susnik fired three more, to make doubly sure, then stepped away from the truck. He glanced up and down the road. There was nothing in sight. Few people used the big road these days. Only smugglers, bandits, and kidnappers; and there weren't as many of those around as there used to be.

He put away the gun. Walked back to the car and shut down the hood. Climbing in he did a casual U-turn then sped off, heading North. He was smiling. Now all the Kozaks were dead, except Arman, and he would die in prison. Altyn was truly safe, his mother was avenged, and by this time tomorrow he would be well on his way to the beautiful city of Prague. Life was good.

63

ONE MONTH LATER

We sat in the new Gazebo. Watched the rain blowing in from the Channel. On the glass-topped table sat a bottle of Pinotage with two, half-filled, wine glasses. A third glass stood empty.

Alex was playing with Lucy. Throwing a ball that squeaked loudly each time the little terrier clamped it in her jaws. I was working on a text message. *Alison back home with her family. Thanks for your help. T. Dutton.*

'Who's that to?' asked Alex.

'A cafe owner in Manchester. I'd forgotten to thank her for helping me to find you.'

Things were getting back to normal. Tony Hale had accepted the half truth we gave him. Though he was clearly unhappy about the Russian involvement.

'When you say *taken care of* by Susnik,' he had remarked, 'I hope that doesn't mean what I think it means. We all know how the Russians 'take care' of things.'

'I don't suppose we'll ever know,' I said. 'He's out of the country now. So unless bodies start turning up in someone's back yard it doesn't matter, does it?'

'As long as it's not my back yard,' he said, pointedly.

Dorset police, too, had wound down their murder enquiry. Fallon's body had been discovered less than a week after Ballinger had dumped it.

Some days later DCI Ryan called me into his office. He told me that a London gangster had been found shot to death in his own car, in Uxbridge. He asked if I had any thoughts on that.

When I told him I had not, he went on to disclose that the dead man's car had contained the firearm that was used to murder Bianca's friend, Gary. Moreover, the dead man had both my home and office addresses. Written on a piece of paper found inside his wallet.

'Looks like our killer met his come-uppance,' he stated.

I asked if that meant the case was closed.

'Not closed,' he said. 'Officially the case will remain unsolved. But we won't be looking for anyone else. I've taken it upon myself to inform Bianca's and Gary's families that, in my opinion, the man responsible for both of their deaths is now, himself, dead. Hopefully it will give them some closure.'

'Thank you,' I said.

'I hear your wife's back home?'

I nodded.

'I'm pleased for you. Your Superintendent Hale tells me there was some Russian involvement in all this?' He looked at me steadily. 'Oddly enough, Fallon also had links with the Russian Mafia.'

'Who?' I asked, dodging the trap.

'Joey Fallon. The dead man in the car. Do you still think the break-in had something to do with your wife's disappearance?'

'Yes I do. Although I don't suppose we'll ever know for sure, will we?'

'No,' he agreed giving me a last, searching, look. 'I don't suppose we will.'

He stood up. Reached out to shake my hand. 'Take care Mr Dutton. I don't think I'll need to see you again. Can't speak for the Met, though. They might have a few questions for you.'

'Right,' I said. 'Well you know where I am: and thanks for keeping me informed.' And that was it. In the event, I heard nothing from the Met. I figured they had put Fallon's death down to just another gangland killing.

I checked my watch. Looked at Alex sitting there on the cane settee, Lucy on her lap. 'He's late!' I remarked. The words were barely out of my mouth when the doorbell chimed. I walked quickly across the short, covered walkway and into the house.

When I opened the front door Ballinger stood there, looking slightly damp. 'I've brought this,' he said, holding up a bottle of Montepulciano. 'It's Italian.'

Also by

J M Close

The biographical Novel

Long Ride On A Ghost Train

Michael Tully's world has been reduced to the size of a hospital bed. His future can be measured in weeks. The only human kindness he can count on comes from the amiable fire fighter who pulled him from his burning flat, and the young Irish nursing sister with a soft spot for a grumpy old man. Stuck in death's waiting room, Michael seeks refuge in the past. He recalls the journey he took from childhood, through adolescence, to manhood. Rejoins his vaguely delinquent friends as they blunder their way through the austere, cold-war world of the nineteen-fifties. Once more Michael finds companionship, romance, and heartache too, in an age when the teenager was invented, rock and roll was king, and the good really did die young

They called themselves the gang of four.

There was Eddie: Sexually abused – and confused. One of fate's victims. If it could possibly go wrong, it would go wrong for Eddie.

Then there was Dodge: Of dubious parentage and a naturally truculent demeanour. A smile was a notable event with Dodge.

Next came Mig: The one with the money and the looks. The one who always got the girl. Sadly for everyone else, there is a Mig in every rat pack.

And there was Michael: Cynical beyond his years, yet a true romantic at heart. Inclined to fall in love at the drop of a hat, and far too often for his own good.

Along with his friends, Michael felt ready for whatever the world had to throw at him. He was just too young to know how merciless, and indifferent, the world can be.

Soon to be released in *JMP* paperback